ALSO BY KERRY WILKINSON

The Andrew Hunter series

SOMETHING WICKED | SOMETHING HIDDEN

Standalone novels

TEN BIRTHDAYS | TWO SISTERS

THE GIRL WHO CAME BACK | LAST NIGHT

THE DEATH AND LIFE OF ELEANOR PARKER

THE WIFE'S SECRET

The Jessica Daniel series

LOCKED IN | VIGILANTE

THE WOMAN IN BLACK | THINK OF THE CHILDREN

PLAYING WITH FIRE | THICKER THAN WATER

BEHIND CLOSED DOORS | CROSSING THE LINE

SCARRED FOR LIFE | FOR RICHER, FOR POORER

NOTHING BUT TROUBLE | EYE FOR AN EYE

SILENT SUSPECT

Silver Blackthorn

RECKONING | RENEGADE | RESURGENCE

Other

DOWN AMONG THE DEAD MEN

NO PLACE LIKE HOME

1

Andrew Hunter blinked his eyes closed in a momentary effort to escape the strobing lights that were pummelling him. As onslaughts went, certainly when it came to torture methods, this was pretty good. Not only were the blinking, flickering coloured bulbs above doing their best to disorientate him, the thumping music left him unable to hear anything other than bass and the singer's vague warblings.

There had to be laws about this sort of thing. Wasn't there a Geneva Convention? Something about human rights? It wouldn't be quite so bad if he hadn't paid ten quid for the privilege of losing two of his five senses.

Andrew opened his eyes again, but the lights were still battering a headache his way. As they winked on, it gave him a fleeting view of the rest of the nightclub. There were three levels. He was at the top, leaning on the banister and peering towards the dance floor on the ground. A mass of bodies writhed into one another, arms flailing into the air. Others were flapping around as if they were all having a fit at the same time.

The second level was some sort of VIP lounge thing,

where it cost another tenner for admittance. From what Andrew could see, it was all leather couches, martinis and blokes in suits. It had that wanker vibe to it.

The top level was for the hardcore drinkers. There were bars at opposite ends and, though the music was still abysmally awful, not to mention thunderously loud, it was *almost* bearable.

Andrew started to turn towards the bar, just as a cheer erupted from below. The song had changed, but was that a reason to celebrate quite so loudly? He didn't get nightclubs – he never had. Even when he'd been in his teens and early twenties, places like this were a mystery. He was all for a pint in the pub, bit of a chat, that sort of thing. Who could possibly enjoy this sort of sensory deprivation?

The floor was uncomfortably sticky, lathered with spilled drinks and who knew what else, as Andrew crossed towards the bar. If that wasn't bad enough, he couldn't remember the last time he'd sweated so much. Possibly back at school when they did cross-country on the hottest day for twenty-eight years. If not that, there was the best-forgotten incident in the sauna in Riga.

Andrew squeezed past some rugby sort with big shoulders and a square head, finding himself a spot at the bar.

'Oi, mate, whatcha after?'

Andrew swivelled, accidentally brushing across the sleeve of the man standing next to him. The reveller's white shirt was translucent with sweat, giving Andrew a lovely, clammy palmful of strange-man perspiration.

Andrew wiped the contaminated hand on his trousers, though the sweaty man didn't seem to notice. The barman was still staring at Andrew, wanting a response. 'Bottle of sparkling water, please,' Andrew said.

The barman shot him a look of bemusement before crouching and opening one of the fridges. He told Andrew the price, which would have been extortionate even if the water had been retrieved from the moon and then carbonated via the process of trained monkeys blowing bubbles through straws. Andrew handed over the money anyway and then the barman disappeared off to the till.

Water in hand, Andrew shuffled away from his spot, moving to the other side of a slumped girl to get a better view of the other end of the bar. When he was close enough, he turned around, leaning back onto the varnished wood and holding the bottle to his lips. He stared up towards the large screen that was showing either music videos or porn – hard to tell these days – while half-watching the couple underneath.

The man was eighteen or nineteen, with hair that was swished sideways as if he'd been caught in a vicious side wind. He was wearing tight jeans and a slim-fit top, showing off solid upper-arm muscles. He leaned over the woman next to him, bottle of bright blue somethingoranother clasped in his hand, smiling at her with perfect teeth and then whispering enough to make her giggle.

Jenny Mays worked as Andrew's assistant at his private investigator's office and he wasn't used to seeing her giggle, not like this. This was an act. Whatever Windswept Boy had said hadn't been funny at all. She was dressed for the occasion. Her dark hair that was usually in a ponytail was up in a perfect bun or bob-type thing that only women could manage. Andrew wondered how they learned to do such things without it all falling out. Were there pins involved? He had enough trouble getting a comb through his.

As well as having done something to her hair, Jenny was in some sort of flared flirty red dress that Andrew would usually associate with 1950s diner waitresses. He wasn't sure what to make of it. Jenny didn't really do dresses. It was usually flat shoes or Doc Martens, skirts with tights, or jeans – or, some-times, usual office-wear. She was playing with a dark bracelet, looping her finger underneath and twiddling it in a circle. It was perfectly natural and yet, somehow, she was making it an act of seduction. She was a chameleon, adjusting herself to fit into wherever she was needed.

Jenny was breaking the rules – even though he'd gone through them with her in his car before they'd got anywhere near the line to enter the club. Rule one: Don't be alone with Max Grayson.

Broken – they were in the corner together, at least a couple of metres from anyone else.

Rule two: No touching Max Grayson.

Broken – Max had the hand with the bottle brushing Jenny's arm, the other touching the hemline of her dress, rubbing an area that wasn't quite knee but wasn't quite thigh, either. He was leaning in, talking into her ear, with Jenny reciprocating by whispering back into his. Not to mention flashing Max that pinball ding-ding dimple-ridden get-out-of-jail smile along with the big brown-eyed aren't-I-wonderful stare.

Andrew realised he'd been looking at them for too long, so angled himself up towards the big screen again and took a sip from his water. He wondered when he might step in, given Jenny was already breaking rules one and two. Would he wait until Max the octopus had a hand on Jenny's backside? Her breasts? Would she stop him? Would he?

If he *really* thought about it, he was pimping her out, wasn't he? She might have volunteered, might have cut him off and said she'd do whatever when he brought this up, but it was still his idea at its core. What was *wrong* with him?

Jenny laughed loudly and, when Andrew glanced back to them, Max was whispering in her ear again. It had to be done, so Andrew took out his phone, pointed it towards them and snapped a picture. He checked over his shoulder, making sure nobody was watching, and then clicked three more as Jenny and Max switched positions, with her talking into his ear. It might have been the angle, but from where Andrew was standing, it looked like Max had a couple of fingers underneath the hemline of Jenny's dress. Definitely more thigh than knee.

Andrew knew he had to move. This was too much. He had to come over all fatherly, give it the old, 'Time to leave' rigmarole.

Before Andrew could move though, Jenny did. She slipped underneath Max's arm, taking his free hand with hers, guiding him around a table towards the darker reaches at the back of the club. Andrew followed while trying to make it look like he wasn't following. It was a tough act to pull off, mainly consisting of him bobbing his head somewhat in time to the music while sipping his water. It probably looked like he had some sort of medical condition.

Jenny led Max down the stairs, still holding his hand. They passed the second floor VIP entrance and kept going towards the ground. Andrew couldn't work out why they were heading to the dance floor, but then it turned out they weren't anyway. As he squeezed apologetically between a pair of young women, Andrew saw Max and Jenny disappearing through the door of the disabled toilet together. He arrived just in time to hear the click of the lock slotting into place.

Okay, this was bad.

He should have probably come up with a rule three: No sneaking off to toilets with Max Grayson, but he generally thought that would have been covered by both rules one and two. With Jenny, it was hard to know how much she'd taken on board and by what amount she was going to go off and do her own thing anyway.

Andrew was in a dim corridor that smelled of stale sweat. It was so rancid that it was close to wiping out sense number three. If the club could find a way to get rid of his taste and touch, it'd be a clean sweep.

Somewhere towards the dance floor, there was the sound of glass breaking and then another cheer.

Andrew thought about knocking on the door. Perhaps faking a limp and pretending he needed the disabled toilet? Maybe he should kick through the door, action-hero style, riding to Jenny's rescue?

Or perhaps, as she had displayed so many times before, Jenny didn't need him in order to get the information they wanted.

Andrew leaned against the wall and then regretted it. The surface was coated with either condensation or sweat – *hopefully* the former. Three more girls passed, shooting him awkward 'who's-the-granddad?' looks, so Andrew had to style it out, offering smiles and nods, while leaning into the damp-ridden wall.

Was this a new low? It was hard to tell. There was the time he'd accidentally thrown food over the woman who later became his wife. Then the occasion where he proposed to the same woman on one knee, barely a metre from a freshly piddled puddle of piss. They were sort of bittersweet memories; this was all bitter. Then the whole thing with her becoming his ex-wife.

Just as Andrew was wondering if he should try to find a manager somewhere, there was a click and then the door popped open. Max's head emerged before the rest of him. He checked both ways, straightened his shirt and then headed off through the open door on the other side of the corridor into the throbbing mass on the dance floor.

Andrew watched him go and then, a couple of seconds later, Jenny's head poked out, closely followed by the rest of her. She eyed Andrew and then winked, before breaking into a full-on grin. The music was so much louder on the ground floor that he couldn't hear her, but she mouthed 'okay?' and

Andrew nodded. She cracked a grin that felt both relieving and dangerous.

Moments later, she was pushing through the fire exit at the far end of the corridor, Andrew just behind. She skipped – *actually* skipped – across a patch of wasteland until she was in an alley that passed between two houses. By the time Andrew had caught up, she was holding her hand out towards him.

'Got it,' she said.

Andrew looked down at what she was offering him – a small polythene bag filled with white powder.

'What is it?' Andrew asked, taking the bag and holding it up to the nearby street light.

'Max said it was cocaine – so it's either that or mashed-up paracetamol.'

Andrew opened the bag and sniffed it. It didn't really smell of anything, but then he wasn't sure if cocaine had an odour anyway. That wasn't the point. He strode to the nearby drain and turned the bag upside down, emptying it all and then pushing the bag into the adjacent bin.

Jenny was next to him and was soon strolling towards his car, which was parked a few streets away. At least, Andrew assumed that was where she was headed. He wasn't sure where he'd left the car and all the streets around this area of Manchester looked the same.

'Jen,' he called.

She waited until he was at her side and then they walked together. 'What?' she replied.

'It's cold – take my jacket.'

Andrew went to drape it around her shoulder but she shrugged him off. 'Don't be daft.'

Not wanting to be the only one of them properly clothed, Andrew draped it over his arm and continued walking. 'We've got to have a very serious word about sticking to pre-agreed rules,' he added.

'Pfft.'

'And about that. You can't keep going "pfft" to get out of things.'

'I bet I can.' She laughed, not like the giggle she'd offered Max in the club, but for real. Andrew could see the creases in her cheeks.

'Fine,' Andrew said, 'but it could have been dangerous. You put yourself in a vulnerable position and I blame myself because I let you.'

'It's fine.'

'Jen, it's not fine.'

She batted a hand towards him and then stopped, one hand on her hip. 'I did this for you and you don't even trust me enough to tell me why Max is so important.'

Andrew felt a couple of inches tall. She was right. She *had* done this for him without needing to know the reason. And that was after he'd promised her she wouldn't ever have to do this sort of honeytrap work. He was a scumbag.

'It's not because I don't trust you, Jen.'

'Then why is it?'

He couldn't face her. 'It's because I've made a terrible mistake.'

It was no surprise that Jenny was in the office ahead of Andrew the following morning. He often wondered if she had some sort of tracker on him, enabling her to set off just in time to get there first. He generally aimed to be in for around half past nine, but even when he got in *at* nine, or earlier, there she was.

Their argument from the previous night – if it could be called that – was seemingly forgotten as Andrew switched on his computer.

'Wanna brew?' Jenny asked. She was fresh-faced and wide awake, despite their late-night escapades.

Andrew was feeling rough and he'd not even been drinking. It was hard to tell quite why he felt so bad, but it was probably the combination of the music and the lights. He felt like he'd lost a fight with a glitterball.

Jenny glided across the room effortlessly, hair back in its usual ponytail, dress replaced by tight semi-smart jeans and a plain top. She'd not asked about the nature of his mistake the previous night and he'd not expanded. He was embarrassed by his own decisions.

As he slumped into his chair, Andrew started to feel his temples thumping. He definitely had a headache on the way. Jenny pottered behind him, flicking the kettle on and then fiddling with teabags and milk.

Andrew watched her humming to herself as she fingered through the wall calendar, crossing something off and writing a few things onto various dates in the future. He'd worked fine by himself before hiring her and yet now he couldn't remember what it was like to be on his own in the office. She'd somehow ended up doing much of the admin he hadn't liked in the first place.

She was more than an employee, she was a mate, someone he trusted implicitly. But he wanted to ask *who* she was, what was going on in her head. He frequently wondered why she worked for him when it was clear she was capable of so much more. Despite that, he didn't want to push, not after discovering the handful of incomplete, patchy details about her past. He didn't want to admit he knew any of it and make it seem like he'd been spying. It wasn't long ago that she'd lunged for a thug more than twice her size, raining blows down on the back of the man's head until Andrew had pulled her away. She'd been fearless that day, as on many others. Fear*some*, even. All because that man had called her a psycho. Andrew wanted to know why she had been so triggered, yet he didn't.

What's more, even though Andrew *knew* Jenny was keeping things from him, he was also hiding details from her – not least the reason they'd been in the club with Max Grayson.

Before Andrew could become too immersed in the other things going on in his life, the 'I heart MCR' mug was plonked on the desk in front of him. The postcard that was angled against his monitor fell over, photo side down, leaving the message on the back clear to see. Jenny glanced at it but said nothing, righting the card and then heading to her own desk.

On the front was a photo of a beautiful golden tiger,

surrounded by greenery and a clear, perfect lake, with the word 'THAILAND' over the top. On the back was the address of Andrew's office on one half, with three words on the other: *I need time*.

Andrew was drifting, thinking of the person who'd written the message, when he was interrupted by a knock on the door. He called 'come in' and a woman appeared. Considering some of the people who came asking for help, she was distinctly normal-looking: jeans, plain jacket, non-wild dark hair, a bag that could be designer but was probably knock-off from the market.

She looked between Andrew and Jenny, settling on Andrew. 'Are you Andrew Hunter?'

'Yes.'

'And you're an, um...' She left it hanging, possibly too embarrassed to say what Andrew's job was.

'...Private investigator,' Andrew said.

She gasped and nodded too quickly. 'Right and you, erm...'

'...Investigate stuff.'

She nodded some more. 'Right, I um...'

The woman seemed confused, but Jenny leapt into action, offering her a seat close to Andrew's desk and then delving into her own bottom drawer and emerging with a packet of chocolate Hobnobs.

'Biscuit?' she asked.

The woman batted her hand.

'Brew?'

'Okay... that'd be nice. Just a bit of milk.'

Jenny was soon in the back corner, giving the kettle yet another early-morning workout.

Andrew turned back to the woman. 'How can I help you, Mrs...'

'Applegate. Anna Applegate. It's a bit awkward, I'm afraid. You're not the first investigator I've visited.'

'Right...'

There was another moment of silence in which Andrew wondered if he should know the identity of the woman. Her last name seemed vaguely familiar, but he couldn't place it.

'Are you a football fan?' Mrs Applegate asked.

Andrew shook his head. 'Not really.'

Jenny chirped a 'me either' from the back of the room, which the woman didn't seem to mind.

Mrs Applegate shrugged. 'I don't get it myself, but you know what it's like round here.' She sighed, but there was more to it than a simple gasp for breath. She sucked in her cheek and started to chew on the skin, waiting until Jenny had placed a mug of tea on the desk in front of her. She nodded a 'thank you' and then offered a slim, sad smile. 'You know Man City, don't you?' she added.

'Yes.'

Mrs Applegate flicked her temple with her middle finger. 'Course you do. Everyone does. Sorry. It's my daughter, Michelle, she...'

As she tailed off, the memory of where he'd heard her name before clicked into Andrew's mind.

'The canal...' he whispered.

She nodded, cradling the mug near her mouth. 'Last September, they found my daughter's body in the canal near the Turing Memorial. Her name was Michelle and her boyfriend is a footballer.'

'Jack Marsh.'

Another nod. 'Right. Jack Marsh.' She said the name as if it was a swear word, then added: 'You remember it?'

'It's hard to miss anything even vaguely related to football in this city,' Andrew replied.

'So you know all about his alibi, then?'

Andrew scratched his head. He remembered it being a big story for a few days and then it had slipped off the agenda. A

lot had happened in the seven months since. 'Bits and pieces –
it's better if you fill me in.'

'Marsh claims he was in a hotel with his teammates at the
time my Michelle ended up in the water. He did a big interview – going on about how the death of his girlfriend had
affected him – but it's all rubbish. I *know* he was involved.'

Andrew opened his top drawer and removed a pad and
pen. He wrote the name 'Jack Marsh' at the top.

He looked up, locking eyes with Mrs Applegate. 'How do
you know he did it?'

'Have you heard the rumours about him?'

Andrew shook his head. 'Even if I have, let's pretend I
haven't.'

She sipped her tea, squinting slightly, apparently sizing
him up. For a moment, Andrew thought she was going to stand
and walk out. He'd seen it before – some clients didn't like
being questioned themselves, wanting their version of events
to be taken as nothing but the whole truth.

'He pushed her down the stairs,' she said quietly. 'She had
her own place, but I think he was paying the rent, or at least
giving her the cash to afford the rent. It was hard to get details
from her at the time. I didn't even know until I went round to
see her one morning.' Mrs Applegate put the mug down and
separated her hands as if she was holding a balloon. 'Her ankle
was out to here and she couldn't walk on it. Told me she
tripped – the usual.'

At that she gulped back a sob, her voice cracking. Jenny
slipped around her desk, offering a box of tissues that was
accepted with a tear-ridden smile.

Mrs Applegate continued talking as she dabbed her eyes.
'It was only a few weeks before that when she came round
mine with a black eye, plus he'd punched her so hard in the
kidney that she was weeing blood for a weekend. I wanted her
to go to the doctor, but she wasn't having it. Kept saying it was

an accident. There's no official record any of it happened. She wouldn't even let me take photographs. There were always bumps and bruises. I stopped asking where they came from in the end because she'd only say it was a door handle or corner of a table. It wasn't just that – he cheated on her all the time, tipped a pint of beer over her head on her birthday when he was pissed – I could go on, but... no point, is there? You either believe it or you don't.'

Andrew hadn't added to his single note. In one way – the biggest way – even if all of that was true, all it showed was that Jack Marsh was a special type of scum. It didn't mean he was a killer.

'What about the night she died?' he asked. 'Why do you think he killed her?'

Mrs Applegate blew her nose and then balled up the tissue, dropping it in the bin next to Andrew's desk and apologising. 'She was out with one of her friends, doing what young girls do. They say she died of alcohol poisoning and then ended up in the canal, but I know it was him. When the police got involved, Marsh said he was with his teammates in a hotel in the centre. Apparently the team often stay in the same place the night before a match. His friends covered for him and that was that. They said they couldn't prosecute.' She swirled her hand. 'No evidence.'

Andrew was about to ask something else when the door to his office banged open. At first he thought it could have been the wind, but, when he turned, the light in the stairwell behind silhouetted a beast of a man.

Iwan's last name was a mystery to Andrew, but he was the hired thug who had been a constant shadow in his recent life. Iwan was easily over six foot, with monster shoulders, a puffed-out steroid-freak chest and a squat dumpling head on top.

Andrew got to his feet, taking a step towards the door. 'I'm with someone,' he said.

Iwan glanced around Andrew towards the woman sitting at the desk. He ignored Jenny, though he didn't budge from where he was standing. 'I need a word.'

'It'll have to wait.'

'I don't have time for that. Now.'

Andrew took another step forward, resting on Jenny's desk in an attempt to hide the fact his knees had wobbled. 'I'm with a client. You'll have to wait outside.' He almost sighed with relief that his voice hadn't quivered.

Iwan glared down on Andrew and, for a moment, Andrew was certain he wouldn't move. He considered his options. Calling the police? Yeah, right. Physically ejecting a bloke who was twice his size? No chance.

Iwan's eyes narrowed and then there was the merest hint of a nod. It was hard to tell what happened next because, before Andrew knew it, Iwan was back in the hallway and the door was closed. He was pretty sure Iwan hadn't turned, hadn't allowed his eyes to stop boring into Andrew, and yet he was gone.

Andrew had his back to Mrs Applegate and took a breath, giving himself a second or two to try to get his heart rate down. He soon turned, all apologetic smiles.

'Sorry about that,' he said. 'Misunderstanding over times. You were saying that the police were unable to prosecute Mr Marsh...'

Mrs Applegate didn't seem to have realised anything was too amiss. She nodded. 'Right – they said his alibi checked out, that he hadn't left the hotel all night. They'd spoken to him, his teammates, staff, checked CCTV – that sort of thing.'

Andrew leaned back in his seat, chewing the end of his pen, trying not to think of the man outside his office door. 'I hate to be blunt, Mrs Applegate—'

'Anna.'

'Sorry, Anna. I'm just not sure what exactly it is you want me to do. You said your daughter died of alcohol poisoning... are you questioning that?'

'No – the coroner said that. I've no reason to doubt him.'

'Then where do I fit in...? Don't get me wrong – if I was a certain type of person, I could take your money, read some papers, type up a report and come back to you to tell you what you already know. I'm not going to do that, though.'

'That's precisely why I want you.'

'Sorry...?'

'The other investigators I went to almost bit my hand off, promising all sorts. They said they'd get police files, they'd contact the football club, interview Marsh – all that. They were after easy money, but you...' She glanced towards Jenny, then back to Andrew. 'You've said everything I wanted. I know you might not be able to do any of that. But I *also* know Marsh killed my daughter. I want someone with an open mind who isn't just in this for the money.'

Andrew took a moment to think, still biting the end of the pen. 'You want me to prove Jack Marsh killed your daughter?'

'I know there are holes in his story, but, for whatever reason, they've been missed.'

Andrew looked to Jenny, whose lips were tight. She raised her eyebrows as a reply. He turned back to the woman: 'I... um, look, Mrs— Anna. I'll tell you what. I've got a couple of things to finish off and then we'll do a bit of digging this afternoon. If I can find an angle or an inconsistency in the coverage of what happened to your daughter, even something small, then we'll see how far we can take things. I don't want to give you false hope and I don't want to rip you off. We'll be in touch later in any case. If this is something I feel we can look at properly, Jenny will talk rates with you then and she'll take a few more details. Okay?'

Mrs Applegate stood and shook his hand. 'That's all I wanted. I don't want ridiculous promises.'

Andrew led her to the door and opened it. Iwan was resting against the railing outside, but Andrew ignored him, escorting Mrs Applegate down the stairs and showing her onto the street. He took a few seconds to compose himself, waving to Tina who worked in the office opposite, and then headed back inside towards the office.

Iwan was in the doorway, cracking his knuckles, sporting a sinister smile.

'I need a word,' he said.

'So I gathered.'

3

As Andrew squeezed past Iwan to get into his office, he noticed the crinkled scar across the top of the man's bald head. His skin was the dimpled pink of a regular drinker, but the blemish was seared white – the result of Andrew cracking a tyre iron across the other man's skull. It should be an action of which he was ashamed and, perhaps, in some ways, he was. It came after Jenny had leapt onto Iwan's back and hammered her fists into his head because he'd called her a psycho.

Andrew sat at his desk and swivelled the chair around, trying to appear calm, as if Iwan was just another man, not a behemoth with a grudge.

Iwan didn't look at her, but he nodded sideways in Jenny's direction. 'Get lost for a few minutes, eh, darling?'

Jenny didn't move.

'Don't talk to my staff like that,' Andrew said, heart chundering.

Iwan grinned lopsidedly. 'You want to do this in front of your tart?'

'Don't talk *about* my staff like that... especially not when she's someone who's kicked your arse.'

Jenny remained silent and Iwan still didn't acknowledge her, instead glaring at Andrew.

'You get what you were asked for?'

Andrew let the silence hang for a few seconds, wishing he'd been brave enough to resist the task he'd been given in the first place. 'We got it,' he replied. 'Max Grayson deals drugs on the side. Definitely cocaine and possibly other substances.' Andrew pulled a cardboard wallet out from underneath his keyboard and passed it across. 'There are photographs in there, as well as an audio recording on a pen drive.'

Iwan opened the folder and flicked through the photographs from the night before. When he was satisfied, he snapped the cover closed and slipped it under his armpit. 'Well, well, well. Little Max is off to the naughty step.'

Andrew didn't reply, waiting to see if Iwan would expand. When the larger man took a step to the door, Andrew called after him. 'Hey.'

'What?'

'We're clear now, right? No more requests.'

Iwan moved back into the office, bowing ever so slightly to ensure Andrew could see the scar on his head. '*Clear?* You reckon everything's equal?' He thrust a pudgy finger in Andrew's direction. 'Things are equal when Mr Braithwaite says they are. Got it?'

'I'm not your lapdog to do jobs whenever you want.'

Iwan took another step towards Andrew, towering over him and grinning. He motioned to throw a punch, stopping himself but making Andrew jump anyway. 'We'll be in touch.'

He waited for a second or two and then finally headed out the door and down the stairs.

Andrew remained in his seat for a few seconds, listening for the sound of the outside door before getting up to close the door to his office. He hovered next to it, biting his bottom lip, before turning to Jenny.

'I should've told you,' he said.

She motioned at the door. 'We were following Max last night because *he* wanted you to?'

Andrew nodded. 'I'm sorry.'

'*He's* your terrible mistake?'

'Sort of. Not him – his boss. Thomas Braithwaite thinks I owe him a favour.'

Jenny didn't reply instantly – she knew who Braithwaite was as they'd stumbled across him while investigating the case of a young couple who'd been shot in broad daylight. He owned an importing and exporting business and yet there was more to him than that. He had an enormous house close to Liverpool and had been linked to various bribery allegations. Andrew and Jenny both had their suspicions over what sort of criminal activity with which Braithwaite might be involved, but, from her point of view, their connection to him finished when the case ended. That was months ago, yet now Iwan had shown up in the office.

'Why do you owe him a favour?' Jenny asked.

'I don't... it's a long story. He thinks I do and that's enough for him.'

Jenny licked her lips, eyes narrowing as she stared at Andrew. It only took a couple of seconds, but then she was nodding, fully accepting what Andrew had said. 'Braithwaite wanted you to look into some drug-dealing kid?'

'Max is the son of Steven Grayson, who sits on Liverpool's city council. I don't know – I didn't ask – but I'm guessing Braithwaite wanted dirt to use against Steven. I didn't want to use you and I know I shouldn't have, but—'

'I don't mind.'

'But *I* do – and so should you. I thought this would be the end, that it would all go away.'

He stared at her, riddled with shame. He'd misled someone he liked – *really* liked – in order to manipulate Max

Grayson into a position that would allow some gangster to blackmail his father. What sort of person did that make Andrew? He'd asked himself that question so many times recently that he wasn't sure any longer. At one time, he thought of himself as a good guy, now he didn't know.

Jenny opened her bottom drawer and offered him the Hobnobs. Her solution to everything.

Andrew shook his head.

'What do you think's going to happen now?' she asked.

Andrew ruffled his hair. 'I have no idea.'

4

Andrew felt his eyes clouding over as lunchtime approached. The sentences on his screen were blending into one another to form one much simpler word: BORING.

As he stifled a yawn, Andrew spun in his chair to face the other desk. 'Save me, Jen.'

She didn't always wear glasses and he'd never quite figured out if she actually needed them, but Jenny nudged them to the end of her nose and peered over them towards him. 'Save you from what?'

'I'm finishing that background check for that accountancy firm last week.'

'And... what's their potential new boss like?'

'He doesn't earn the salary he claimed on his application form, but, other than that, he's the most boring person I've ever looked into. Everything checks out – wife, two kids, house, car, holiday to Disneyworld, no ropy investments... Boring, boring, boring.'

'Never killed a prostitute then?'

'Only the one – but we've all been there.'

Jenny took off her glasses and swivelled her chair to face him. 'You ready to hear about Jack Marsh?'

'Anything that gets me out of the world of accountancy.'

She clicked something on her computer and then turned back to the screen. 'When this happened last year, there was loads of coverage. I've ignored some of the unsubstantiated stuff for now.'

'Any obvious places to start?'

Jenny bobbed her head from side to side. 'Maybe... there are people we could talk to.'

'Let's have it then.'

'The Man City players were staying in the Radisson Hotel in the city centre on a Saturday night ahead of a Sunday game.'

'Manchester city centre?'

She looked up. 'Right – from what I can gather, even if they're playing at home, the team will often all be in the same hotel the night before a match. It's probably team bonding, or so the management can keep an eye on them – something like that.'

'Fair enough.'

'According to the reports, the police checked security cameras at the hotel and interviewed staff. From what it says, Jack Marsh was sharing a suite with another player and didn't leave his room. It says they were playing cards and then they went to bed.'

'It's going to be hard to check that alibi in any more depth than the police have but we might be able to find a staff member or two.'

Jenny clicked through a couple of screens on her computer. 'There are a few other places we can start.'

'Go on.'

'Pretty much everything Michelle's mum said is what the

reports say. She was on a Saturday night out and then the next thing anyone knew, she was being pulled out of the canal on Sunday. Coroner labelled it as accidental death, with the specifics that she ended up in the canal at some point in the early hours of Sunday morning and died through alcohol poisoning. There's another bit saying the water temperature would have contributed.'

Andrew took a moment to think it through, then said: 'So she drank enough to kill herself – and *then* stumbled into the canal?'

'I guess – she was out with a friend, but they became separated and no one's too sure what happened then.'

'If she was walking close to the canal, she could have fallen in if she'd stopped to be sick or something like that. Or stumbled in? She wouldn't be the first person to do that. People are always going on about a phantom pusher around here. How old was she?'

'Twenty.'

He puffed out the required 'so young' breath. 'Who's the friend?'

Jenny looked back to her screen. 'The last person to see her was Chloe Kilgallon. According to her Facebook page, she works as a waitress at Harvey's Diner on Deansgate. She posted about an hour ago that she was off to work.'

She waved Andrew across and he stood at her shoulder, looking at the photo of the two girls.

'They've not got those tans from Manchester,' Andrew said.

Jenny pointed to the young woman in a red dress. 'That's Michelle,' she said.

Michelle Applegate looked nothing like her mother. While the older woman was easily missable in a crowd, Michelle went out of her way to be *un*missable. She had long blonde hair – likely extensions – claw-like nails, big heels, bigger hair, eyelashes larger than a butterfly's wings, a tiny red dress and tangerine orange skin. Chloe had black hair with a black dress but was otherwise similarly kitted out for an ankle-breaking night out.

'When was this taken?' Andrew asked.

'July last year – a couple of months before Michelle died.'

Andrew peered closer at the photo, taking in the tattoo that looped around Michelle's left wrist. It looked like some sort of stylised Chinese writing. Chloe had something similar around her ankle. It was easy to sneer, but they were two young women looking to enjoy themselves. Nothing particularly wrong with that.

'What else have you got?' Andrew asked.

'An interesting one. Jack Marsh's childhood sweetheart was a girl named Megan Halfpenny. They were going out when they were both fifteen or sixteen. They grew up on the same estate together. He's lived in the city his whole life, played his way up through the youth teams, that sort of thing. He has the accent, knows the city and he used to kick balls against garages across the road from his house. It's why the fans love him so much now. There's article after article about it. There was talk a couple of years ago about knocking down those garages to build more houses, but a group of locals kicked off, saying it was where all the local kids gathered to play football. There was a big debate about spaces for young people to play in the *Herald*. "Where will the next Jack Marsh come from?" – all that. Anyway, before that, when Jack got his first pro football contract and then made his debut, there was a lot of stuff about Jack and Megan being football's new prince and princess, king and queen – that type of celeb magazine stuff. He was getting it from all sides. The sports sections were all over the local boy-come-good stuff; the showbiz pages wanted to hear about him and his girlfriend.'

Jenny clicked onto an article from a few years previously, showing a young couple in their school uniforms. Poor old Jack was riddled with a peppering of acne around his forehead and a shirt that was too big for him, the large flappy arms making his head look tiny. Megan had soft gingery hair in a ponytail and, contrary to her boyfriend's clothes, was wearing a blouse at least one size too small. Andrew felt uncomfortable even looking at the photo, knowing how young she must be.

'How old are they here?' Andrew asked.

'Fifteen, I think – it's hard to know – but Jack got pulled out of school at some point. I think the clubs do a sort of home-schooling. Jack and Megan broke up once he got properly famous – I think it happened when he was about eighteen. There are photos of him falling out of a club with a girl on his nineteenth birthday, so I guess they were done by then.'

'How old is he now?'

'Twenty-three.'

'Have you found Megan, too?'

'She works in a local clothes shop. It's not just her, though. There are all sorts of rumours around the web – posts on forums and the like. There are so many young women – always women – saying he's done odd things.'

'Like what?'

'It's all tittle-tattle. One person might give a story that's either true or close to it, but somebody else wants to feel important, so they embellish their own encounter, or make up something entirely. It's hard to verify anything.'

'But...'

'There's a woman who says she met Jack in a club one night. They ended up in some hotel room and, when she woke up the next morning, he'd disappeared – and so had all her clothes.'

'What? He'd nicked them?'

'I don't know – it's posted by a random username on some football gossip forum. The IP is from Manchester, but that doesn't mean much. Could be made up, could be someone who wants to get something off their chest. No way of tracing it to a person. I found an article from the *Herald* with one of Jack's old neighbours, saying his car got trashed by Jack and a couple of drunken players. It was all denied and that was that. Most of this stuff is a couple of years old. It sounds like, if any of it *is* true, that he's calmed down.'

'Or – if anything Anna Applegate says is true about him beating up her daughter – he simply started doing it indoors.'

'I guess.'

'Anything criminal?'

'He was done for speeding twice but kept his licence. There are a couple of stories about him getting into fights with people in clubs, but never any charges. Hard to tell if it's true or just paper talk. Nothing really.'

Andrew glanced back towards his own screen and the details of Mr Boring and the accountancy firm. He still had a couple of days on that.

'How about you call Mrs Applegate?' he said. 'Tell her we'll start digging and see if she has anything else we might need. She might have a password for her daughter's old email account or something like that. When you're sorted, how do you fancy a wander?'

'Are we off to a certain restaurant on Deansgate?'

Andrew patted her on the shoulder. 'How'd you guess?'

5

The month of April in Manchester, perhaps England in general, had always given off something of a schizophrenic vibe. Some days the wind howled, the rain lashed, the apocalypse descended; other times the tabloids proudly declared that the country was hotter than a random place in the Mediterranean – as if there was some sort of competition going on. The chances of Greek papers ever printing stories saying their temperatures were higher than Manchester's for a day chosen completely at random seemed unlikely.

It felt like a summer's day as Andrew and Jenny walked through the streets of Manchester. Those lucky enough to not be working were strolling around in sandals, shorts and T-shirts. Pasty, bare flesh was on display everywhere Andrew looked and it felt like it might be half-term or some other sort of school holiday. Either that or people were getting younger, which was an altogether more concerning issue.

Andrew and Jenny passed through a packed St Ann's Square, emerging onto Deansgate. The stores lining the mile-long road were overflowing with people stocking up on summer clothes, convinced the sunshine would be around for the foreseeable future.

Harvey's was an American-style diner towards the southern end of Deansgate. A row of tables and chairs adorned the pavement outside, with half a dozen people sitting around eating. A couple had a pushchair slotted in next to them. The man had his top off, displaying flabby mounds of tattooed flesh, while the woman was emptying the contents of a ketchup bottle onto her mountain of fries. Behind them was an Asian family: grandparents, parents and kids sitting around two tables, chatting and enjoying the sun as the shortest boy raced his toy cars across the pavement. On the furthest set of seats underneath a large parasol were two vest-clad, skinny jean-wearing tanned young men, one sitting on the other's lap. They were feeding each other fries and laughing. It was Manchester in a nutshell.

Andrew stood at the window closest to the door that had a menu pinned to the inside glass, listening to the 1950s rock bursting through the open door.

'They do great ice cream sundaes here,' Jenny said, slotting in next to him. 'Plus they have milk and cookies. Not just normal cookies – they're the size of a plate. You can get chocolate chip, M&M, or half and half – plus you get unlimited refills on the milk.'

Andrew turned to look at Jenny, who stared up with big brown eyes.

'What?' she said with a shrug.

'Do you judge a restaurant solely by its desserts?'

'Who doesn't?'

'Normal people.'

'Pfft. Normal people are boring. There's this cake place in the Northern Quarter. Slices the size of your head.' She held her hands apart as if Andrew couldn't comprehend the size of a human head.

Andrew hadn't been looking at the menu anyway. He twisted back, peering through the glass towards the counter. 'Can you see Chloe inside?'

Jenny joined him, squinting through the slightly tinted glass before stepping sideways to look through the open door instead.

'She's serving a table at the back,' she said.

Andrew and Jenny headed inside, standing next to the 'please wait to be seated' sign. Chloe was serving burgers to a table of teenagers in the furthest corner. She was wearing a pink uniform with a dress that had a flared skirt, white ankle socks and flat shoes. She seemed younger than in the photo Andrew had seen.

When she turned, Chloe spotted Andrew and Jenny. She smiled and held a single finger up, then left her tray on the main counter and crossed to them, grinning even wider.

'Afternoon, guys – table for two?'

Andrew nodded towards the corner where Chloe had been serving. 'Can we sit by the window?'

'Absolutely!'

Chloe spun and led them to a booth a couple along from the teenagers and asked about drinks, calling them 'guys' again for good measure. Kids these days and all that.

'I already know what I'm getting,' Jenny said before Andrew had a chance to reply.

Chloe seemed surprised but pulled a small notepad from a pocket on her hip.

'Milk and cookies, please,' Jenny said. 'Half chocolate chips, half M&Ms.'

Chloe skitched a note and then turned to Andrew. 'And you, sir?'

'Just a Coke... er, diet.'

'Coming right up.'

Chloe disappeared off towards the kitchen, leaving

Andrew and Jenny by themselves. Andrew realised he was frowning.

'What?' Jenny asked.

'I wasn't planning on staying.'

She shrugged. 'This way we get to examine Chloe in her own habitat.'

'She's not a safari animal.'

'Fair enough – this way we get a bonus afternoon cookie.'

'*We?*'

Jenny grinned. 'I didn't stop you ordering anything.'

'I didn't get time to look at the menu!'

They were interrupted as Chloe returned, placing an empty glass in front of Andrew and pointing him towards the drinks fountains near the counter. Jenny's milk was in a frosted glass, with condensation already dribbling along the side. Andrew felt thirsty just looking at it.

'Your cookie will be right out,' she said.

Jenny pointed towards her name tag. 'You're Chloe, right?'

Chloe glanced at her tag and then nodded, though one eye had narrowed. 'Right.'

'Can we ask you about Michelle Applegate?'

Andrew had planned on at least getting to the whole paying-the-bill part first, but sometimes it was better to let Jenny do her thing. She was only two or three years older than Chloe, which immediately gave her an advantage over him.

Chloe's eyes narrowed to slits, lips pouted as she turned from Jenny to Andrew and back again. She checked over her shoulder, and when she replied, her voice had lost its chirp. 'Who are you?'

'Private investigator,' Jenny replied, then nodded at Andrew. 'Well, he is. I just sort of hang about and get in the way.'

Chloe rocked onto her heels, nodding. There was a ding of a bell from behind and she stepped away, nearly walking into the other waitress. They apologised to each other and then Chloe headed into the kitchen. A moment later and she was back out again, pizza-sized cookie in hand. She placed it in front of Jenny and then turned to her colleague.

'Can you cover for five mins?' she asked.

The other waitress shrugged, not appearing overly enthused but not refusing either.

Without being asked, Jenny shuffled along the soft bench, taking her cookie with her. A gentle trickle of steam was seeping from the top and Andrew couldn't help but flash back to being a child. He remembered being in the kitchen of his Aunt Gem's flat, back when the estate on which she lived wasn't so run-down. He'd lick the bowl and spoon after making a mess on the counter, then sit in front of the oven and wait for the cookies to start turning brown.

'You here because of 'Chelle's mum?' Chloe asked, still standing.

Andrew had been so lost in the memory that he could only cough, flailing like an amateur. He managed to nod and Chloe slipped in next to Jenny, who was picking at the cookie with her fingers.

'I went through everything with the police,' Chloe said.

'We're looking to see if there are any alternative angles,' Andrew replied.

'What are you trying to find out?'

'I guess we won't know until we find it.'

She sighed, glancing out the window towards where the other waitress was cleaning the now empty table where the topless man and his ketchup-obsessed partner had been sitting. 'What do you want to know?' she asked.

'You were the last person to see Michelle...?'

'Right.'

'Were you good friends?'

Chloe glanced back to the counter, making it clear she was

looking at the clock. 'I've only got a few minutes. 'Chelle and me had known each other since primary school – so, yeah, we were good friends. We saw each other pretty much every day and generally talked or texted on the days we didn't. Can you get on with it?'

She didn't sound aggressive, more frustrated. Andrew guessed she'd been through all of this many times before.

'How about Jack Marsh? Did you know him?'

Chloe shook her head. 'Not really. Only through 'Chelle – and not even then.'

'But he was her boyfriend?'

'It was complicated. He'd only be free on certain evenings and sometimes for just a couple of hours at a time. He'd say "hi" to me and then disappear off with 'Chelle.'

'Did you mind?'

Chloe turned towards Jenny, who was a quarter of the way through her cookie.

Jenny answered for her. 'It was fine because you had lads on the go as well, right?'

Chloe's nod was slow and deliberate. 'Something like that.' She motioned towards Jenny and Andrew noticed her nails were a lot shorter than in the photographs. No longer glorified weapons. 'You part of the crowd?' she asked.

'Which crowd?' Jenny replied.

'I'm sure I've seen you out once or twice. You have a familiar face.'

Jenny had a mouthful of cookie but nodded. 'I get around.'

'But you're not one of us, are you?'

Jenny shook her head, leaving Andrew to feel as if he'd missed something. Both girls turned to Andrew. On the surface their features were the same, but it felt as if they were about to explain some piece of new technology to Granddad on Christmas Day.

''Chelle and I had gone out on the Saturday night,' Chloe

said. 'She knew Jack was staying at the Radisson but he'd told her not to go to the hotel. 'Chelle was in a mood about that, so we went to the bar in the Hilton instead.'

Andrew pointed towards the northern end of Deansgate. 'That one?'

'Right – but it was dull in there and they had this creepy barman on.' She turned to Jenny: 'Y'know the type, all chest hair and waxed eyebrows.'

Andrew didn't *personally* know the type, but he nodded anyway. Jenny did the same.

'We moved on to this champagne place near Great Northern. Sometimes they get footballers or actors in. 'Chelle was always going on about it.'

Suddenly Andrew got it – Michelle and Chloe were fame-chasers. Chloe had been asking Jenny if she was part of the crowd. To Andrew, it seemed ridiculous. Of all the people he knew that might crave attention, Jenny would have been bottom of the list – and yet she'd not denied it outright.

'Wasn't Michelle going out with Jack at that point?' Andrew asked.

Chloe glanced at Jenny, then back at Andrew. 'So?'

'But she wanted to go to the champagne place because there might be celebrities there…?'

Jenny rolled her eyes and batted a dismissive hand towards him. She twisted until she was sitting sideways, facing Chloe. 'What was it – lads' mags? Papers?'

A glimmer of a grin crept onto Chloe's face. 'You name it. At first she wanted to marry an actor to get into *OK!*. She was keen on this *Corrie* bloke for a while. We kept seeing him out, but I think he already had a girlfriend – some scally skank. Then she gave her number to this lad who used to be on *Hollyoaks*, but he never called. For whatever reason, she thought it would be easier to go out with a footballer.' Chloe reached into the curve at the front of her top, pulling a mobile phone out from her bra and tapping at the screen. She turned it for Jenny to see. 'Look.'

When it was Andrew's turn, he could only make out a photograph showing a series of balloons and lines drawn onto a sheet of paper.

'This was 'Chelle's masterplan,' Chloe added. 'She had this step-by-step guide. She wanted to find a lad, get married, sell the rights to a magazine, get an advice column and then some sort of book deal. She was obsessed by those hardbacks that come out every Christmas. She'd get her mum to buy her them and then only look at the pictures.' Chloe paused, then added quickly: 'She wasn't stupid. She could read.'

'What then?' Andrew asked.

'She wanted a TV show – ITV2 or Living. Either that or *Big Brother*, something like that. She was always going on about it.'

Chloe tucked her phone back into her bra and turned to look at the clock again. Their five minutes was almost up, but the other waitress was standing at the counter, chatting to a lad in a red bow tie who either worked there or dressed particularly extravagantly.

Jenny had eaten half the cookie and licked her finger clean. 'Celebs not your thing?' she asked.

Chloe shrugged. 'Sort of... not really. 'Chelle would follow all these people on Twitter, Instagram and whatever else. She'd see where they were going out in the city, then we'd follow. I went along more to keep an eye on her. She wasn't the only one – but I've not been part of that crowd since the night she, well... y'know...' She swallowed, then added, 'It was exciting, though.'

There was a sparkle to her voice and, for a moment, Andrew felt that excitement. The draw of money and fame. He didn't interrupt and neither did Jenny. Chloe seemingly felt compelled to fill the gap.

'I think I always knew it was a bit of fun,' she said. 'I'd work here during the day, then go out at the weekend. It was a distraction from real life. For 'Chelle, it *was* real life.'

'What happened on the Saturday in the champagne bar?' Andrew asked.

'Not much. It was quiet. You can never judge it. Sometimes, you go out and there are famous people all over. Actors, footballers, sometimes even a movie star. When it's Christmas and there are pantos on, you get all sorts. Other times, it's just a bunch of normals. We'd been drinking for a few hours and I was ready to get a taxi home.'

'With Michelle?'

Chloe shook her head. 'No, I'm still with Mum and Dad. 'Chelle had her own flat. Sometimes I'd stay over when she first got it – but then she started getting a bit funny, saying she couldn't have Jack round if I was there. It wasn't a problem.'

'Where was her flat?'

'Hulme way. I can't remember the address, but it was near the Asda, on the same road as some church. It was re-let about a month after. The landlord was a right bell. 'Chelle's mum wanted to pick up her stuff and he made a right fuss over letting us in. He kept going on about how busy he was. Eventually he arranged to see us one Sunday morning, but then he was annoyed because we couldn't clear everything into 'Chelle's mum's car. He said he'd keep the deposit for cleaning, as if it was a big deal. I told him to piss off and stop being a knob.'

'Can you remember his name?' Andrew asked.

Chloe glanced out the window towards the Asian family. 'I'm not racist, like.'

'I'm not saying you are.'

'Yeah, but you know what it's like. You say a bad thing about someone who isn't white and then you're automatically racist.'

'I'm only asking for a name.'

Chloe chewed her lip and folded her arms. 'Something Bose – like the speakers. He owns a bunch of flats round there. He won't talk to you, though.'

She looked over her shoulder again and said she'd be right back. It took Chloe a few minutes to deal with the teenagers at the back, clearing their table and then showing the patience of a saint as they divided up the bill, each paying with a selection of coins. Chloe dumped the money in the till and then had a brief chat with the other waitress before returning to the table.

'I've only got a couple more minutes,' she said.

'We could talk properly another time?' Andrew replied.

Chloe shook her head. 'No... It's not you – but I thought this was all done months ago. I can't keep going over the same things. Just ask what you want.' She turned to Jenny. 'More milk?'

'If you can.'

She returned quickly with another frosty glass for Jenny and then slotted in alongside her.

'It was quiet on the Saturday you were out,' Andrew said. 'You wanted to go home but Michelle wanted to remain out. So what happened?'

'I hung around for another hour or so because 'Chelle wanted. It was about half twelve and then we went outside. I thought 'Chelle was going to get in a taxi – but she said she was going to stay out for a bit. I thought about doing the same, but, well...' She tailed off.

'Where did you get the taxi from?' Andrew asked.

'Close to the champagne place near Great Northern. You can flag 'em down, even if they're pre-book only.'

'You left but Michelle stayed out?'

Chloe turned away, gazing through the glass at the front of diner. 'It's not like I knew what was going to happen.'

'I know, I wasn't—'

She glared at Andrew, a mix of anger and regret. 'It happened most weeks. I'd normally call her on Sunday to see if she wanted to go for lunch. Don't make me a bad friend.'

Andrew didn't reply immediately, learning his lesson. He didn't think Chloe was a bad friend. 'Which direction did she go when she left?'

'Towards the Radisson.'

'Did she say—'

'She didn't say nothing. She just walked away. The police asked all this. They said she wasn't caught on any of the hotel's CCTV, so what do you want me to say? That's the way she walked. I got a taxi that went the other way.' Chloe pushed herself up and adjusted her cleavage. She placed a bill on the table, looking at Andrew. 'That's for whenever you're ready. I've got to go.'

'Can you answer one more thing?' Andrew said quickly. 'Was Michelle seeing anyone other than Jack?'

Chloe turned to look at the clock again. 'She weren't no slag.'

'I'm not—'

'Look, I don't know you and you don't know me.' She turned to Jenny, lowering her voice. 'They weren't exactly exclusive, but it was what it was. 'Chelle couldn't believe her luck with Jack. She had her plan about magazines, TV and all that.' Chloe clicked her fingers. 'She would've married him like that.'

'Did he ever hit her?' Andrew asked.

Chloe bit her lip again, stepping away from the booth. She stared at Andrew, eyebrow twitching. She took a deep breath and then sighed the reply, 'Sounds like you already know the answer.'

6

Jenny finished her cookie and Andrew left a twenty-pound note on the table. He couldn't wait to get away from the diner, striding into the side alleys that led away from the shopping area. Only locals or the occasional lost tourist used the cobbled cut-throughs and shadows hung from the surrounding buildings, leaving a slight chill, despite the warmth of the day.

'What do you reckon?' Andrew asked.

'Good cookie,' Jenny replied.

'I meant about Chloe and Michelle.'

Jenny nudged him with her elbow. 'I was only joking.'

'Sorry,' Andrew said, unsure why he was annoyed.

'I knew girls like Michelle,' Jenny said. 'At school and uni – we weren't friends or anything, but I reckon most teenagers probably know one or two people like that. At some point they either marry someone famous or they grow out of it. I guess Michelle didn't get the chance.'

'It wasn't a flattering picture though, was it?' Jenny didn't reply, leaving Andrew to ask, 'What?'

'You're being a snob,' she said.

'Huh?'

They emerged onto a street with a small park across the road. Jenny crossed between two parked cars without waiting for Andrew. When he caught her, she was heading for a bench on the edge of the green. She sat, patting the space next to her and then pulled out a Dairy Milk from the satchel she was carrying.

'Want some?' she asked.

'You just ate a cookie the size of a car wheel.'

'Your point?'

Jenny unwrapped and bit into the chocolate, before offering it to him.

Andrew shook his head. 'Why am I a snob?' he said.

'Because you're looking down on Michelle just because she had a certain plan for her life.'

'Not much of a plan, is it?'

Andrew wasn't trying to be mean, but he got The Look anyway.

'Right,' Jenny said, sounding annoyed. 'Say you had a daughter. She studies hard at school, she goes to college, then university. Perhaps she does a Master's. She spends years and years working as hard as she can, then, at the end, she gets a job working in some massive company. She's incredibly successful and makes loads of money. Are you proud of her?'

'Of course.'

'Say you have a second daughter. For whatever reason, she's not as driven as the first. It doesn't matter why, because people are different. She drops out of school but meets someone who she really likes. They have kids and he ends up being really rich and famous. Both your daughters end up with the same amount of money in their bank accounts, so who's your favourite?'

'It's not just about money.' Andrew was trying not to sound annoyed.

Jenny held up a finger to stop him. 'Exactly. For whatever reason, Michelle Applegate was looking for a shortcut. You're assuming it's because she was stupid, but perhaps she's the smart one? Maybe, if everything in her master plan works out, she gets to have everything she wants. Someone could work seven days a week; ten, twelve hours a day, give everything they have to their careers and end up with the exact same thing as Michelle. Nice house, car, holidays, whatever they fancy. Who's the smart one? Michelle who's written that plan and devoted herself to getting what she wants, or the other person who studied every moment for twenty-odd years and then works every day?'

Jenny bit off another chunk from her chocolate bar, leaving Andrew to stare at her. Things had really gone full circle if she was lecturing him about the nature of people.

'Were you ever part of that celebrity-hunting crowd?' Andrew asked.

Jenny swallowed. 'Before I knew you – but not really. Not my thing.'

Andrew wondered if he should follow it up but figured Jenny would tell him if she wanted. He couldn't imagine her on the arm of someone famous, not because she didn't have the looks, more because she'd be the centre of attention without trying.

'I wasn't being snobbish,' Andrew said, more quietly. 'Or, I wasn't trying to be. I suppose I figured... well, I don't know.'

'If everyone was some high achiever, life would get pretty boring very quickly,' Jenny said. 'Not everyone wants to sit around sipping chai and talking about nineteenth-century literature.'

'Not everyone wants to sit around reading celebrity magazines, either.'

Jenny jumped up. 'Good – so we're agreed. There's room for everyone, no need to be snobby.' She squeezed the final chunk of chocolate into her mouth and dropped the wrapper in the bin. 'What now?' she asked.

Andrew joined her, suitably chastened. 'Probably the Radisson. I've never been in but I want to see the layout.'

The Radisson Hotel in the centre of Manchester was on Peter Street, stone-throwing distance from the main Bootle Street Police Station – if the thrower had a good arm.

First, Andrew and Jenny walked the route that, according to the papers at least, was roughly the way Michelle Applegate had headed. They strode along Peter Street, passing the hotel and then continued past the square next to Manchester's Central Library. They turned on Portland Street, passing the 'genting club' – a term that Andrew had always thought sounded particularly appalling. What exactly did 'genting' mean? And, if it was what he assumed, did that imply watching strippers was something all 'gents' should do? They followed the row of back-to-back hotels, heading towards the bright lights of Chinatown and then turning right onto Sackville Street.

At the corner, Andrew and Jenny peered up at the CCTV camera, which was the final time Michelle had been spotted. The image of her stumbling past was still on the websites of the police and the *Morning Herald* – grey and fuzzy but undoubtedly Michelle.

After that, her exact movements were unknown. It was a five-minute walk along Sackville Street to the Gardens, the Turing Memorial, and, ultimately, the canal in which Michelle had been found. Andrew and Jenny followed the road, which was particularly bland compared to the blinking lights behind. There were a couple of pubs, but neither seemed the type that would be particularly busy at one o'clock in the morning when Michelle would have been passing.

Although it took them five minutes, given Michelle's apparent state of inebriation, there was every chance it would have taken her longer – and that was if she'd gone in a straight line.

Having walked the route, Andrew and Jenny paced the edge of the canal. The main road was a bridge over the water, but from both Canal Street and Sackville Gardens there was only a climbable fence that separated them from the plunge.

Canal Street was the heart of Manchester's Gay Village, with a long row of pubs displaying rainbow flags. The exact place where she was found might have been well populated by revellers at the time Michelle was there – but there was every chance her body had drifted to its resting spot.

With no way of knowing what happened after the final CCTV sighting of Michelle, Andrew wasn't sure what else they could do by tracing her route. The police would have spoken to bar owners, servers and pub-goers, not to mention checking the security cameras. Too long had passed for Andrew to be able to double-check any of that. If someone who'd been drinking outside the pub at the time was unable to help the police, there was little chance of Andrew getting any assistance many months on.

Jenny took a few photos anyway and then they made their way back to the Radisson. They headed into the reception area, which was largely what Andrew expected – tall ceilings, lots of white, people in suits, some bloke in a top hat for an unspecified reason, and a widescreen television next to the bar showing the BBC News channel. The lift needed a key card to open, as did the adjacent door that led to the stairs. With Top Hat Man hovering, Andrew had little choice other than to approach the reception desk.

'Can we have a room for tonight?' he asked.

The man behind the computer screen peered at Jenny and then Andrew. He had a slim smile fixed on his lips that had a knowing look about it. 'Absolutely, sir,' he said. 'Twin, double or suite?' His gaze flickered to Jenny once more, no doubt taking in that she was a decent age younger than Andrew and that they had no luggage.

'Suite,' Andrew replied, sliding his credit card from his pocket and not asking the price. The receptionist went through the rigmarole of taking Andrew's address and not raising an eyebrow at the fact it was ten minutes down the road. He took Andrew's phone number, email address and a host of other details he had no reason to know. Pretty much the only thing he didn't ask was Andrew's inside leg measurement. By the time he'd handed over a pair of keycards, Andrew had long since switched off.

They were in the lift heading to one of the upper floors when Jenny finally spoke. '*Suite?*' she said.

'You said the footballers were in nice rooms.'

'Good point.'

The doors pinged open and they stepped into a hallway lined with a springy carpet and moody lowlighting. Andrew headed along the corridor until he reached their room. The key card slot flashed red the first three times he tried it, finally plipping green and allowing him in on the fourth. Those things never worked first time.

The room was massive – at least as big as Andrew's flat. The living room had a bar in the corner, plus a wide window that looked out over the city below. There was a wet-room bathroom and a bedroom almost as big as the living room, with a four-poster bed and eighteen pillows; Jenny actually counted.

Andrew tried the windows, but they wouldn't open any further than a few centimetres. 'Famous or not, the hotel don't trust you to not jump.'

'Do you reckon that's why rock bands throw TVs *through* the windows?'

'Probably.'

'So, no way out of the room...?'

Andrew pressed himself against the glass and peered down. 'No – and it would be quite the plummet. The lift has that camera pointing at it on the ground floor. If Jack Marsh left his room, it would have had to be down the stairs.'

They moved back into the corridor, walking in one big loop around the floor. Neither of them spotted a security camera and the only thing of any real interest was a fire door at either end. Both had a sign reading 'warning: this door is alarmed' above. They soon found themselves back near the lift. The stairs were adjacent and no key card was needed to open the door.

Andrew was out of breath by the time they'd descended four floors. He rested on the banister, staring up and around. The walls were whitewashed, the steps hard – nothing to see. No reason for guests to use them instead of the lift. Jenny said nothing about Andrew's lack of fitness, waiting until he was ready again and then they continued down. When they reached the first floor, Andrew motioned Jenny through the door and they did another loop. There was a window at the end of one of the corridors, but it didn't open any further than the one in their room. When they reached the door again, they headed back into the stairwell and continued down to the ground floor.

As well as the door that opened into reception that needed a key card from the other side, there was a space underneath the stairs, sealed by a locked door that read 'Maintenance Only'. There was another door opposite with a red and white no entry sign and the words 'Staff Only'.

Andrew turned to Jenny. 'What do you reckon?'

'You know me.'

Jenny was through the staff door before Andrew could say anything – not that he was going to stop her. It led into a far darker corridor with the outline of a door at the end. Andrew moved ahead and opened the second door, which led into another corridor, this one clanging with the sound of pans and voices. It smelled of something spicy and meaty.

'Can I help you?' a voice asked.

Andrew turned to see a young woman in an apron and cook's hat. She had been smoking an e-cigarette that was hastily being pocketed.

'We're a bit lost,' Andrew said.

She eyed him and Jenny suspiciously. 'There's only the kitchens back here.' She nodded to the door behind her. 'Reception's that way, or the door you came through, obviously.'

'Is there a way to get outside?'

'Through reception.'

'Yes, but is there *another* way?'

'Why?'

Andrew was beaten, but Jenny jumped in, gripping his arm firmly. 'My husband likes to know where all the fire exits are. He gets a bit panicky.' She squeezed him and gazed up adoringly. 'Poor love.'

The kitchen worker peered between them again, though her features softened. She pointed past them towards the direction of the noise. 'There's a fire exit that way.'

'Is it alarmed?' Andrew asked.

'Yeah, but no one's going to bother about that if there's a fire.'

She stepped to one side, freeing the door that would lead back to reception. Andrew took the hint and passed through it, finding himself in the bar. Once closed, it was almost impossible to know it was a door at all. It was covered with the same dimpled padding as the walls around the bar and, from what Andrew could see, only opened one way.

They headed back to the lift, but couldn't say much as there was already a bickering couple inside, arguing about how much money they'd spent in the Arndale Centre.

When the lift opened at their floor, Andrew and Jenny headed to the room. Once they were inside with the door closed, Jenny sat on the bed, bouncing up and down. 'Do you reckon Jack Marsh could have left by the fire door close to the kitchen?' she asked.

Andrew rested against the wall. 'Maybe. It doesn't mean he's involved in anything that happened to Michelle, but it *is* a way out. The police would know about the door, though. They would've asked staff about it, wondering if anyone saw him around – plus it's alarmed. And how would *he* know about it? If he was determined to do something to harm his girlfriend, it seems like a weird plan. Wait until he's holed up with his teammates in a hotel, then sneak out a back door. Even if he did, how would he get back in?'

'Hmm...' Jenny didn't seem quite so sure.

'There's every chance Michelle simply fell in the canal,' Andrew added. 'There are a few every year.'

Jenny motioned to the room: 'Why are we doing this then?'

They looked at each other and Andrew didn't have an answer. Perhaps, because numerous people *did* drown in the canal, there was the odd one that police didn't investigate properly, especially when the victim had copious amounts of alcohol in his or her system.

'Do you reckon the alarms on the fire exits work?' Jenny asked.

'I suppose.'

'Have you ever thought about it, though? All these places – hotels, offices, shops and so on. They all say their fire exits are alarmed because they don't want people to exit through the wrong place – or because they're worried of some potential break-in. Imagine how much all that would cost. You could stick up a sign *saying* there's an alarm and no one will bother to open it because of that – or you could *actually* install the alarm system. One costs a lot more than the other but the outcome is the same.'

'I think—'

Andrew didn't get a chance to finish his sentence because Jenny was bounding away from him, out of the room, towards the opposite end of the corridor. He called after her first and then started jogging, but it was already too late. She arrived at the fire exit a moment before he did. There was a horizontal bar across the door and it looked like it opened onto a set of metal stairs.

'Ten quid says there's no alarm,' Jenny said, one hand on the bar.

Andrew tried to sound firm: 'Don't open the door, Jen.'

'Twenty?'

'We've already aroused the suspicions of the guy checking us in because I live down the road – then the cook because she knows we went through a staff-only door. What's going to happen when that alarm goes off?'

'You're assuming there *is* an alarm.'

Andrew glanced up towards a small metal box that was pinned to the wall above the door. 'That looks like an alarm to me.'

'Pfft. If Jack Marsh left this hotel, he could've gone out through the fire exit, down the stairs and he'd be on the road,' Jenny said. 'Easy-peasy. The police wouldn't bother checking because why would they? Something says it's alarmed and you believe it.'

'Jen—'

Too late.

Jenny heaved the bar down and shoved the door open. A

split-second later, an ear-piercing shriek rattled through the corridor, making Andrew wince. He stuck his fingers in his ears, but it barely dimmed the racket, which was so loud it actually hurt.

'Oops,' Jenny mouthed.

7

Andrew weaved around the escalator and found himself at the end of a long tunnel in between two stores. Shoppers passed on either side of him, but the Arndale Centre was nowhere near as busy as he'd seen it in the past. Being the biggest shopping centre in the middle of Manchester meant it was bedlam in the run-up to Christmas, not to mention the Boxing Day sales. Not so much in April.

Jenny quickly caught him, bouncing excitedly on her heels as Andrew nodded towards the fire door at the end of the tunnel. 'Do you reckon that one's alarmed?' She grinned. 'You're never going to let me live this down, are you? You cause one little evacuation and suddenly you're the person who sets off alarms.'

'I thought they were going to throw us out of the hotel.'

'We're not even staying there! Anyway, I reckon that deputy manager bought it that I was suffering from low blood sugar and collapsed. He definitely seemed concerned.'

Andrew raised his eyebrows. 'The one thing you're definitely *not* suffering from is low blood sugar.'

At the mention of sugar, Jenny turned towards the American candy shop that hadn't been there the last time Andrew had been in the centre. The window was filled with boxes of hyperactivity-inducing cereal, the colours of which were so luminous, Andrew felt slightly dizzy looking at them.

'No way,' he said.

Jenny grinned as she set off, nodding towards the next rank of shops. 'C'mon, it's over here.'

Andrew followed until they reached the type of clothes shop he would have normally been too intimidated to even look at, let alone enter. The window was full of skinny, stick-like mannequins dressed in barely there outfits which would no doubt cost something in the region of a small principality's gross domestic product. Jenny had no such issues, breezing inside and heading straight for a rack of short dresses. Andrew had little option but to follow. He stood at her shoulder, wondering if he seemed more like her weird father or a creepy older boyfriend. Neither was a good look.

Jenny removed something short and purple from the rack and turned, holding it in front of herself. 'Megan's over there,' she said, nodding towards the other side of the store.

Megan Halfpenny had changed a lot from the picture Andrew had seen of her in school uniform alongside Jack Marsh. Her gingery hair was now a much brighter red and had been woven into some sort of physics-defying cross between a plait and a bun.

There was another member of staff talking into a phone behind the tills, with Megan off to the side, chatting to a customer and doing a lot of nodding.

Jenny took something silvery from the rack and headed towards Megan carrying both dresses, chirping a 'come on' in Andrew's direction.

'Stunning,' Megan was in the middle of saying, still nodding at the other customer. 'You look utterly stunning in that.'

The woman to whom Megan was talking definitely did not look stunning in the dress she was trying on. She turned sideways to look into the full-length mirror but that didn't stop the dress being a snot-coloured green, with weird puffy bits around the arms. It wasn't her fault, but the outfit made her look as if she'd been partially inflated. With Megan still nodding enthusiastically, the customer also started nodding.

Andrew figured day one of training to work in a clothes shop must be nodding and complimenting customers while pretending said customer didn't look like a dropped blancmange in an appallingly ill-fitting pink dress.

After even more nodding, the customer turned back to the changing rooms. 'I think I'm going to get this,' she said.

The woman disappeared, while Jenny held up her two dresses, smiling at Megan and saying she was going to try them on. A moment later, the two women were off in the changing rooms, leaving Andrew alone with Megan. She smiled awkwardly at him and he smiled back – or tried to, at least. It might have been some sort of grimace. Sometimes it felt like his face did its own thing and he was left dealing with the consequences.

At least one ice age passed before Jenny and the other woman emerged. The one with the snotty dress thanked Megan and then headed to the tills, while Jenny stood in front of the mirror and turned to Andrew. She was wearing the purple dress, which looked as if it had been made for her. It clung perfectly and she did a small curtsy.

'Well,' she said to Andrew, 'what d'you think?'

'It's, er, purple...?'

She rolled her eyes, turning to Megan. 'He's useless. What do *you* think?'

'Stunning,' Megan said. 'You look utterly stunning in that.'

Jenny smoothed down a crease that wasn't there. 'Yeah, it's not bad...'

'If you buy today,' Megan said, 'you get ten per cent off in our sale – plus, if you sign up to our mailing list at the counter, you get another ten per cent off.'

Jenny turned back to her, padding forward in bare feet, changing tack with astonishing ease. 'Can we have a quick word about Jack Marsh?'

There was a pause in which Megan stared at her open-mouthed. 'Um...'

'It's not what you think,' Jenny added hastily.

'I already said no to the papers.'

'We're not journalists. We want to stick up for Jack.'

'Who are you?'

'Private investigators.' Jenny nodded at Andrew. 'Well, he is. He's got the ID card and everything. I'm Jenny and he's Andrew.'

Megan glanced quickly towards the counter, where the first customer was typing her PIN into the card machine. She opened her mouth to say something, but then stopped herself. 'How are you sticking up for Jack?' she asked.

'People are saying he's done something and we're looking into how true it is.'

Megan frowned slightly. 'How do you think I can help? I've not seen him in three years.'

'You can give us some background, though.'

The first customer called 'thank you' and waved towards Megan, then headed out of the shop.

Andrew shuffled awkwardly on the spot, unsure how he could help. Standing up to gangsters twice his size: no problem. Young women: not a chance.

'I can take a break in half an hour,' Megan said. 'There's a food hall on the top floor and we could maybe talk then...?'

'Okay,' Jenny replied.

'It's just...' There was a pregnant pause in which Megan looked at Jenny and Jenny looked at Andrew. Eventually,

Megan decided to spell it out: 'I'm on commission,' she said, almost apologetically – though not quite.

Jenny nodded, continuing to look at Andrew, having apparently figured that out already.

'How much?' Andrew asked as reality finally dawned.

'Three hundred,' Jenny said.

Andrew half-coughed, half-choked.

'Minus the discount,' Megan added.

'So still two hundred and fifty odd,' Andrew replied, recovering.

Neither of the women replied initially, until Jenny lofted her satchel. 'I don't have any money on me.'

It was, of course, typical. She'd carry around chocolate, cakes, biscuits, a picnic for five people – but money? Why would a person need that?

'Fine,' Andrew said, removing his wallet from his pocket and handing it over. 'But, technically, that dress will be mine.'

Jenny winked. 'You'll look stunning in it.'

Andrew couldn't figure out what the food hall smelled of. It was definitely something fried, and might have been meaty, though there were also hints of rotting carcass. Jenny had already eaten a fresh doughnut and had taken to untying and retying her shoelaces, presumably to give herself something to do with her hands that didn't involve eating.

Megan appeared a little after thirty minutes had passed. She bought three tacos loaded with oozing brown meat, fluorescent green guacamole and sour cream.

'How did you know where I worked?' she asked, sitting at their table. She didn't sound too concerned.

'Facebook,' Jenny replied. 'Plus Instagram and Twitter. Pretty much everywhere, really.'

Megan shrugged. 'Do you know Jack?'

Jenny shook her head. 'Not directly.'

'So what *do* you want?'

'To ask you about the Jack you knew.'

Megan started picking at her food, scooping the guacamole out first with her fingers. 'What are people saying he's done?'

Jenny glanced to Andrew, who offered the tiniest shake of his head. 'We can't really say,' Jenny replied.

'So you want me to tell you what I know, without you saying why?'

'I suppose...'

Megan crunched into the first taco and then wiped her mouth with her finger. She chewed and swallowed, then added: 'It's to do with a girl, isn't it?'

'Why do you think that?' Jenny said.

She shrugged. 'What else is it going to be?'

Jenny was unfazed. 'When did you first start going out with Jack?'

'Thirteen or fourteen. We'd been at the same schools all the way through from when we were five. It was one of those things that happened almost just because. I don't even remember him asking me out, or the other way round. We were hanging about all the time and then we were boyfriend-girlfriend.'

'Didn't he end up leaving school at some point?'

Megan cracked open the rest of the tacos and started to eat with a fork. She had a mouthful of beef but nodded, making an 'mmm' sound. 'I think it was the year we did our GCSEs. He was too young to sign a proper football contract, but they had his parents sign this thing that meant he got this special tutoring. I don't remember properly. You'd have to ask him.'

'Were you still going out then?'

'Yeah. He said we'd stay together forever, but I guess that's the type of thing you say as a kid. I think I knew it wasn't going to last.'

'What changed?'

Megan squished her lips together and puffed out a breath. 'He did – but it wasn't really his fault. I was annoyed then, but now I reckon it was always going to happen. He had all these people around him – agents offering him money and cars, older players talking about things they'd get up to, journalists making him feel important.' She paused, licking her lips. 'Other girls as well.'

Jenny continued: 'Were the women a problem?'

Megan shook her head. 'Not then. It was more his mum being in his ear all the time. She'd tell him I wasn't good enough for him. I was some council-estate chav and he was going to be a superstar. She was terrified I was going to get pregnant and that he'd be stuck with me.'

'You didn't get on with her then?'

'We never really met, and when we did, she hardly said anything. I found out most of that through Jack. He used to laugh about it. I think he just liked spending time with me because his mum disapproved.'

Jenny took that in, offering a quick glance to Andrew before continuing. 'When did you break up?'

Megan ate a couple of forkfuls of her food and then leaned back in her seat. 'Do you really need to know this?'

Jenny shook her head. 'Perhaps not. It's up to you.'

She chewed another mouthful, seemingly considering it. 'It was on my nineteenth birthday. I know that makes it sound like we'd been going out for five years, but we hadn't really. We'd break up and make up, plus there were times when I wouldn't see him for a week or two because he'd be off touring, or playing or whatever. Things drifted and then he didn't turn up to my party – didn't even call to say he couldn't make it. I ended up phoning him and saying we were done. I got a text about a week later saying "sorry" – but that was it. I've seen him out and about a couple of times since – but only to say hello to.' She paused, smiling and even giggling slightly. 'He did buy me a birthday present in the end, though.'

Megan waited for Jenny's inevitable question and then added: 'He bought me a brand-new car. That was four years ago and I've still got it. I guess it was a sort of goodbye gift, too. I never asked for it, but Jack could be weird like that. He was on a lot of money and he'd pick an expensive place for us to go out and eat. He'd make a big deal about having to pay for it – even though it was his choice and he knew I'd never be able to afford anything. He'd go on about that for ages, then turn around and buy something crazy a week later. As well as the car, he got me a ring the Christmas before, too. I ended up selling it a year ago and it was still worth two grand then, so I've no idea what it cost new.'

'Do you regret breaking up with him?'

Megan shook her head. 'It would never have worked. I'm surprised we were together that long.'

'Why?'

It was subtle, but Megan's posture changed. She'd been relaxed: leaning back and tolerating the conversation, if not slightly enjoying the memories. After Jenny's question, she ate some more food but then leaned forward, elbows on the table. She sighed and looked at Andrew, perhaps wondering why he was there given he'd said little.

'Jack wasn't always nice.' Megan's voice was a whisper, almost lost among the chatter of the people around them. She glanced up, making sure they'd heard and then focused on her food again.

'What did he do?' Jenny asked.

Perhaps subconsciously, Megan brushed her right eye. When she realised Andrew was watching, she quickly moved her hand away.

'Did he hit you?' Jenny asked.

The reply didn't come immediately, but, when it did, it was even quieter than before. 'Once.'

'You don't have to tell us anything you don't want to.'

There was another pause, leaving Andrew to think about how he would never have said that. The biggest problem with this job was that people didn't need to speak to them. There were no warrants, no compulsion. Any information paid for could be compromised, even though, indirectly, that was what had happened with him buying the dress. Actually telling Megan she didn't have to talk to them could've broken the spell and encouraged her to stand up and walk away. Instead, Jenny had made it sound like she cared. Perhaps she did? Andrew was never sure with her.

Megan nodded, breathing through her nose. 'I'd spilled some nail varnish and a bit got on these new trainers he'd bought. I didn't see it coming.' She rubbed her eye again. 'He bought me a necklace to say sorry. I've still got it.'

'How old were you then?'

'Seventeen, I think.'

'And that was the only time…?'

Megan shrank in front of them, cradling her arms across her front. 'It was partly my fault again. I got mud in his car and…'

There was a long pause in which Andrew wanted to jump in and say it wasn't her fault, but the conversation was little to do with him.

From nowhere, Megan shunted her chair back with a loud screech. 'Look, when he gave me the car, he also gave me a piece of paper from a lawyer saying that if I spoke to the papers or whatever, he'd be able to sue me. I don't really want to say any more.'

Jenny and Megan continued watching each other, but there was another long pause in which neither of them spoke. Andrew thought about the implications of the gagging contract

Megan had been asked to sign. That could be why she hadn't sold a story to the media. Perhaps the car was what she got for signing it, or maybe it was a genuine gift?

Andrew eventually broke the silence, speaking slowly and deliberately. 'If you think he could sue you, why talk to us?'

Megan stared at him briefly and then turned away. Her voice was croaky and soft. 'Sometimes it's nice to have someone that'll listen.'

8

Jenny was eating a bowl of Sugar Puffs at her desk when Andrew got into the office the next day. 'Brew?' she asked, before he'd sat down.

'I'll do it.'

Andrew dumped a spoonful of instant coffee granules in his mug and clicked the kettle on, then leaned against the fridge, watching Jenny eat. If she felt self-conscious, then she didn't show it, crunching her way through her breakfast and then drinking the leftover milk by tipping the bowl upside down and emptying it into her mouth.

'It's hard to beat a good bowl of Sugar Puffs,' she said, with a satisfying gasp.

'I've never really been into cereal. I'm more of a toast sort of person.'

'Do you know there's a café in London that serves only toast?'

'Really? Why?'

Jenny shrugged. 'Who knows? That's London for you. Anyway – I've got us an appointment for later.'

'At the toast place?'

No! We're looking to rent a flat out Hulme way, so we have a viewing.'

It took Andrew a couple of seconds to realise what she was implying. 'Good stuff,' he said. 'I was going to get to the land-lord. What time?'

'Two o'clock – but there's something else you need to see first.' She waved him over to her desk and swivelled the monitor so the light wasn't reflecting quite so brightly. 'I should've found this earlier, but it was so obvious, I almost missed it.'

The screen was showing a large photo of Jack Marsh playing football. Instead of the sponsor's name on the front of his shirt, it had been altered to read 'danger'.

'What's this?' Andrew asked.

'Anna Applegate's blog. It's one long list of libels.'

She clicked onto a page marked 'The Truth'. At the top was a photo of Jack sitting with a pretty blonde woman in a restaurant somewhere. They were chatting amiably, obviously unaware the photo was being taken.

'Did Anna take that?' Andrew asked.

Jenny shook her head. 'It's from a magazine – one of those "spotted" column things. The woman he's with was in *Emmerdale.*'

Andrew peered closer at the picture but didn't recognise the blonde. Jenny scrolled down and pointed at the screen.

CITY SLICKER! *Soap siren Hannah Bertram was out and about last weekend, smooching with Premier League footballer, Jack Marsh. A witness says the blonde bombshell was tucking into a carb-loaded plate of penne. She must not know our golden rule: Forgetti da spaghetti.*

'Is that from the magazine column?' Andrew asked.
'Yep.'

'Who writes this?'

Jenny wagged a finger at him. 'Snob. Anyway, that's not what's libellous.'

'Who cares what someone else is having to eat?'

Jenny ignored him, scrolling to the next passage of text.

CITY STRIPPER! *Soap siren Hannah Bertram was taking her life in her hands last weekend, smooching with Premier League simpleton, Jack Marsh. A witness says the blonde bombshell was being lined up as Marsh's next victim after a string of sex attacks. She must not know our golden rule: Don't Turn Your Back On Jack.*

'I'm not sure I get what's going on,' Andrew said, having read it through twice.

Jenny clicked onto a second page, this one showing Jack Marsh wearing a Santa hat. He was in a hospital, next to the bed of a grinning but ghostly pale child and handing over a large Christmas present.

'Anna Applegate's going through the papers and magazines, finding anything she can about Jack and then uploading it to her site. She leaves the original caption or story, but then adds her own twist. Everything's about him being some sort of sexual predator or a danger to women.' She pointed at the picture of Jack with the sick child. 'You don't want to read this one.'

Andrew took Jenny's word for it. 'Anna didn't tell us that when she was here.'

'No... I'm surprised it's not been shut down. You know what lawyers are like.'

'How did you find it?'

'Someone had linked to it on a football forum.'

'Is it easy to search for?'

Jenny didn't reply, instead trying it out. She typed in a

dozen different search combinations revolving around Jack's name, his club, football and the like. Anna Applegate's libel-ridden blog didn't appear on the top page for any of the search terms.

'I guess that if they launch some sort of legal complaint, it'll draw attention to it,' Andrew said. 'More people will see it if they make a fuss – this way, it's just a woman ranting to a handful of people.'

He sat on his chair and swivelled to face Jenny.

'Does this mean we shouldn't do any more work on the case?' she asked.

It took Andrew a few moments to reply. 'Probably...'

'She thinks he killed her daughter – we knew that then and we know it now.'

Andrew spun back to his desk, drumming his fingers on the tabletop. 'It's one thing to be angry, another to do this. I think we both have an inkling Jack Marsh might not be very nice – but what if everything he says is true? He had nothing to do with Michelle's death. Imagine if you were innocent and you knew all this was out there...?'

He was expecting a smart reply but instead Jenny was staring at him. When she realised he was watching her back, she spoke quietly. 'It's not nice to have people spread lies about you.'

She was right, of course – but it didn't feel as if she was expressing an opinion. There was recognition there.

'Are you all right?' Andrew asked.

Jenny blinked and then the dimple in her cheek returned and she was smiling again. 'Yeah, sorry, spaced out for a second. What are you going to do?'

Andrew lingered on her for a moment longer and then picked up his phone. 'I'm going to let Mrs Applegate choose whether she wants us to continue looking into things or if she wants that site to stay up. She can't have both.'

. . .

It took Andrew fifteen minutes to persuade Anna Applegate that she couldn't keep the anti-Jack site live *and* continue to employ him to look into her daughter's death. He'd expected her to tell him to get lost, but, when she realised he wasn't going to budge – and that he didn't care about her money – she wilted. She told him the site would be offline by the end of the day and then asked if he'd found anything. Andrew gave it the usual 'don't want to get any hopes up' line and she seemed satisfied enough.

He felt exhausted by the time he hung up, leaning back in his seat and yawning as if he'd just woken up. Jenny was flitting around, sorting the recently arrived mail.

'Yours,' she said, putting a padded envelope on his desk and then continuing through the stack. 'Yours, yours, mine, bin, bill, yours, bin, bin, bill, yours, bin.' She finished by flicking the final piece of junk mail into the bin along with the others and then nodded at the Thailand postcard that was still resting against his monitor. 'No new postcards.'

'Okay.'

'Were you expecting another…?'

Andrew picked up his pile of mail, pretending he hadn't heard. The first was the water bill, which was typically exorbitant considering they only used the tap to fill up the kettle, plus flushed the toilet a few a times a day.

Jenny took the hint, returning to her desk and tapping away at her computer.

The next letter was something from the bank, then more junk mail cunningly disguised as non-junk because it had his name on the front. By the time he got to the padded envelope, Andrew was wondering if he could recall the last time he received anything interesting. He remembered being a child, writing out stamped-addressed envelopes to enter competitions on television. Every once in a while, he'd get something himself from a relative on holiday. Getting and sending letters was a thrilling experience, now it was another in life's long list of mundane happenings.

He was about to rip it open when he noticed there was no proper address or stamp on the front. It simply read: 'Mr Andrew Hunter, Private Investigator' in felt-tip-etched capital letters.

Andrew turned and held it up. 'Jen – was this with the rest of the mail?'

She peered up from her desk and shrugged. 'Everything was in a pile on the doorstep.'

There was nothing written on the back and the envelope was new, sealed with the glue it came with, rather than any sort of tape. Andrew pulled one of the ends apart at arm's length, not sure what he was expecting. He couldn't remember having anything hand-delivered before. When nothing leapt out, he peeped inside but was unable to see anything. Still at arm's length, he tipped it upside down onto his desk, whereby two rectangular pieces of thin cardboard dropped.

Andrew picked them up, glancing at the first and then reading the words on the second. It was handwritten, the characters topped and tailed with elegant swooshes and curls, the neatness of which Andrew couldn't have managed if his life depended on it. His eyes darted along the paragraphs and then returned to the start again, reading the note over and over.

'Andrew.'

Jenny's single word brought him back into the room and he spun on his chair, coughing and blinking because of the light.

'What?'

'You've not moved in three minutes. Nearly four.'

Andrew held up the first piece of card. 'I've been sent an invite for Man City against Everton tomorrow. There's a spot reserved for me in an executive box.'

Jenny pouted out her bottom lip. 'Very nice. If you're going to watch something you're not bothered about, you may as well be in comfort. I've heard you get free food, free drink, the lot. Who invited you?'

Andrew switched the cards around, showing her the second that had been handwritten. 'Thomas Braithwaite.'

'Oh.' A pause. 'I thought getting those pictures of Max Grayson dealing in that club meant everything might be even again...?'

'Me too...'

'Do you think it's because he knows something about Jack Marsh?'

Andrew didn't reply, instead rereading the card.

'Because, if it is,' Jenny continued, 'then how does he know what we're looking into?'

Andrew wasn't listening. He was focusing on the final three words, which had been underlined: *Don't be late.*

9

Manish Bose was late.

Jenny was in the passenger seat of Andrew's car tapping away on her phone as he sat and watched the front door of the flat they were supposed to be viewing.

'What time did you arrange?' Andrew asked.

'Two.'

'It's ten past. Did you definitely arrange for two?'

'Definitely. Scout's honour.'

'Were you in the Scouts?'

'No – I was only interested in joining when someone said they didn't let girls in. When I found out they *did* accept girls, it all seemed a bit boring.'

Andrew found that unsurprising. 'I'm going round back,' he said. 'Call me if he turns up.'

After getting out of the car, Andrew slipped into the alley that skirted the rear of the flats. Everything was one- or two-bedroom, red-brick and new-build – but it still had a look as if no one chose to live in the area – they were forced to through circumstance. The lane was covered with moss and black bin bags, plus someone had dumped a pizza box against a gate, leaving a red and yellow gooey mess mashed into the gutter. Someone a few streets over was playing some sort of booming crime against music, the brain-frying bass doing its absolute best to annoy anyone in a half-mile radius.

Andrew wasn't sure in which flat Michelle Applegate had lived, but it wouldn't make a great deal of difference given everything looked the same. The lane cut between a row of small houses on either side before opening back onto the narrow road, where yet more identikit Lego buildings had been plonked. Andrew had a peep over the back gate of one of the houses, but there was little to see because the space was so small. The bathroom in his Radisson suite had been larger than the play area any kids would get here.

As he reached the main road, Andrew's phone started to ring. He saw Jenny's name, so didn't bother to answer, instead quick-stepping around the corner until he was back where he'd started. Jenny was leaning against his car, chatting with an overweight Asian man, who was dressed in a long, cream thobe with sandals.

'Here he is,' Jenny said, pointing towards Andrew and offering a friendly wave. 'This is Mr Bose,' she added, indicating the man and then introducing Andrew. They all said hello and then the man unlocked the nearest flat and let them inside. It was even smaller inside than it seemed from the outside, a reverse TARDIS effect. What Andrew thought were small two-bedroom houses were instead minute one-bedroom flats. The living room and kitchen occupied the same space, with a small cupboard that was actually the bathroom and then a bedroom that could fit a bed and little else.

The landlord, perhaps as expected, introduced each room as if it was a wing of a palace before they ended up back in the living room. Jenny and Andrew nodded politely, as if they were actually interested. There was so little to see that the tour took barely two minutes.

'What do you think?' Mr Bose said, checking his watch.

Jenny spoke before Andrew could. 'Not bad,' she replied. 'How do you take payment?'

'Bank transfer or cash. No cheques.'

Jenny turned to Andrew, speaking absent-mindedly as if it had just come to her. 'One of my old friends used to live round here actually. I can't remember exactly where. I've not seen her for a couple of years.' She turned back to the landlord. 'You might remember her – Michelle...?'

He frowned slightly. 'I have lots of tenants.'

Jenny was unfazed. 'Michelle Applegate.'

His eyes narrowed and then widened. 'Applegate...?'

'Right. I visited her once, but that was ages ago. We fell out of contact.'

Mr Bose turned and waved a hand towards the opposite side of the street. 'Your friend owed me money.'

'Oh.'

The man bounced on his heels and puffed his chest up, making himself appear marginally taller. 'Her friend had a foul mouth, too.'

'Really?'

'And the neighbours complained, not to her – to me. So much noise. Noise, noise, noise. Music every night.'

'Are you sure that was Michelle?'

He clapped his hands and started to wag a finger at Jenny. 'Loads of rubbish, too. You have to pay for this stuff, you know? It costs money to go to the tip. She owed me money and then I had to pay more money to dump her stuff.' Mr Bose opened the door and motioned for Andrew and Jenny to exit. 'No more, I say. One was enough.'

'Sorry?'

'If you're a friend of her, then no.'

Jenny was in the doorway, level with the landlord. 'No what?'

'No rent. I've had it once, not again. You'll have to find somewhere else.'

'But—'

'No, out you go.'

At that, he pushed Andrew in the shoulder, sending him bumbling into Jenny and leaving them both on the short path outside. He slammed the door shut and then strode past them towards his van.

'I'm sorry for what happened to your friend,' he said, 'but not again. No, no, no.'

Mr Bose got into his van, closed the door and took out his phone. As he began to speak into it, Andrew and Jenny returned to the car and he started the engine.

'That was weird,' Jenny said.

Andrew eased away from the kerb and headed to the first T-junction, waiting even though there was no traffic. He eyed the van in his mirror, watching Mr Bose pull out without indicating and then drive with the phone to his ear. Andrew turned left and so did the van, so he immediately indicated left again, heading back along the street parallel to the flat they'd viewed. When his mirror was clear, Andrew pulled over to the side of the road again. He left the engine idling, still watching his mirrors.

'What are we doing?' Jenny asked.

'When you mentioned Michelle Applegate and he worked out who you meant, he waved a hand towards the row of flats opposite where we were. She probably lived in one of them, so let's knock on a door or two.'

'Sounds like she didn't get on with her neighbours,' Jenny replied. A van turned onto the street, but it was a different colour to Mr Bose's. 'How many landlords do you know who'll turn down money like that?' she added. 'Michelle must have been a really bad tenant if that's how he feels.'

'All the more reason for someone to remember her.'

Andrew checked his mirrors one final time and then switched off the engine. Jenny followed as they made their way back to the street they'd just left.

They walked the line of the flats opposite, waiting until they saw movement in one of the front windows and then knocking.

A woman with tufty, greasy brown hair answered, hoisting a young child who was sucking a dummy onto her shoulder. She looked as if she'd been expecting someone else as she took a half step back. 'A'ight...?' she said.

This time, Andrew did the talking. 'Hi,' he said, 'we're looking for someone named Michelle Applegate.'

She turned between the two, eyebrows creasing into a frown. 'Who are you?'

'Old friends,' Jenny replied quickly. 'She was in my year at school. I've been trying to track her down and my dad found someone who said she lived round this way.'

Jenny nudged Andrew with her elbow.

The child was fidgeting, so the woman put him down and told him to go and play in the living room. She glanced both ways along the street and then lowered her voice. 'Didn't you hear?' she said.

'Hear what?' Jenny replied.

'Sorry to be the one to tell you, but she died last year.'

'Oh...' Jenny turned to Andrew, her face full of such concern that he would've sworn she was genuinely stunned to discover the fate of her friend. 'I didn't know,' Jenny added.

'Did you know her?' Andrew asked.

The woman half shrugged, half shook her head. 'I don't want to talk ill of the dead and I know you were friends – but she lived two doors down and we didn't get on.' She looked at Jenny and winced slightly.

Andrew placed a hand on Jenny's shoulder. 'Do you want to go sit in the car?' he said. 'I'll be over in a minute.'

Jenny looked at him and then muttered 'thank you' to the woman. She turned and sauntered away in the direction of the car.

'Sorry,' Andrew said. 'I didn't realise.'

The woman batted a hand. 'Not your fault. Wish your daughter could've found out in a different way, but at least you know.'

'How did she die?' Andrew asked.

'In the canal. Drunk, they reckon. None of us here were surprised.'

'Did she drink a lot?'

The woman shrugged again. 'It weren't easy raising a wee baby here with her noise all through the night. Music, noise. Always leaving bottles in her front yard, too. It's hard enough round here, without all that.'

'Did she have any friends on the street we could talk to?'

The woman shook her head. 'What d'you reckon? I think I saw her mum round there once or twice, p'raps a lad or two. I didn't go sticking my nose in though.' She started to close the door and nodded towards the inside. 'I gotta get back.'

Andrew thanked her for her time and then set off back to the car. From what people were saying, it seemed like neither Jack Marsh nor Michelle Applegate were angels.

For now, he had far more pressing concerns – like the fact Jenny thought he could pass for her father and that the woman who'd opened the door believed it.

10

There was a party atmosphere around the vast expanse of tarmac as Andrew skirted through the crowds of football supporters. There were far more women than he'd expected – children, too. He'd not been to a live football match in nearly thirty years and all he could remember were lines of men shouting abuse at the referee.

Despite the warmth of the day, people were still wearing hats and scarves in City's sky blue. It was ninety minutes until kick-off and Andrew had expected the area around the stadium to be largely empty – but there was more to do than watch the game that would take place inside. There was an organised penalty competition for kids going on in one area, plus hot food stands, places to get drinks and all sorts of street traders selling everything and anything as long as it was in City colours.

As Andrew tried to figure out where he was going, there was a loud cheer and he turned to see a coach edging its way towards the stadium. When it stopped and the door hissed open, there was a second cheer. He watched as a man in a tracksuit – presumably a player – stepped down and automatically grabbed a pen from the closest supporter who was pressed behind a barrier. The player signed a dozen programmes with a swishing swirl that took barely half a second to create and then handed the pen back with a nod. Some of the other players did the same, while others kept their heads down and marched towards an open door of the stadium, listening – or at least *pretending* to listen – to music through sets of brightly coloured headphones.

Andrew found himself watching the small group of misfits behind the barrier. They were mainly men, all wearing City shirts, though there were a few women too. Each seemingly knew what they were doing, having arrived with pens, plus items they wanted signing. When an olive-skinned man with long hair stepped from the coach, they started singing a song about shooting and scoring, which drew a wave and smile. One of the fans behind the barrier was singing louder than the others and it was only then that Andrew noticed the fan had grown his hair and probably fake-tanned his skin in order to look more like the player. There was a couple jostling for position, trying to push in alongside him. The woman's shirt was heaving, the weedy man with glasses slotting in underneath her arm as if she was smuggling him through customs. He thrust a programme towards the long-haired player, but it was ignored. Next to them was a man at least a foot taller than anyone around him, wearing the full kit: socks, shorts and all. He wasn't singing, wasn't shouting, wasn't trying to get anything signed. He was simply watching. It was all a bit strange.

Another cheer went up as Jack Marsh stepped down from the coach. He was wearing bright blue headphones and carrying a small leather washbag. He offered a thin smile towards the crowd but didn't stop, striding towards the stadium and disappearing inside.

Andrew had seen enough, so he walked the long way

around the coach until he found a gate marked 'VIP entrance'. A pair of suited men were chatting to one another but went quiet as Andrew approached.

'Hi,' Andrew said, passing the largest one his driving licence. 'I was told to report here with ID. I think I'm in one of the executive boxes.'

The man eyed the ID and then scrolled along a list of names on an iPad. 'You *think* you're in a box?'

'I was sort of invited.'

'Hunter...' He tapped the screen and nodded, before opening the door and stepping aside. 'Someone will meet you at the top of the stairs. Show them your ID and they'll sort you out. Enjoy the match.'

Andrew thanked him and did as he was told, this time finding a woman in a suit who led him along a bright corridor until they reached a light blue door.

'The Braithwaite party is in here,' she said with a smile, not realising how ominous it all sounded, before opening the door for him. Andrew grimaced a near smile and then headed inside, whispering to himself to be calm.

The first person he set eyes upon was Iwan the brute. The white strip lights above made the scar on his head stand out even more than before – a slim line of white against the red of his skin. As Iwan eyed Andrew wordlessly, Andrew couldn't help but stare at it. A tyre iron would do that sort of thing. Iwan continued to say nothing, although his gaze never left Andrew.

The room had one long table close to the door that was piled with food. A pair of slide-open metal serving trays were filled with curry on one side and pasta on the other, with rows of sandwiches and cakes on the tables. There were two ice buckets nearby with wine bottles poking from the top, and a pair of fridges underneath, stocked with bottles of beer.

There were a handful of other men in suits milling around

whom Andrew didn't recognise, but then a voice boomed over them all.

'Mr Hunter, what a pleasant surprise.'

He turned as a hand clamped down on his shoulder and then Thomas Braithwaite was at his side, appearing as if from nowhere. Andrew hadn't seen him in a couple of months but nothing had changed. Braithwaite's black hair was greying but in a gentlemanly way that left him appearing seasoned and wise. He was trim and lean with neat facial hair – but none of that mattered once his eyes focused on a person. They were the blue of the ocean in a holiday brochure, enough to freeze a target to the spot. As soon as Andrew turned, Braithwaite's eyes lasered in on him and he found himself gulping.

Braithwaite clasped Andrew's hand, squeezing tightly as he shook it. 'Nice of you to come.'

'I, um—'

Braithwaite opened his jacket to reveal the dark blue football shirt underneath. 'I hope you're going to join us in being an Evertonian for the day...?'

There was an undercurrent cheer of approval from a couple of nearby men who'd been listening in.

'I'm not a big football fan,' Andrew replied.

Braithwaite laughed, finally releasing Andrew's hand. 'Why am I not surprised?'

He beckoned Andrew away from the food, through the mêlée, until they were at a floor-to-ceiling window. Beyond was the perfect green of the pitch and row after row of largely empty sky-blue seats. Braithwaite slid the glass open and stepped out onto a balcony overlooking the pitch, nodding Andrew through and then closing the door behind them. When Andrew looked behind, he could see Iwan hovering close to the glass, gaze still unwaveringly focused on him.

The seats on the balcony were, unsurprisingly, the same blue as the others in the stadium. Braithwaite sat in the central one, meaning he was almost exactly level with the halfway line. He patted the spot next to him, waiting for Andrew to sit and then putting his feet up on the rail.

'I'm glad you accepted my invitation,' he said.

'It sounded like more of a request.'

Braithwaite pressed back further into the chair and laughed. He reached underneath, emerging with an already open beer bottle and swigging from the top. 'How are you, Mr Hunter?'

'Fine.'

'How's business?'

'That's fine as well.'

'What about your little assistant?' He turned to Andrew and winked. 'She still "fine"?'

Andrew turned away, facing the pitch. 'She's none of your business.'

Braithwaite nodded and then laughed again, louder this time. Andrew said nothing. Below, a group of people in fluorescent tops were trying to wrestle a sponsor's banner into place over the centre circle. Someone had dropped their end and it was flapping in the breeze as they chased after it. No matter what the job, there was always one.

'Fascinating, isn't it?' Braithwaite said after another swig of his beer.

'What is?'

'That you have an interest in Jack Marsh.'

Andrew felt a chill. He said nothing at first, focusing instead on trying to show he wasn't concerned. 'Are you following me?' he asked. 'Spying on me?'

Braithwaite didn't answer straight away, letting the tension build. 'Not really.' He nodded behind, towards the glass. 'Iwan has big ears – and I always keep an eye on my investments.'

'I'm not your investment.'

Braithwaite dropped his feet to the floor, leaning forward

and pressing his fingers into a triangle. He turned to Andrew. 'You keep telling yourself that, Mr Hunter. Remember that unsolved fire near to your aunt's flat? Wouldn't it be awful if the police found a jerrycan with your DNA on?'

Andrew felt his anger flaring. He spoke through clenched teeth: 'I had nothing to do with that.'

'Do you think innocent men never go to prison? We both know that's not the case.'

Andrew turned, locking eyes with Braithwaite. It felt dangerous. 'I've never set fire to any flat,' he said.

Braithwaite smirked as the doors slid open behind them. Andrew feared Iwan, but it was a waitress in a short dark skirt and white blouse. She was defying gravity by lofting a tray loaded with champagne-filled flutes and canapés, somehow managing to keep everything level, even while opening the door, closing the door and then descending half a dozen steps. There had to be witchery involved somewhere. Or invisible wires. Andrew knew being a waiter would have never been a job for him – he'd have been dropping stuff all over the place.

Braithwaite accepted a glass of champagne, plus a couple of the finger foods. Andrew declined everything with an apologetic smile and wave. He was regretting showing up.

After the waitress had returned inside, Braithwaite was quiet as he ate. Below, the players were warming up on the pitch, with a multitude of balls flying in all directions. To Andrew, a multi-ball game seemed a far more interesting prospect than watching an entire match in which only one was used.

'Why am I here?' Andrew asked.

Braithwaite crunched into his final prawn-topped cracker thing and chewed slowly. He dabbed his mouth with a handkerchief that had been in his jacket pocket and then turned to face Andrew once more. 'I've had something stolen – and I want it found,' he said.

'I can give you the number for the police if you want. Dial nine, then another nine – and then one more nine.'

Braithwaite smiled with his lips but not his eyes. Andrew knew he should have shut his mouth, but sometimes – since starting to work with Jenny – there was a tiny part of him that embraced the menace.

'This is a matter in which the police will not be involved.'

'I'm not hunting down drugs or anything like that for you.'

Braithwaite drummed his fingers on the armrest between the seats. 'I'm not sure who you think you're dealing with, Mr Hunter – but I'm a legitimate businessman.'

'Is that why you were talking about jerrycans and house fires?'

The drumming stopped but Braithwaite's eyes didn't leave Andrew. The steely, staring blue burned gravely. 'Thin ice, Mr Hunter.' He let it sink in and then added: 'I had an antique violin imported to a music shop in Manchester city centre—'

'A violin?!' Andrew was unable to stop himself.

'What are you trying to say?' Braithwaite replied harshly.

'Nothing... What's it worth?'

'The money, Mr Hunter, is irrelevant. It was – *is* – my property and it's been taken. I know it wasn't any of the bigger operators in the city, so it'll be some street kids or estate urchins mucking about.' Braithwaite hissed the sentences, becoming clipped and more annoyed.

'How was it taken?' Andrew asked.

'It was at BD Music in the Northern Quarter. The man who owns the shop is renowned for quality repairs and restorations. He's a good friend and is mortified by what happened. I want you to know that I do not blame him in any way for the outcome. Someone broke in from the alley at the back of his shop.'

Braithwaite reached into the inside pocket of his jacket and took out a small silver USB memory stick. He passed it to

Andrew, who flipped it over. Aside from the manufacturer's name, there was nothing written on it.

'What is it?' Andrew asked.

'You'll find out.' He jabbed a finger towards the pitch. 'I don't care how you go about things, but I do not want you talking to the shop owner. Find another way.'

Andrew didn't feel the need to point out that he hadn't actually agreed to find Braithwaite's violin. It wasn't as if he was going to turn him down. He wasn't that brave.

Down on the pitch, the players trotted off towards the changing rooms. The rows of sky-blue seats were now around a quarter filled.

'If I find out who took your violin, what are you going to do to the person who took it?' Andrew asked.

'I don't necessarily need names – I just want what's mine.'

'If I can't talk to the owner and you won't tell me what's on the pen drive, what do you think I can do?'

Braithwaite reached across and patted Andrew's cheek. Although he did it lightly, there was a solidness to his touch, letting Andrew know he was capable of something much harder. Andrew pulled away. 'You're an investigator, Mr Hunter – a good one from what I've seen – with a clever assistant—'

'Don't bring Jenny or anyone else into this.'

'So don't disappoint me.'

There was a thorny silence in which Andrew felt as if everything was at a crossroads. He didn't want to work with, or for, Thomas Braithwaite. He wanted nothing to do with the man – but perhaps, if he could find the damned violin, it would put an end to their business. He had thought the same thing after getting evidence of Max Grayson's drug-dealing.

One more job.

Just one more job.

But how many one more jobs would there be?

'If I do this,' Andrew said, 'we're done. No more "one final thing". No more visits from your ape.'

Braithwaite laughed. 'I'm sure Iwan would appreciate being called an ape.'

'I mean it.'

Braithwaite reached into his other inside pocket and took out a small photograph. 'I don't like failures, Mr Hunter,' he said, passing the picture across.

The photo showed a browny-orange violin. The sides were slightly battered and two strings were missing. It looked old and the only marking that distinguished it was a dark 'LK' scratched into the wood next to the chin rest.

'What does LK stand for?' Andrew asked.

'Louis Kleinholt – the person who made it.'

Andrew spent another second or two eyeing the photo and then pocketed it. The afternoon was not what he'd expected – and the violin made things all the weirder. He stood to leave but Braithwaite held an arm across him, though didn't stand himself.

'Stay and watch the match – free drink, free food. A game of football.'

'Football's not really my thing.'

'Fine – but if you wait around until after the match, if you're *really* lucky, I'll introduce you to Jack Marsh.'

11

Andrew sat on the balcony throughout the match, not entirely sure what was going on. One team scored, then the other, then the other team again. There was lots of shouting and, in the end, Thomas Braithwaite didn't seem too pleased about the result – which was at least one thing Andrew enjoyed about the day. Iwan prowled throughout at the back of the small row of seats. He didn't say a word to Andrew, didn't need to because his beady stare said it all.

After the match, Braithwaite's friends disappeared, full of backslaps and boozy thanks. Braithwaite himself was tipsy, eyes slightly glazed, speech not quite as crisp as Andrew had known before. Iwan was as alert as ever.

Despite his state, Braithwaite knew where he was going. He led Andrew and Iwan out of the box and along a maze of corridors, flashing some ID card to a couple of security types and eventually emerging in front of a door marked 'Players' Lounge'. Inside was a large hall, lined with comfy soft chairs and more tables of food. Large televisions were pinned all around, each showing what appeared to be one long loop of various goals being scored, intercut with a woman in an impossibly tight dress pretending to be excited about it. A wide, well-stocked bar was opposite the door, but waitresses were flitting around with more drinks anyway as old men in suits mixed with the players and their wives.

Braithwaite pulled Andrew to the side, nodding towards an area underneath one of the televisions, where a suited Jack Marsh was tucking into a plate of chicken. In the seat next to him was an older woman with a grey bob of hair and sky-blue trouser suit. On the other side, a tall black man was tapping away on a phone. His suit was so sharp that looking at it was like being punched in the face.

'There's your man,' Braithwaite said.

'Who are the other two?' Andrew asked.

'His mother, Eloise, and his agent. Would you like an introduction?'

Braithwaite stepped forward but Andrew didn't move. 'I'll figure it out,' he said.

With a shrug and a glance to Iwan, Braithwaite replied, 'Suit yourself' and then headed off to the far side of the room, where he backslapped and said hello to a player Andrew didn't recognise. They were soon chuckling away like lifelong friends, which, perhaps, they were.

Andrew found himself a seat in the corner of the room and took out his phone, using it as a shield that allowed him to watch the room while making it look like he was eyeing the device. After a few moments, another player joined Jack by the television. They chatted and laughed together, before the agent stood and hurried from the room, phone to his ear.

On the other side, Braithwaite had found a group of people he clearly knew – a mix of players and older men. Braithwaite continued to drink, with Iwan nearby, watching but saying nothing.

When Jack finished his food, he left the mucky plate on the floor next to his seat, muttered something to his mother and then headed off towards a separate group of largely women. Men outnumbered women in the lounge by at least two to one and, though some of the females were clearly wives and girl-friends, there was also a small number of women seemingly unattached. They were wearing short, identical dresses in the colour of a team sponsor. Jack homed in on them like one dog to another dog's arse, full of smiles and hands-in-pockets boyishness.

When he'd been sitting between his mother and agent, Jack had been surly and silent, but in among the women, he was another person. He'd touch one of the girls on her lower back, then lean in to hear what she had to say, before firing back with something of his own. Some laughed, some either didn't know who he was or didn't care. Eventually he seemed to settle on a woman with long raven hair that curled along her back. He whispered something in her ear and she giggled girl-ishly, playfully pushing him away with her well-manicured fingers and then leaning in herself to say something back to him. Of all the things he *might* be, Jack Marsh was definitely a ladies' man.

Andrew continued to watch for a few minutes, before real-ising that he was in danger of standing out. He was by himself, staring at a phone screen – and if anyone challenged him about who he was, he wouldn't really have an answer.

First, he sidled to the bar, ordering a sparkling water and trying to listen in to whatever Jack might be saying to the woman. All he could make out from them was a series of giggles, which was drowned out by the general hubbub around the room.

Unsure what else to do, Andrew crossed towards the tele-visions and the comfy seats, sitting in the spot where Jack had been a few minutes before. Eloise Marsh glanced up to him, didn't smile, and looked the other way again.

'Hi,' Andrew said.

She turned back to him, eyes narrow. 'Hi,' she replied, offering the most watery of watery smiles before once again looking away.

'My name's Andrew.'

'If you want to say hello to him, just do so. You don't need me to introduce you.'

'Sorry...?'

She spun back, eyes rolling. 'Look, he might be my son, but if you want an autograph or some ridiculous "selfie"' – she made bunny ears – 'then you don't need me to wave him over and make some ludicrous introduction. Just go and say hello.' Eloise glanced over towards where her son still had his hand on the lower back of the raven-haired woman. 'Oh, for God's sake. Well, you might want to give him a few minutes.'

Her tone was pure Manc, dripping with a hint of brick-through-your-window aggression.

'I was more interested in talking to you,' Andrew said.

Eloise scanned him once more, this time lingering on his face. 'Do I know you?'

'No.'

'You a journalist or something?'

'I'm a private investigator.'

She spat out a breath. 'That's a new one. Some wannabe copper, eh? What do you want?'

'I'd like to ask you about Anna Applegate.'

For a moment, everything froze and then Eloise swore so loudly that everyone turned to look.

Andrew only had a moment to act, holding his hands out to show he meant no harm and saying quickly: 'I'm trying to help.'

One of the security officers from near the door was marching across and Jack Marsh had even removed his hand from the woman's back to turn and stare.

Eloise eyed Andrew suspiciously and then held up a hand.

'It's fine,' she called across to the burly bouncer, who frowned and then turned in a circle, seemingly unsure what to do next. Eloise leaned forward, keeping her voice hissingly low. 'If you're working for Anna Applegate, then I am politely asking you to leave – but I won't remain polite for long. That woman is a liar. She's trying to destroy my son's reputation.'

'If you're referring to her website, then, as of last night, I believe it's offline.'

She shuffled to face Andrew properly, once again examining his features, taking her time. 'Assuming that's true, you've bought yourself one minute of my time.' Eloise slipped her sleeve up and peered down to a sparkly jewel-encrusted watch. 'Tick-tock.'

Andrew tried to speak clearly, even though he was trying to get his words out as fast as possible. 'Anna Applegate doesn't believe the official version of what happened to her daughter. I know you might think that involving me means she wants us to dig up dirt on your son, or try to implicate him in some way – but, if you look at it from another way, the two of you actually want the same thing.'

Eloise's neck snapped round like a rubber band pinging. 'She wants to destroy my son.'

'She wants to know what happened to her daughter. If your son is nothing to do with that, then finding the truth will help you both.'

'My son did nothing to that girl. The police cleared him.'

'That's right – but the rumours about Jack haven't gone away. If I can find out what happened, Anna will have her closure and those whispers about your son will disappear.'

She paused, breathing in through her nose and glancing over Andrew's shoulder towards her son. 'What makes you think the truth is anything other than her stupid daughter falling in the canal?'

'I don't know – perhaps that *is* what happened. All I want to do is prove that one way or the other.'

'And you're better than the police, are you?'

Andrew shrugged. 'Sometimes...'

Eloise looked down to her watch again and then dropped her wrist. 'That's your minute.'

'I've said all I have to say.' Andrew dug into his pocket and removed a business card. He passed it over and Eloise glanced at it quickly. For a moment, Andrew thought she was going to rip it up, but she dropped it into the bag at her side and then turned to look past him towards her son.

'You don't seem to be very good at pissing off,' she said.

'Um...'

She nodded at the door. 'Take the hint.'

12

Andrew had fallen into something of a sorry Saturday night routine. Television was full of talent shows in which the word 'talent' was a questionable term, plus Z-listers in sequins. Jenny would likely call him a snob for those opinions, but he suspected she was probably trying to wind him up.

Living in Beetham Tower did at least give Andrew another form of entertainment. It was the tallest UK building outside of London and, though it wasn't quite people-watching given how high his flat was, Andrew had developed a fascination in watching the dots below scuttling from place to place.

By the time Andrew had finished a bottle of beer, he realised an hour had passed. It was a little after eight in the evening and the sun had almost gone, leaving a murky blue haze clinging to the horizon. The street lights were dotted deep into the distance, before the darkness of the countryside took over.

Andrew had been doing his best to forget about Thomas Braithwaite since their afternoon at the football. He didn't want to work for him but had no other solution. What was he going to do? Go to the police himself? He had friends in the force – one in particular – but he wouldn't even know what to tell her.

As he fumbled with his jacket, Andrew found the memory stick Braithwaite had given him. His creaky knees and back had a grumble about him getting up and then he retrieved his laptop. It only took a moment to figure out that the drive contained a single video file.

The first shot was from the inside of a shop, showing the back door. A few frames later, there was an explosion of splinters and then three people burst through. They were each wearing hoods, with scarves across their mouths. One was a bit chubby, another taller and thinner, with the final one somewhere in between.

As the angle changed to a wider one from a different camera, Andrew could see it was from a music shop, presumably BD Music in the Northern Quarter. A piano was against one of the walls, with two shelves of music books adjacent. A full drum kit was set up on a slightly raised platform close to the window, with racks of guitars at the back. There were brass instruments Andrew didn't know the name of, plus a xylophone next to the counter. The xylophone seemed like a hell of a lot of fun.

The chubbier of the men had a hammer, which he instantly embedded in the till. He'd clearly heard the proverb about trying again if a first go wasn't a success, so thrashed away at it another half-dozen times until the drawer exploded with a spray of banknotes. Andrew didn't need to be a crime expert to know that robbing shops had largely gone out of fashion because so many people in current times chose to pay on a card. The robber held up a roll of receipts and then dumped them on the floor, before stuffing what little cash there was into his pocket. Relatively speaking, given the risk they'd taken to break in and the potential prison sentence for doing so, the money wouldn't be worth it. That left the obvious question as to why this trio would be robbing a music shop. There would surely be more lucrative spots to break into?

The footage continued to roll and, as would be expected, there were many items that couldn't be stolen. Wheeling a piano down the road would be conspicuous to say the least – although there were few sights in Manchester that Andrew would find impossible to believe.

He had seen robberies that weren't robberies in the past, scenes in which something wasn't quite right. Here, it felt like three incompetents not realising they'd made a mistake until it was too late. One of the men stopped close to the shelves of music books, plucking off an armful and then saying something to his mate, who shrugged.

Why were they stealing music books? Could they really be that valuable?

The chubby man with the pocketful of money walked with his shoulders hunched forward and his head drooped, as if he hadn't entirely evolved and still had a few strands of primate DNA about him. He grabbed three flutes from a rack behind the counter, clasping them under his arm and then crouching down and standing back up with a trumpet in hand. The taller, skinny man was wearing a hoody so loose that it was almost down to his thighs. On a Milan catwalk, it might be some new look for the season – the flabby backside – but on a slightly grainy CCTV image, it looked pretty silly. He walked along the row of instruments at the back and then ducked out of sight behind the counter. He emerged with a violin case, a second trumpet and a ukulele. The trio looked at each other and then scarpered back the way they'd come.

Andrew rewound the footage and watched the final part again. If the violin had been stolen to order, then the thieves had done a good job of hiding their intentions. They'd not hunted around for the case, it had been almost an afterthought for the man with the baggy hoody. The one who'd robbed the till had already looked under the counter, picking out a trumpet instead of the violin.

Braithwaite had said that the thieves were 'street kids or estate urchins' and it was hard to argue with the sentiment, if not the choice of words. His contacts would largely be in the Liverpool area, so it was perhaps not a surprise he'd come to Andrew to find the culprits in Manchester.

It was still very odd, though. Were kids nicking violins nowadays? In Andrew's youth, it had been cans of lager and porno mags. Perhaps the city's criminals were going upmarket?

Andrew clicked the video back to its beginning and set it to run again. The man with the hammer was just getting tucked into the till when Andrew's phone started to ring with a number he didn't recognise. He swiped to answer and an abrupt woman's voice stung his ear.

'Mr Hunter?'

'Yes.'

'This is Eloise Marsh. I'm calling to tell you that you're on.' She asked if he had a pen and then read out an address to the south of the city in the Wythenshawe area. 'Come to the house tomorrow at six p.m.,' she added. 'This is a one-time offer – so don't be late.'

13

Steam was rising from the leafy golf courses and frosty fields as Andrew drove west on the M56. His Aunt Gem was sitting behind him, her faithful pug, Rory, curled up on the passenger's seat. Andrew had told his aunt that she should sit in the front, but she wasn't having it. The suggestion of putting Rory in the boot was similarly dismissed with an outraged slap on Andrew's shoulder, followed by Gem telling him that she'd sit in the boot herself before putting the dog in there.

Andrew knew that people had to wear their seatbelts when in the front, but he wasn't sure of the law surrounding animals. He was probably breaking a rule somewhere along the line but was getting more grief from his aunt in the back than he was the dog in the front.

'Oooh, so that's the airport, is it?' she said as they passed a signpost that very clearly read 'Airport'.

'Yes, Gem,' Andrew replied.

'And that's where the planes go from, is it?'

'Yes, Gem.'

There was a short silence and then. 'So that's where *we'll* be flying from next month, is it?'

'That's right.'

Another silence.

'I just don't know about it all, Andrew. All this flying lark. It's not natural.'

Andrew fought the urge to turn away from the road. They'd had this conversation roughly five times a week for the past month. Despite being a little into her seventies, Gem had never left the country. She'd barely left Manchester and this was to be her first trip overseas.

'I'm not arguing about it any longer,' Andrew said, trying to sound firm but not angry. 'I'm taking you to Corfu and that's that. You know my friend Craig's going to have Rory for the week.'

'But Reg at bingo was going on about how I'd need special socks for the plane. Something to do with my veins. He said your legs can explode.'

'It's not a problem, Gem – and your legs don't explode. It's called Deep Vein Thrombosis – but it only happens on really long flights. Ours is only about three hours. If you move your legs around, you'll be fine.'

She harrumphed, as if she'd been hoping this was some-thing that could get her out of the holiday. Jenny had convinced Andrew that his aunt really did want to travel abroad for the first time, even though everything she said and did made it seem as if she didn't.

'We're not flying Ryanair, are we?' Gem added. 'I've heard terrible things. Did you know they charge you for a wee? Reg says they charge you for everything. He says oxygen is charged per minute.'

Andrew glanced in his rear-view mirror to see if his aunt was joking. It didn't look like it. 'We're not flying Ryanair,' he replied. 'And, even if we were, they don't charge you for breathing – or weeing.'

Rory pushed himself up and stomped in a circle, creating a

deeper divot in the seat before curling up once more. He didn't seem impressed at the talk of Andrew and Gem abandoning him to swan off to Corfu for a week.

'But the heat, Andrew,' Gem said. 'I've heard it's so hot, you can fry eggs on the pavements out there. I don't think I'm up to it.'

'It's not that hot in May – and you're definitely up to it. Our hotel has air conditioning, so you can sit in the room if it's too warm.'

She batted the back of his seat with her hand, annoyed that her new list of arguments against going had proved fruitless. She'd have something else by the next week – probably Reg at bingo saying the exchange rate was terrible and it would cost hundreds of pounds to get a meal, or that the political situation was unstable and she didn't fancy holidaying in a warzone.

Andrew passed the next junction and there was a merciful period of silence before Gem was off on her next topic.

'How's your little friend?' she asked.

'Jenny?'

'Oooh, she's lovely. I know she's out of your league, but—'

'She *works* for me, Gem. We're not seeing each other.' Andrew wanted to add: 'And she's not out of my league,' but that would only start another argument, which he wouldn't win.

'A little birdie told me you were back in contact with that ex-wife of yours...'

'That was me, Gem. *I* told you.'

'All right, no need to snap.'

Andrew gritted his teeth. He visited his aunt at least once a week and every conversation ended up heading in a similar direction.

Moments later and it was as if the previous part of the exchange had never happened. 'Did I tell you about Marie's cataracts? Poor woman...'

Gem had indeed told Andrew about Marie's cataracts – three times. At least fifty per cent of her topics for conversation seemed to revolve around people and the illnesses they had. Someone she knew had recently had a stroke, there was Reg's osteoporosis, another person was on a waiting list for a new hip.

Andrew ummed and ahhed where it felt like he should. He'd heard it all before and didn't really have a reply then. What could he say other than, 'That sounds nasty'?

Mercifully, they reached the junction towards which Andrew had been heading and Gem stopped listing illnesses, instead pointing out potential hazards. Those included a stationary traffic cone, a horse in a field roughly two hundred metres away and three cars on the opposite side of the road. She also pointed out the speed limit sign, even though Andrew had not only seen it, he'd already slowed.

Andrew followed the signs for the car boot sale, bumping over a ramp onto a field and waking Rory once more. Gem pointed out that they were in a field and then started pointing to gaps between stalls, trying to claim Andrew could park there and then telling him off for snapping when he said it was for stallholders only.

It was a typical morning with his aunt.

Eventually, Andrew parked in a proper spot and then helped his aunt out of the car before putting Rory on a lead. Rory plodded along like a little barrel on stumps as Gem slotted in at Andrew's side. She wasn't much better at barely five feet tall, shuffling along while her feet hardly seemed to leave the ground.

'It's very big,' she said.

'It's the biggest car boot sale in Europe. I did say that when I asked if you want to go.'

'Yes, but you didn't say it was *this* big. I mean there's big and then there's *big*.'

It wasn't long before Andrew was regretting inviting his aunt. It was nice to get her out of her poky flat for a morning, it *really* was, but it was also hard work. She wanted to stop at every stall, regardless of the nature of the tat that was being sold. She wanted to buy a lamp that was broken, solely because the teenager selling it 'had a nice face'. Andrew managed to talk her out of most of the impulse buys, primarily because she'd have to carry it back to the car. In reality, he knew that *he'd* be carrying it back to the car. She wanted a cassette player that had been made forty years previously – plus the fifty tapes it came with. That was all well and good until Andrew pointed out it would be a good fifteen minutes to carry it.

Ultimately, he couldn't talk her out of buying a new set of cutlery that came in a polythene bag for two quid, or Shakin' Stevens' autobiography for fifty pence.

'Are you ever going to read that?' Andrew asked as she dropped it into a bag for life.

'Maybe,' Gem said. 'He had that Christmas song, didn't he?'

'Nobody reads celebrity biographies, Gem. You should come here the week after new year. It's full of people trying to get rid of Christmas presents they didn't want in the first place. Someone else buys one of these books for a couple of quid and then they never read it either.'

Before he knew it, Gem was walking Rory and Andrew was carrying two bags for life overloaded with tat.

Gem stopped for a sit-down every few minutes, with the spring sunshine just about the only redeeming factor.

It was at the fourth sit-down close to a stall selling polystyrene cups of tea for fifty pence that Andrew finally saw the thing he'd come for. He bought Gem a drink and a cookie and left her with the bags, while he and Rory headed off towards a stall that had been set up next to a battered BMW. Three tables had been pushed together, with rows of slightly squished boxes at the front. There was the usual hotchpotch of market fare – notepads, pens, cleaning supplies – but the items that had drawn Andrew's focus were at the far end of the stall.

The stallholder was busy trying to find change for a customer at the other end of the tables, so Andrew picked up the violin and flipped it over. It was the only one he'd seen at the boot sale. He took out the photograph Braithwaite had given him, comparing the violins. There was no 'LK' etched into the wood of the one on the stall and it had all the strings – but, otherwise, from what he could tell, they were similar. The wood grain looked alike and the varnish was the same chestnut brown.

Andrew pocketed the photo and waited for the stallholder to notice him.

'Where'd this come from?' Andrew asked, as the man strolled across.

The man behind the tables was skinny with a too big tracksuit and a face like a chipmunk. 'House clearance, pal.'

His accent was so broad that Andrew needed a few seconds to understand what he'd said. Andrew pointed at the flute in an open case next to the violin. 'This too?'

The stall owner swept a hand towards the pile of instruments. There were two recorders, a tambourine, a bongo, plus a triangle for good measure. 'Everything came from the same place, pal,' he added.

'You got anything else?'

He shrugged. 'Whatcha after?'

Andrew pointed at the violin. 'Any more of these? I'm looking for more than one.'

The human chipmunk scratched the bum fluff on his chin. 'I'd have to make some calls. Come back next Sunday and I'll see what I can do.'

'Any chance of getting one sooner?'

The man eyed Andrew and then peered down at Rory. He continued scratching his chin and then shook his head. 'Nah. No way, pal. I prob'ly can't get any more, like. Don't find many of them in clearances, y'know?'

Andrew didn't know. He hoisted up the violin. 'How much for this?'

The stallholder didn't even look at it. 'Fifty quid.'

Andrew flipped it around and held it to his chin, acting as if it might be for him. As if he didn't have fingers like cheap supermarket sausages. He knew he should probably haggle, get the guy down to thirty quid or something, but he couldn't be bothered. He dug into his wallet and fished out the money, handing it across, where chipmunk face snatched it like a man who couldn't believe his luck.

14

After a long, long morning, Andrew dropped a well-walked Rory and Gem back at their flat. They lived on the first floor of a housing block that wouldn't have looked out of place if it was surrounded by high-chain fencing topped with barbed wire, enormous floodlights and a lookout tower for escaping prisoners. He hefted Gem's bags for life up the concrete steps and then followed her to her front door as she told him how some nice little ginger kid had been round days previously, offering her half a dozen frozen beef Wellingtons for a fiver. Andrew wondered whether, deep down, Gem knew about the amount of nicked goods that got traded around her, or if she was genuinely naive to it all. He liked to think she was simply trusting of everyone.

Rory toddled past Gem into the flat, no doubt ready for a lengthy lie-down. Gem, meanwhile, fiddled with trying to get her shoes off before crossing the threshold.

'I'll put a lamb joint on,' she said.

'I can't stay for dinner,' Andrew replied. 'I've got to work today.'

'But it's a Sunday!'

'I know – but I still have things to do.'

Gem dotted the four points of a cross on her front, even though Andrew had never known her go to church. 'Even God rested on the seventh day, Andrew.' She poked at his ribs. 'And you're getting so thin. Just look at you.'

Her opinion on his weight was not one shared by the scales in Andrew's bathroom. 'I'll come round in the week,' he replied. 'I'll take Rory out for a walk and then we can eat together afterwards. I'll call you.'

'You'll do no such thing. I know how much it costs to call from those mobile things.'

'We've had this conversation, Gem. It's not that expensive.' Andrew stepped away, knowing that if he hung around much longer, he'd get drawn inside as inevitably as a spider gets stamped on. 'I'll call you in the week,' he said, still walking backwards.

He somehow managed to get away without being ticked off for snapping and then Andrew set off away from the estate on foot. He passed through a familiar selection of ginnels and lanes that snaked around the blocks of flats, until he passed under a set of double arches. He crossed a paved forecourt that was overgrown with moss and then reached a row of small bungalows that looked utterly out of place among the surrounding identikit towers.

Before Andrew could knock, one of the doors was flung open, revealing a chunky, tall man with rugby-player shoulders, squat ears, thin blond hair and a granite jaw. Craig was one of Andrew's friends and wearing his ever-present Doc Martens, with jeans and a Henley T-shirt.

'Got your text,' Craig said, stretching out his hand for Andrew to shake.

They turned and headed towards the arches, walking on autopilot.

'What it is this time?' Craig asked with a laugh.

'Huh?' Andrew replied.

'You only turn up when you want something.'

'Not always but, er...'

'I don't mind,' Craig said. 'Keeps me busy.'

They passed a small huddle of teenagers under the arches who hadn't been there a few minutes before. They each nodded in Craig's direction and one of them risked an 'all right', which was returned.

'I wish I could do that,' Andrew said. 'Whenever I see kids hanging around together, I always think I'm going to get mugged.'

'Have you ever been mugged?'

'No.'

'So what is there to be afraid of? Too much *Daily Mail*. Not all kids are bad – in fact hardly any of them are. Not all adults are bad, either. If you see a bunch of mothers hanging around the school gates, do you think they're going to mug you?'

'No.'

'So there you go.' Craig spoke with a matter-of-fact laugh – but it was easy for him to say. He'd been in the army and was built like a shed. Not even one of those cheap sheds from B&Q that blow over at the first sign of a bit of wind – a proper one with bricks, foundations and a general sense that a nuclear blast wouldn't take it down.

'How's Gem?' Craig asked.

'Same as ever. I just took her and Rory for a ride to the car booter out Bowdon way. She wanted to buy half the stuff there, broken or not.'

Craig laughed. 'Your aunt's an absolute cracker. You're lucky to have her.'

'Aye, I know.'

They continued walking, passing a play park in which all the equipment was miraculously still in place, and then finding a bench near to the swings. Craig sat, so Andrew followed, even though the voice at the back of his mind urged him to go for one of the swings. They weren't being used, after all.

On the far side, some lads were playing football, using their coats as goalposts and taking it far too seriously, given the way they were sliding in on one another.

'So...' Craig said. 'What is it?'

'It's a weird one,' Andrew replied.

Craig pressed back onto the bench and stretched his legs.

'Have you heard anything about stolen musical instruments?' Andrew asked.

Craig snorted in confusion, rather than humour. 'Instruments? Like flutes and all that?'

'Specifically a violin – but there might be other things, too. A keyboard, recorders, trumpet. Anything like that.'

Craig ran a hand through what little there was of his hair. 'Instruments? I thought you were some big-shot investigator. Suicidal girls, nutters in woods, shootings in the city centre... now you're trying to find some instruments?'

Andrew didn't have a defence because he felt the same way. 'I wouldn't ask if it wasn't important...'

Craig leaned forward and then turned to Andrew, apparently now convinced he wasn't being wound up. 'A violin...' He spoke almost with a sigh, nodding back towards the way they'd come. 'Look, I love this area as much as anyone. This is my home and always will be – but I'm not going to pretend this is the type of area where you'll find a nicked violin. At best, you'll have some kids strumming a guitar and hoping to be the next Oasis.'

'Can you ask around anyway?'

Craig shrugged apologetically. 'Course – but don't hold out much hope. You'd be better off asking around the music schools, that sort of thing.'

'It's got to be hush-hush.'

As his eyebrows rose, Craig placed a hand on Andrew's shoulder. It was a gesture so unexpected that Andrew shivered, before apologising.

'You in trouble?' Craig asked. It felt like the air had been sucked from Andrew's lungs.

Andrew shook his head.

'Anything I can do?' Craig added.

'Ask around. If you hear anything, come back to me.'

Craig spent another few seconds examining Andrew before turning to face the footballers. They were setting up what at first glance appeared to be a penalty competition – except that, rather than a goalkeeper, some poor sod was standing in the centre of the goal, bent over with his arse as the target.

'Why this estate?' Craig asked.

'I've seen the CCTV of the break-in and I don't think it's pros. Just blokes in hoodies thinking they might be able to nick things more valuable than they end up with. I wondered if the violin might have been stolen to order but... I don't think so. I might be wrong.'

'So you reckon that it'll just be blokes with goods to get rid of?'

'Probably. They wouldn't risk eBay, so it'll be pub car park, or tower block stairwell – that sort of thing. It's not every day people will get offered hooky musical instruments, so it'll stick in memories.'

Craig was nodding now. He was so well respected on the estate that if anyone had heard anything, he'd be able to find out. 'Any other details?' he asked.

Andrew thought about mentioning the markings on the violin but figured it wouldn't make much difference. If someone had been offered a nicked violin, they'd remember regardless. 'Not really,' he said.

The first shot whistled past the bent-over lad's backside, missing him and sending the watching kids off to fetch the wayward effort. Their laughs and jeers echoed around the park as Craig stood.

'Fancy a Sunday afternoon pint?'

Andrew shook his head. 'I have somewhere to be in a while and I've got to drive.'

Craig offered a 'fair enough' shrug. 'She still in Thailand?'

'Yep. Got a postcard about a month ago.'

'She ever coming back?'

Andrew turned and started to walk back towards Craig's house. 'I wish I knew.'

15

Andrew's car engine idled as Jenny checked the map on her phone.

'This is definitely the place,' she said.

She probably didn't need the phone to tell her that.

The gates to Jack Marsh's house were closed, although the giant 'JM' that had been welded into the metal posts was the giveaway.

They were on the furthest edge of a housing estate, close to the airport but largely surrounded by fields and dead-end cul-de-sacs. It was a strange area in that there were hundreds of houses a minute's drive away and yet, on the road outside Jack's house, surrounded by high hedges and fields, it felt like they were in the middle of nowhere.

Or, it would do if it wasn't for the half-dozen fans wearing sky-blue shirts who were gathered by the gatepost.

A wall that had to be three metres high surrounded the property, but Andrew could see Jack's house through the gates. It was two storeys and big – but not overly extravagant and nowhere near as large as Andrew might have suspected. He'd visited vast mansions with stables in the field at the back – and, aside from the gates, this was far more normal.

Jenny put down her phone and wriggled so that she could see past Andrew through the driver's window. 'Who are that lot?' she asked.

'Probably fans.'

'Imagine waking up every day to that. I'd go crazy. What do you reckon they want?'

Andrew put a hand to the glass, shielding the glare from the early-evening sun. He wondered if any of the misfits from the stadium were there, making a weekend of it. That was probably a thing – Saturday: go to the football; Sunday: stalk the players.

'An autograph, maybe? Selfie? Who knows? It's almost six on a Sunday and they're standing outside someone's front gate.'

'So are we.'

Andrew switched off the engine and turned to grin at Jenny. 'Except *you* don't have to be here. I only called because I thought you'd be annoyed if I didn't.'

'I had nothing on.'

'Why not? It's the weekend – you're young. When I was your age, I was...' Andrew tried to think back but all he came up with was playing fantasy board games on Sunday afternoons. 'Well, I can't remember, but I wasn't doing this.'

'I broke up with my boyfriend last night.'

'Oh.' Andrew stared at Jenny, wondering if she was going to expand. She tugged a loose strand of hair from her face but shrugged. 'He was boring me.'

'That's brutal.'

Another shrug. 'He must've seen it coming. I'd been putting it off for weeks.'

'Right.'

Andrew wasn't sure what else to say. Jenny had never been

one to talk about her relationship – or relationships – and on the rare occasion she did, she only ever referred to the poor lad as her 'boyfriend'. Andrew didn't even know his name. Not that it was any of his business.

'Is everything... okay?' he asked.

'Fine. Shall we get on with it? It's two minutes to six.'

Andrew checked the dashboard clock and then climbed out of the car. The fans stopped to turn as one in his and Jenny's direction, perhaps wondering if he was anyone important. When they realised he wasn't – and that he also wasn't a fan like them – they turned back towards the house.

As they neared the gates, Andrew noticed that there were light blue ribbons tied around some of the metal posts towards the edges. Someone had looped a scarf around too, plus there was a small teddy bear wearing a light blue bobble hat that was sitting on the floor.

The fans were standing at the opposite gatepost to the buzzer. Next to it was a small sign that read 'deliveries only'. Andrew was about to press it when he noticed the small huddle of fans eyeing him and Jenny. There were five men and a woman.

'What's going on?' Andrew asked.

One of the bigger blokes glanced at Jenny, then Andrew. 'You not 'eard?'

'Heard what?'

The man dug into a rear pocket and removed a screwed-up newspaper, holding it up so they could see the back-page headline: 'JACK-POT: Spanish giants in for Marsh.'

'He's leaving?' Andrew said.

'So they reckon. Off to Madrid or something. You never know with the papers.'

The woman pushed past him, jabbing a finger towards Andrew. She was wearing a football shirt that was way too tight. 'He ain't going if we 'ave anything to say about it.'

As Andrew continued talking to the fans, Jenny stepped around him and pushed the buzzer, muttering 'It's six o'clock' quietly enough that only he would hear.

'You shouldn't do that,' the man said, nodding at Jenny.

'We've been invited,' she replied.

There was a silence in which it felt like everything had stopped. All six of the fans stared at Jenny open-mouthed.

'*Invited?*' the woman eventually managed.

'That's right.'

'You were *invited*?'

'That's why we're here.'

There was a low 'ooooh' and a collective widening of eyes as Andrew suddenly wanted to be somewhere else. He wasn't even famous – far from it – and yet the way the fans were ogling him left him cringing. For the first time, he felt a twinge of sympathy for Jack Marsh. When could it ever be normal to wake up and find people standing at the bottom of the driveway wanting to say hello?

Andrew turned to avoid the stares, peering through the gates as Eloise Marsh appeared in the doorway of the house and then started to walk towards them. Her bob of grey hair looked more silvery in the sinking sun and she was shorter than she'd appeared when she was sitting in the players' lounge.

When she got to the gates, she nodded towards the group of fans, offering a crisp but polite 'good evening'.

One of the fans couldn't hold his tongue, blurting out: 'Is he off to Spain?'

Eloise smiled tightly but said nothing, instead opening the gate just enough to let Andrew and Jenny slip through. She closed it behind them and then set off along the patch, waiting until they were out of earshot before speaking.

'I usually open the gates remotely from the house – but I didn't want any of the lunatic fringe getting in. If I'd known they were going to be around, I'd have given you a different time.'

'Do you get many fans hanging around?' Jenny asked.

Eloise stopped and stared at her, making Andrew and Jenny halt too. Andrew hastily explained that Jenny was his assistant and the older women pursed her lips, seemingly annoyed at something, though not saying what. 'Sometimes,' was all she said, before turning and striding to the house.

Inside, there was a large tiled reception room loudly echoing their footsteps. The walls were covered with various football shirts, some with Jack's name on the back, others with the last names of players so famous even Andrew knew who they were.

Eloise closed the door and led them through to a carpeted study, where the walls were decorated with rows of glittering trophies and medals. The corner of the room was given over to a shelf containing a collection of hardback books that all seemed to be about football. A large ceiling fan whirred above, though it was largely moving around already warm air.

Eloise sat in a wide leather armchair and then motioned for Andrew and Jenny to sit in similar seats.

'Is this Jack's house?' Andrew asked.

'More of a family house, you could say.'

'Is it just you and Jack here?'

Eloise said nothing at first and then offered a small nod. It was all a bit odd. Jack was twenty-three years old, yet seemingly living in this large place with his mum. When Andrew thought about it, he hadn't seen many other people in the players' lounge who could've been a parent. It was partners and children – except for Jack, who had his mum at his side.

'I was questioned, you know,' Eloise said.

'Sorry?' Andrew replied.

'About that Applegate girl's death. When she was found in

the canal, the police came to the house. They talked to both Jack and me.'

'Okay...'

'I know how you types think and I can only imagine what that girl's mother has said to you. You did at least keep to one thing – that hateful cow's website has disappeared, which is why you're here.'

'What did you tell the police?' Andrew asked, realising he was pushing it.

'The truth.'

'Which is...?'

Eloise fixed Andrew with a glare so forceful that he had to will himself not to shrink into the chair. Dealing with Braithwaite was bad enough but now there were two people seemingly wanting to harm him with looks alone.

'I assume you already know that Jack was in the hotel with his teammates on the night that Applegate girl ended up in the canal?'

'That's what the police say.'

'That's what *happened*. The police asked about me, too – but I was here by myself that night.'

Eloise held up a hand to indicate the room. It was the little things that gave away the wealth – the thick rug in the corner that didn't look as if anyone had ever stood on it; the lack of dust on any surface. There would be a cleaner – *cleaners* – who came in every day to keep everything looking as new as possible. Even the doorknobs gleamed as if they'd never been touched.

'You think it's easy just because we have money, don't you?'

She spoke as if it was a challenge.

Andrew could have told Eloise that he *also* had money. Lots of it. Enough that he never had to work a day if he so chose. That was a story in itself – and a large reason of why his once wife was now his ex-wife.

Eloise wasn't waiting for a reply anyway. She flapped a hand towards the front window. 'You saw that lot outside. Today's are almost sensible, but you should see some of them. We've had people try to come over the gates. One woman got stuck trying to squeeze between the bars. They only want to say hello, or shake Jack's hand, but it's too much. If Jack scores at the weekend, especially if it's in the derby or something like that, you should see them out there. The men hero-worship him. They want to buy him a pint, be mates, that sort of thing – but it's the women...'

Her gaze shot spitefully towards Jenny and then moved back to Andrew again.

'That slut who ended up in the canal was like all the others. At the least, they're desperate to get photographed with Jack. They think that if they get in the papers, or on one of those trash websites, that they'll be made for life. Someone Jack knows was tricked into getting one of these girls pregnant.'

'How—?' Andrew didn't get his question out because Eloise talked over him.

'Word's gone round that players should use only their own condoms. This girl had one in her bag, but she must have tampered with it. Next thing you know, the dirty slag is on the front page of the *Sun*, saying how some horrible footballer has knocked her up and then abandoned her.' Eloise glanced at Jenny again, speaking with a hissed fury. 'It's a different world out there.'

'I'm not sure why you're telling me this,' Andrew said.

Eloise snarled her top lip. 'Because I've seen it all before. Someone threw themselves in front of Jack's car as he was leaving the training ground a couple of months ago. He wanted compensation, saying Jack had run him over. Jack already had a dashcam to stop all that. You can see the guy jumping off the kerb for no reason and then the car doesn't touch him. Whatever that woman's told you is because she wants a payout. Compensation culture – that's what the world's like nowadays. She doesn't care that her stupid drunk bimbo of a daughter fell in the canal, she just wants money. *Jack's* money. She's using you to rake up old details. They're all at it.' She leaned forward, thrusting a finger towards Andrew. 'I'm not having it. You might think you're doing something noble, but she's tricking you. When she ends up using some insignificant detail to try to get a payout from Jack, don't say you didn't know.'

Andrew gave her a few seconds to calm down, but the ceiling was so high that her words echoed on. The room suddenly felt very small.

'I think you might have misunderstood what I'm trying to achieve, Mrs Marsh.'

'*Really?*'

'I'm only interested in if there's something that was missed. The police say Michelle Applegate died from alcohol poisoning and that, at some point, she ended up in the canal. I'm not trying to stitch him up – but Jack was going out with Michelle. He might know something about what she was like, or why she was near the canal. They might have had a conversation that he's forgotten about how she liked to go to the park and watch the water – that sort of thing. If you can arrange it, I'd really like to talk to Jack one-on-one.' He nodded towards Jenny. 'Perhaps two-on-one—'

'He's got a lawyer for that sort of thing.'

Andrew shook his head. 'I'm not police. There are no summons, no warrants, nothing like that. Just a chat. He might not know anything more than he's already said – but perhaps there's a small detail I can stir that will end up exonerating him completely. You think I'm trying to work against you, but, if the official version of what happened to Michelle Applegate is wrong – and I can find out the truth that it's nothing to do with Jack – then many of these rumours about him will go away.'

Eloise's gaze flickered to Jenny once more. 'I'll ask him,' she replied. 'But I'm not making any promises.'

At that, she stood and stepped towards the door, their time seemingly done. Andrew and Jenny followed back through the echoing hall until they got to the front door. Next to it was a large bulging, grey sack with 'Royal Mail' on the side. It was open at the top, with a mound of letters and parcels spewing.

Eloise smirked a knowing, wicked grin and then delved through the sack's contents before pulling out a large padded envelope. 'Jack Marsh' was written on the front in pink swirly characters. The address simply read 'Manchester' – yet it had arrived.

'Here,' Eloise said, handing Andrew the package.

'What?'

'Open it and you'll see what these girls are like.'

The parcel felt soft and squishy. It weighed hardly anything. Andrew carefully unsealed the top, eyeing the crowned figure on the stamps gazing up at him.

The waft of sickening perfume hit as soon as the envelope was open. It was a cross between something fruity and congealing vomit, but edging closer to the vomit end of the scale.

'Go on,' Eloise encouraged, her smile spreading.

Andrew reached into the package and pulled out half a dozen photographs. A glimpse of the first had him blinking in stunned disbelief, coughing for breath.

Eloise peered over the top of the envelope, looking at the picture upside down and laughing. 'Not a hair on her,' she said.

Jenny was on tiptoes, smirking. 'She must've done gymnastics as a kid.'

Eloise forgot her hostility towards Jenny and laughed at that. Andrew realised he was essentially looking at hardcore pornography while surrounded by an aggressive older woman and his assistant, but, at Eloise's insistence, he flicked through the rest of the photos. They somehow became more graphic.

'You see what these girls are like?' Eloise said with a sneer.

'I wish I could *un*-see,' Andrew replied.

Eloise took the parcel from him and then handed it back, saying he'd not finished going through the contents. Andrew reached inside tentatively, emerging with a silky pink thong, which he held at arm's length between his thumb and forefinger.

'Used,' was the only word Eloise said, which prompted Andrew to drop the garment and wheel away.

'That is rank,' Andrew said, ignoring Jenny's grin.

Eloise nodded at the bag. 'There'll be at least another half-dozen like that. Probably more. We get a sack of mail like that every other day.'

Andrew put the envelope down, wondering if he should ask if there was a sink somewhere where he could wash his hands.

'You might have a low opinion of my Jack,' Eloise said. 'You might have read things, you might think he's all about the money – but what would you do if you had women throwing themselves at you? If you got letters like that every day?'

Andrew gulped. 'I'd probably get a bigger washing machine,' he said.

16

Jenny was sitting on the low wall outside her house when Andrew pulled up in his car the following morning. The sun was already simmering over the tops of the buildings, with wispy white clouds bobbing across the brilliant blue sky.

Manchester was outdoing itself for once.

Jenny jumped into the passenger seat, mischievous grin on her face. 'Got any more dirty knickers in the post?' she asked.

'I thought about bleaching my fingers last night just in case. I could still smell that perfume, even after having a shower.'

'You loved it really.'

Andrew pulled away from the kerb and edged towards the main road. 'I really didn't.'

'What about those photos?'

'I think I'm scarred for life. It was like looking at a butcher's counter.'

Jenny giggled and then unzipped her satchel, fishing out a cereal bar. 'Want one?'

'No.'

Jenny had it unwrapped and had devoured half the bar before Andrew could get away from the junction.

'Eloise Marsh called last night,' Andrew said. 'She's given me the address for the training ground and says Jack will talk to us at lunchtime.'

'I didn't expect that.'

'Me either.'

'Where are we off to now?'

Andrew indicated and turned off the main road, heading towards the estate where his Aunt Gem lived. 'My mate got back to me last night, too, saying he knows someone who's been offered a flute.'

Jenny giggled. 'Is that a euphemism?'

'For what?'

'It sounds like something Jack Marsh might receive a photo of. Anyway, I thought you had to find a stolen violin?'

When Andrew had told Jenny of his meeting at the football stadium with Thomas Braithwaite, she'd reacted with the same bemusement as Craig.

'I do. You can have a look at the video from the pen drive later, but the thieves nicked a few things – including three flutes. If someone's been offered one, it might be by a person who has everything.'

Jenny was back in her bag, digging out a second cereal bar and munching her way through it as Andrew headed through the backstreets of Manchester. He made good time, arriving on the estate that bordered the one on which his aunt and Craig lived. It was depressingly similar, lined with grimy two-storey blocks of flats that stretched a long way past a slushy patch of unmown grass. A pair of taller towers eclipsed much of the light, casting thick, cold shadows across an expanse of gritty wasteland. There was an abandoned mustard yellow skip on the side of the road overflowing with rubble and dust. An intermingled mess of graffiti tags was sprayed onto the side.

After getting out of the car, Andrew checked the address Craig had given him and then headed into the closer of the two towers. From the relative warmth of the sun through the car windows, it was chilly enough to raise the goosebumps on his arms.

The tower block was around a dozen storeys high, with an echoing, concrete-clad entrance that offered the choice of solid steps, or a lift that had the F-word graffitied across the front in thick black letters. There was a low groaning from the shaft beyond, as if the spirits were warning of a likely death trap.

'Stairs?' Andrew asked, turning to Jenny.

She eyed the metal doors as the elevator creaked once more.

'Stairs,' she replied.

The flat they were looking for was on the third floor, or – as Jenny put it – sixty-four steps up. She'd only reached eight when Andrew felt as if counting the steps was putting him off from actually climbing them.

When they finally got there, the floor had two long rows of peeling dark blue doors. There was a flickering white strip bulb above but no other windows. It was a few dead flies away from being the setting of a horror movie. Some of the doors had numbers, some didn't. The one immediately by the staircase had a large crumpled dent in the lower half that was distinctly foot-shaped.

'If I say I wouldn't want to live here, does that make me a snob?' Andrew asked.

Jenny's nose was twitching, probably from the undercurrent of bleach that was masking who knew what. 'I'll let you off this time,' she said.

There was no flat thirty-one as such – though there was an unmarked door between thirty and thirty-two. Andrew knocked and waited.

And waited.

He felt as if he was being watched, as if there was a dot on his back on which someone was focusing. When he turned, there was no one there. Jenny felt it, too, because she was peering over her shoulder and returned his curious gaze with a nervous smile.

Andrew spun back as the door opened, revealing a man in loose tracksuit bottoms, a T-shirt with two holes in the front, scruffy dark hair and a beard that had a *couldn't-be-bothered-shaving* vibe to it.

The man stepped forward and peered past Andrew along the empty corridor. 'Who are you?' he asked.

'I'm Andrew. I think my friend told you I was coming...?'

The man continued looking from side to side and waved them in with a flick of his head. Andrew chose the wrong moment to breathe in, gagging as the reek of cigarettes punched the back of his throat. The walls and dimpled ceiling were a throwback to pubs of days gone by, with sticky brown tar clinging to the once-white paint, creating a mucky mosaic of filth.

'I'm Griff,' the man said, shuffling past Andrew and leading them along the hallway into a kitchen that mercifully had the window open. Not that the view was much – the window faced the sibling tower block, meaning almost all of the light was blocked. Aside from a potential glimpse of other people through their windows, Griff had the view of a life prisoner.

The inside wasn't much better. Griff's kitchen furniture looked like it had come from someone's back garden. It was white moulded plastic, with the feet of the table crusted brown. He sat in the only chair, leaving Andrew bobbing awkwardly in the doorway, Jenny at his side.

'You want a tea?' Griff nodded at a kettle that was covered with the same brown filth as the rest of the house. Next to it sat a mug that was more chips than ceramic.

'We're fine,' Andrew replied.

Griff shuffled his chair towards the sink, using it as an ashtray after lighting a cigarette.

'Craig reckoned you were after a flute or summat like that...'

'Not exactly,' Andrew replied. 'He said you'd been offered something second-hand for sale.'

'Aye.'

'What?'

Griff puffed away on his cigarette, flicking a chunk of ash towards the window. He nodded at a photo that was attached to the fridge with a magnet. Not a fridge magnet – an actual red and silver horseshoe magnet. On it was a girl in a crisp navy blue school uniform. She was standing rigidly in the way kids do when an official photographer is around.

'That's my daughter,' Griff said. 'Lives with her mam. Good girl – goes to school every day, does her homework. That sorta thing. She was round here last weekend telling me how she wants to join the orchestra. I 'eard this fella's got some instruments on the go, so thought I'd see what I could get.'

'What did he have?'

Griff gasped another breath of his cigarette. 'I was only after a flute. Reckoned he could do me one for fifty quid – but I don't have fifty quid. He reckoned he had another buyer lined up, so told me it was that or nuffin'. Ended up being nuffin'.'

'Did this fella have any other instruments for sale?'

Griff shrugged and then smiled, flashing a row of yellow-brown teeth. 'Dunno. Didn't ask.'

'Can you give us his name?'

He scratched his stubble, eyeing Jenny and then looking back to Andrew. 'I can tell you where he is and that, but y'didn't get it from me, right?'

'Didn't get it from who?' Andrew said.

Griff's brow furrowed. 'You didn't get it from *me*.'

Andrew was momentarily confused. 'I was trying to make a joke. Like *I* didn't know who the name came from – even though you'd tell us.'

'But it *would* come from me...?'

'I know that.' Andrew turned to Jenny for help, but she was smiling to herself, enjoying the spectacle. 'If you tell us, I'll then forget it came from you,' Andrew said.

Griff's eyes narrowed, though Andrew still wasn't sure he got it. He wished he'd never tried to joke in the first place.

'Darren Wiley,' Griff said. 'Lives out Moss Side. I'll give you the address.'

Griff wrote the address on a pad and then handed over the top sheet. His handwriting was as poor as Andrew would have predicted.

'You didn't get it from me, right?' Griff said.

'We didn't get it from you,' Andrew confirmed.

17

Andrew was parked across from the gates that led to the football club's training ground. It was almost in the shadow of the main stadium, with acres of crisp grass surrounded by tall fences. A steady stream of expensive-looking cars and 4x4s with tinted windows were pouring from the gates, with burly bouncer-types standing nearby, eyeing Andrew as if he might be a terrorist.

'All this for a violin,' Jenny said for the third time since they'd left the block of flats.

'What do you want me to say?'

'Something weird's going on.'

'I know that – but if I can find the damned thing, we can take it from there.'

There was a sputter of diesel and then a sporty-looking silver 4x4 roared out of the car park, clipping the kerb as it accelerated away. There was another small group of fans hanging around on the opposite side of the road from the training ground gates. Some were clutching autograph books but most were taking photos of the departing vehicles on their phones.

Andrew checked his watch and then got out of the car, heading to the gates. The bouncer-type looked at Andrew as if he was a yappy little dog that had just peed on his shoes, standing with his arms folded. It took five minutes for him to accept that they'd actually been invited – and another fifteen for a similarly clad gorilla to march out to the gates in order to escort Andrew and Jenny inside.

They ended up in the lobby of what was a cross between a hotel, a posh gym and a restaurant. The walls were covered with framed photographs of various football teams and there was moody lowlighting, with soft carpets. The smell of something meaty and delicious drifted from nearby.

When Jack Marsh jogged his way down a set of steps, it was almost underwhelming. He was a figure Andrew had seen in numerous clippings, a person idolised by many and demonised by some – and yet he was just a man. He had short dark hair that was gelled forward and was wearing a tracksuit in various shades of blue. There were headphones around his neck that were so chunky, it was like he was wearing a neck brace. Without the suit he'd been wearing in the players' lounge, he seemed... normal.

Jack nodded at the bouncer-type and then turned to Andrew. 'You're an investigator, then?'

Andrew offered his hand. 'Andrew Hunter.'

Jack ignored it, turning to Jenny and breaking into a smirk. 'I didn't realise there'd be something to look at.'

He offered his hand and Jenny started to shake it. Before she could do anything, he lunged forward and lightly kissed her hand.

'What's your name?' he cooed.

'Jenny.'

'Jen... knee...' Jack rolled it around his mouth and then grinned. 'Very nice,' he said.

Andrew was being ignored, but Jenny took control

anyway. 'Is there somewhere we can talk in private?' she asked.

Jack nodded towards the stairs. 'We'll find a corner in the canteen. C'mon.'

Jenny removed her hand from his and then wiped it on her skirt when his back was turned. She and Andrew followed Jack up the stairs, emerging into a wide hall that was filled with rows of tables and chairs. At the far end was a huge serving counter that reminded Andrew of the kitchen front at his old school – except there was no ladle-carrying head cook with a face like a cement mixer scowling at the passing kids. There was also no undercooked pizza or ropy tubs of baked beans, let alone the weird smell that school kitchens always seemed to give off that was one part food to five parts gag reflex. Instead, there was a menu pinned to the wall that listed chicken dishes, along with pasta, rice, noodles and all sorts of other foods that seemed generally healthy.

Jack headed towards the table in the corner, plopping himself down and sitting with his legs splayed wide. He scratched his crotch, unknowingly giving off something of a lice problem vibe, and then nodded at Jenny. She acted like she hadn't seen it, taking a seat next to Andrew on the other side and using the table as a barrier.

'Did your mother tell you why we wanted to see you?' Andrew asked.

Jack's eyes reluctantly left Jenny and focused on Andrew. 'Summat about Michelle? People never shut up about her. You've heard the songs…'

Probably naively, it hadn't even occurred to Andrew that fans of rival clubs might get onto Jack about the rumours surrounding him. Andrew could imagine the lyrics, though.

'I know the police spoke to you about this at the time,' Andrew said, 'but I was wondering if we could hear it from you about what you were up to on the night Michelle died.'

Jack nodded along, as if in agreement before his top lip turned into a snarl. 'You think I did it, don't you?'

Andrew remained calm. 'I don't think anything.'

'I know your type. You read things about me, hear things about me. You think you know me.'

Andrew was about to reply when Jenny leaned in, a knowing, cocky smile on her face. 'He didn't know who you were.'

Jack turned to look at her, frowning. 'What?'

Jenny touched Andrew's arm. 'He's not a football fan. When Michelle's mother came into our office, he didn't know who you were.'

It wasn't exactly true, but it had the desired effect. Jack's ego shrank in front of them. First his head rocked back as he turned between them, momentarily unable to believe someone wouldn't acknowledge his fame, and then he was swallowed by his seat as he closed his legs and focused a bewildered stare on Andrew.

'Oh...' was all he said.

Now Jenny had given him the upper hand, Andrew jumped back in, finding the authoritative tone with which he so struggled. 'I'm not interested in stitching you up, Jack, nor in getting one over on somebody. I don't care about any rumours involving you and I care even less about football. I was in the players' lounge on Saturday – and that's the first football match I've been to in almost thirty years. All I'm worried about is finding out what happened to Michelle Applegate – and that's if there's anything to find out. Okay?'

Jack's façade had dropped with his ego. He looked like a confused young man as opposed to a cocky cover photo of a lads' mag. He glanced over Andrew's shoulder, making sure no one was nearby, and then nodded slightly. 'A'ight.'

'So, what happened on the night Michelle ended up in the canal?'

Jack sighed. He unclipped the headphones from around

his neck and placed them on the table next to his phone. 'I told them and I'm telling you, bruv, I was playing cards in the hotel all night. The gaffer don't let us out after dinner. Everyone'll tell you that. 'Chelle called a coupla times, but I didn't answer. We weren't really going out then.'

'Weren't you?'

He shrugged. 'We were and we weren't. She always thought it was more serious than it were.'

'What was your relationship like?'

Jack sucked on his top lip, exposing a row of perfect white teeth that probably hadn't originated in his mouth. 'All right.'

'You were both equally happy? All going well?'

'Well...' He glanced at Jenny and then back to Andrew. He was hard to read, but there was perhaps a hint of embarrassment. '...I s'pose I was only really in it for one thing. Y'know what I'm sayin'? I dunno about 'Chelle – but she liked being seen out and about with me. I guess we both got something from it.'

'Not a long-term thing, though?'

Jack answered with a subtle shake of his head.

'You know what I have to ask you next.'

For the first time, Jack made full eye contact with Andrew. It was only a moment and then he blinked and turned away, gazing towards the wall instead. In that moment, Andrew could see that there was hurt there, pain at the things that had been written and said about him.

Jack lowered his voice as he leaned in. 'Look, I ain't no angel – but if you reckon I could shove her in the canal, then you're an idiot. People say things about me – that I beat up women or whatever...' – another glance at Jenny – 'I mean...' He gulped, not knowing what to say. It took him a few seconds and then he continued, 'All right, I've done some stupid things – but you show me some eighteen-, nineteen-year-old who ain't. It's different now.'

'Did you ever hit Michelle?'

Jack reeled back as if he'd been hit by a blunt object, rather than asked a blunt question. For a moment there was another snarl of the lip; a cocky, legs-wide objection about to be hurled back. But then the self-esteem fell away again.

His reply was barely audible over the cleaning up that was going on in the kitchen behind. 'Why don't you ask if she ever hit me?'

'Did she?'

There was a microscopic nod and then Jack rolled up the sleeve of his tracksuit top, showing a large scar that ran from an area slightly above his sparkly, chunky watch, all the way to his elbow. 'One of her nails did that.'

'But you sometimes hit back?'

Jack didn't answer. He rolled his sleeve back down and slumped in the chair. He pointed at his arm. 'If you tell anyone about this, I'll say you made it up. My mum's got guys in the newspapers. They'll look into you, find out all your dirty little secrets. See how you like it.' He spat the words like a scorned child, but Andrew didn't doubt there was truth in what he said.

'Anything you say won't go beyond here,' Andrew said.

Jack snatched his headphones from the table, snapping them back around his neck, apparently ready to go. 'Anything else?' he asked.

'You've not really told us about your relationship with Michelle.'

Jack threw his hands up. 'Look, what do you wanna know? She didn't like other girls talking to me. She'd go mental. This one time, we were in a club in London. She'd gone to the toilet but was off for ages. While she were away, this other girl came and said hello. That were it – "hello" – but 'Chelle went mental. Threatening to kill this other girl, kill me – all that.

There were witnesses. What d'you want me to do? Lots of people – guys and girls – wanna say hello.'

It was as if the side of him he'd been suppressing made another bid for freedom as Jack turned to Jenny again, giving her the eye as if to say she *must* be sensing the pheromones in the room and know what he was talking about.

He turned back to Andrew: 'She'd go out with her mates, too. She'd text, saying some lad off the telly was eyeing her up. She'd send me photos of her hanging onto some bloke. She was always trying to make me jealous.'

'She can only make you jealous if you cared for her in the first place.'

It took a second or two, but there was another barely there nod.

'Her mum wouldn't let me go to the funeral. We might've had differences, but we were together for over a year. Then she dies and that's it? How would you feel?' He nodded at Andrew, demanding an answer.

'Not good,' Andrew replied.

'Right – yet *I'm* the bad guy. I've got people calling me a murderer in the street. I've got people singing songs about me.' Jack opened his legs wide again and had a scratch for good measure. 'We done?'

'Just one final time – to be absolutely, one hundred per cent clear – you did not leave the hotel on the night Michelle died...?'

Jack shook his head vigorously. 'I told you, bruv. No way. We were playing cards.'

He scraped his chair back and stood, taking one small step towards the stairs before bobbing back. He grinned at Jenny, the old cockiness returning.

'Hey,' he said, 'can I look at your phone?'

'Why?'

'It's a surprise.'

Jenny frowned but removed it from her satchel anyway, unlocking the screen and handing it over. Jack's fingers danced back and forth and then he handed it back with a grin. Andrew was only half surprised.

'What have you done?' Jenny asked.

He winked. 'You've got my number now, babe. Just in case you're ever feeling lonely. Nice earrings, by the way.'

18

Andrew had only just pulled away from the training ground when his phone's Bluetooth started to ring. The dashboard told him it was a redirected call – which happened during the day when the office was empty. Someone was calling the number listed for his business rather than his actual mobile.

He was ambling along in a 20mph zone and pressed the button on the steering wheel to answer. There was a crackle and then a man's voice said hello.

'This is Hunter Investigations,' Andrew said. 'Can I help?'

'Is Jenny there?'

The voice was slightly squeaky, but it was hard to figure out if that was because of the way it was being broadcast through the car's speakers. Andrew glanced to Jenny, who took a moment and then shook her head.

'She's not in the office. Can I ask who's calling?'

'Um... don't worry.'

There was a plip and then the radio cut back in as the call dropped.

'Who was that?' Andrew asked.

Jenny was uncharacteristically silent. She was holding onto a Jaffa Cake but not eating it, which was even stranger.

'No one ever asks for me,' she said.

'Did you recognise the voice?'

'I don't think so.'

Andrew pulled into the main flow of traffic. 'Could it be Jack Marsh?'

Jenny still hadn't bitten into the Jaffa Cake, which was creeping Andrew out. She was very much see-food, eat-food. 'No, he gave me *his* number. I don't think he took mine – and even if he did, it'd be my mobile.'

'Boyfriend?'

'I doubt it.'

Andrew eased onto the accelerator, wondering if he should ask outright. In the end, he simply went for it: 'Are you ever going to tell me his name? If you've broken up, it doesn't matter now.'

'I would have told you before.'

'Why didn't you?'

'Because you never asked – not properly. Anyway, his name's Oliver... well, Ollie. Ollie Raphael. His name reminded me of the painter at first.' She cut herself off by finally eating the Jaffa Cake. 'That or the Ninja Turtle,' she added.

When Jenny took out her phone and started tapping away, he figured she didn't want to talk about it any longer – which was fine with him. It had been a very strange few minutes.

Britain as a nation had never quite got the hang of building roads in a straight line, instead preferring to create bizarre labyrinth-like housing estates, from which nobody but those who lived there knew how to escape.

This particular area of Manchester was an exception.

Jenny helped Andrew navigate the backstreets of Moss

Side, trying to read Griff's handwriting. He'd given them Darren Wiley's address, saying that's where he'd been offered the second-hand flute. There were long straight rows of red terraces spread into a grid, with narrow ginnels running parallel along the backs of the houses. Cars were parked half on the pavement, half on the road along both sides, their wing mirrors folded in, leaving a tight space along the centre for cars to weave in and out. If that wasn't bad enough, speed humps were dotted along the road – but the markings were so worn that they were hard to spot. Andrew's first indication was when he accelerated into one, sending the car lurching upwards and his head into the ceiling with a whump.

'Speed hump there,' Jenny said.

'Thanks.'

The houses were unerringly similar, with faded white window frames and brown doors, offset against the murky red of the buildings. Almost every one was decorated with a burglar alarm and a satellite dish. Andrew moved from one street to the next, but it all looked the same.

Jenny eventually pointed to a gap between two cars and Andrew spent four minutes and seven seconds parallel parking. He knew that because Jenny had a stopwatch on her phone running and was helpfully telling him that he was 'close' or '*really* close' to the cars in front and behind.

Darren Wiley's door was double-glazed and grubby, with a flimsy piece of golden tinsel dangling from the top corner. There was no doorbell or knocker, so Andrew rapped hard on the plastic. Moments later, it was wrenched inwards, revealing a porky man in a black Iron Maiden T-shirt.

'Are you Darren?' Andrew asked.

The man looked at Jenny, then Andrew. 'Aye. What ya after?'

'I heard you had some instruments for sale.'

Andrew expected some questioning about who he'd heard

this from, but Darren acted as if this sort of encounter was normal. He turned and headed along a hallway, shoulders hunched forward, head drooped.

Andrew and Jenny followed through the hallway, which was lined with boxes, and then into the kitchen. Andrew only knew it *was* a kitchen because of the way the fridge was buzzing like a swarm of annoyed bees. The floor and counter-tops were covered by an array of battered boxes. There were toasters, blenders, kettles, slow cookers, at least four microwaves, two coolboxes, three mini beer fridges, a dozen or so knife sets complete with wooden blocks, a food mixer and a small television. Probably a partridge and pear tree somewhere.

That was just what Andrew could see.

The doorway into the living room was open and there were mountains of more boxes dotted in the murk.

'I got an eBay business,' Darren said, answering the unasked question. 'Raking it in, mate.' He nodded towards the living room. 'You after a PlayStation? I just had a bunch come in over the weekend.'

Andrew didn't want to know where they'd come in from, though he could guess. 'I'm only really interested in any musical instruments you might have.'

'You sure? I can do you a deal on a fish tank?'

'I don't have any fish.'

'Yeah, but if you have a tank, you could get some.'

'I don't think I'm much of a fish person. I'd forget to feed them and then I'd feel guilty...'

Darren gave a 'suit yourself' shrug. 'What instruments you after?'

'What have you got?'

For the first time, there was a hint of annoyance in Darren's face. His grin slipped, which made his jawline appear far more solid than before. He stared at Andrew, keeping his voice level. 'What are you after?'

'A violin...?'

'I ain't got no violin.'

Andrew wasn't about to question him, but it was hard to back down now. 'How about a flute? My daughter, she—'

He didn't get a chance to expand on the lie because Darren wasn't bothered. He cut Andrew off with a 'wait here' and then pushed past him, heading back along the hall and then clumping upstairs.

Jenny waited until the sound of his booming footsteps were echoing from above. 'How can the police not know about this lot?' she whispered.

Andrew looked at the mass of boxes littering the kitchen. He knew Darren's type better than he liked to admit. 'Some of this might be legit – a mix of nicked stuff and cheap gear he got from a mate. Perhaps the police *do* know? Sometimes they'll sit and watch a bloke like Darren because they're more interested in if there's someone else higher up the chain. Either that or he's a very lucky boy.'

There was a thump on the ceiling and then more footsteps banging down the stairs until Darren re-entered the kitchen, out of breath and gasping like he'd just been up Kilimanjaro. He thrust a long, rectangular case towards Andrew and then opened the fridge, removing a can of already open lager and a plate containing three-quarters of a Sara Lee chocolate gateau. He shuffled a couple of the boxes aside and then put the plate down on the small area of counter. Under Jenny's watchful, envious eye, Darren tucked into the cake with nothing but a fork.

Andrew clicked open the case and tilted it so that Jenny could see. It contained a silver flute split into two parts. There were no distinct markings that might indicate it had come from

BD Music, but it was an odd thing for Darren to be selling given the nature of his other goods.

'Where'd it come from?' Andrew asked.

Darren had a mouthful of Sara Lee. He twirled a finger around while flashing a row of chocolate-coated teeth.

Quite the catch.

When his mouth was clear, Darren shook his head. 'Dunno, mate. I get stuff in all the time. Probably some sort of house clearance.'

Jenny chirped up before Andrew could add anything, the only surprise being she wasn't asking for a piece of cake. 'Have you got a toilet?' she asked, pushing her knees together and hunching over slightly.

Darren had another chunk of cake on his fork as he eyed her suspiciously. He put it in his mouth and chewed as he continued to watch her, eventually swallowing and telling her it was upstairs, first door on the left. Jenny offered a cheery 'thanks' and then disappeared out of the kitchen.

Unlike Darren, Jenny's footsteps were barely audible as she padded up the stairs – just as Andrew's phone started to ring. The screen gave the office number, so Andrew held it up, asking 'You mind?' and getting a shrug from Darren, who seemed more interested in setting some sort of record for inhaling a gateau.

Andrew quickly headed along the hall until he was by the front door. He swiped to answer, muttering a quick 'Hunter Investigations'. There was no answer, so he repeated himself, before turning up the volume. All Andrew could hear was the sound of someone breathing.

'Hello?'

More breathing. It sounded wheezy and nasal – not that it particularly meant anything, considering altering a voice on a phone call was easy enough to do.

'Who is this?' Andrew tried.

Nothing.

Andrew hung up. When calls redirected to his mobile, it gave the office number – but he'd be able to find out who'd called once they got back to the office.

By the time Andrew got back to the kitchen, the cake was no more and Darren was washing it down with the lager. He nodded towards the flute. 'You want that, pal?'

'How much?'

'Forty. You sure you don't want anything else? I can do you a deal. I've got those remote-control things that turn your lights on and off. Going like hotcakes on the booters at the moment. Got some mini drones on the go, too. Give yourself a sneaky peep into your neighbour's window.'

He winked.

'I'm all right,' Andrew replied.

'I've got a mate who reckons he can get his hand on a hot tub. Might have to wait a week, but I know another guy who can fit it.'

'I'm sorted for hot tubs, thanks.'

Andrew took out his wallet and handed over two twenties. Darren's greedy eyes lit up and he dispatched the notes into his pocket with a piggy grin.

The sound of the toilet flushing echoed through the house and then Jenny re-emerged. 'We sorted?' she asked.

Andrew nodded to the door. 'Let's go.'

19

As soon as the car doors were closed, Andrew and Jenny both spoke at the same time.

'He's our guy!'

They went silent, waiting for the other to elaborate and then again spoke over one another. Eventually, Andrew started the engine and told Jenny to go first.

'Did you see the way he walked?' she said.

Andrew reversed the car and started to find his way back off the estate. 'I knew he was our bloke the minute he started shuffling along the hallway.'

'There was a dark hoody hanging on the bedroom door as well. Did you keep on at him about buying other instruments?'

'No point – if he'd had something to sell, he'd have been keen enough to hand it over. He's one of our robbers, but there are two others we don't know. When we get back to the office, see if you can find out who his mates are. After that—' Andrew was cut off by the sound of his phone ringing over the car's Bluetooth. The office number showed up on the dashboard.

'You gonna answer that?' Jenny asked.

'No.'

'Do you want me to?'

Andrew didn't reply, letting the phone ring off instead. 'I had a call while you were upstairs in Darren's house,' he said eventually.

'Who was it?'

'No reply, just loud breathing. That's *my* first job – check the call logs. Something weird's going on.'

When Andrew had been looking for offices to rent, there was one major reason he'd gone for the one he had. Location was one thing – it was central, yet on a quiet street and close to a couple of nice cafés. The biggest reason, though, was the parking space that came with the office. A good car parking spot in central Manchester that didn't cost more than the vehicle itself was rarer than a government minister pootling up to the city when there wasn't an election on.

The space was around the corner from the office, barely a minute's walk away. Andrew could – and frequently did – walk to work, but he often left his car in the office space so that it was easy enough to get out and visit clients or witnesses. If someone had offered him a naked supermodel who had eyes only for him at the expense of losing the parking spot, he'd take the spot every time.

At least he had a good idea of what to do with a parking space.

The shadow of the surrounding buildings left Andrew tugging his jacket tighter as he and Jenny walked along the cobbled street that intersected with the one that led to the office. He was lost in his thoughts – trying to weigh up Jack Marsh and his mother, wondering if he believed them. On balance he probably did, though he felt there was more to it than either was letting on.

Then there was Thomas Braithwaite and his weird obsession with some violin. Was there something hidden *inside* the instrument? Or was it valuable? Searches online for the engraving 'LK' or the apparent maker, Louis Kleinholt, had thrown up very little. If Kleinholt was a specialist, then he hid it well. Andrew suspected the only reason Braithwaite was so infuriated by what had happened was because he couldn't stand the idea of someone stealing from him. He used other people, not vice versa – which was why Andrew was still stuck in his clutches.

As they neared the junction, he spied Tina through the glass front of the building opposite his. She was the receptionist in a place that housed half a dozen businesses. She glanced up towards them and, though he wasn't sure she'd actually stopped typing, she somehow managed to wave at the same time, flashing a row of sharp, rainbow nails. It was like she had three hands. Andrew and Jenny returned the wave and then Tina somehow answered the phone too. Did she have *four* hands? It was extraordinary.

Andrew was so mesmerised that, as they rounded the corner next to the office, he didn't realise Jenny wasn't at his side any longer. She was lagging a few steps behind, slowing and falling further behind.

Andrew stopped and turned. 'You all right?' he asked.

Jenny was tight-lipped, nodding past him towards the office.

Andrew had been looking at his feet as they'd turned but followed Jenny's eyeline until he spotted the person sitting on the steps of his office. She was wearing a thin sweater and tight jeans, arms folded around her knees.

She stood, offering a narrow smile. 'Hi.'

Andrew took a breath, not certain his eyes were telling the truth. He turned between the newcomer and Jenny, before settling on Jenny. 'Can you hold the fort for a couple of hours?' he asked.

Jenny hoisted her key aloft and bounced on her heels before striding past him. 'When I was a kid, I built forts out of boxes, so holding one? No problem.'

The woman across from Andrew was wonderfully familiar and yet intoxicatingly different. Her blonde hair was shorter than the last time he'd seen her, no longer a bob, now tousled and slanted to one side, with a wide green headband across the top. Her skin was slightly browned from her time away. There was still the dot of a birthmark near her mouth, too – but it had gone even darker from the sunshine.

The café doors were open, allowing a steady breeze to billow around the warm insides. There was chatter, too. The sound of shoppers shopping, workmen working. Somewhere in the distance, a pneumatic drill was being put to good use. Well, hopefully good use. Every few minutes, the coffee machine inside would whoosh and pop, then the till would ding.

Andrew only had eyes and ears for his ex-wife, though.

'How long have you been back?' he asked.

'Five days,' Keira replied. 'Maybe six. It's a long flight. I went via Dubai, then I wasn't sure whether I'd gone forward or back in time.' She paused, fingering her cappuccino mug but not drinking. 'I've had a few things to do. Six weeks is a long time to be away. You should see my mail pile – mainly bills, of course. I've not got through it all yet.'

Andrew was finding it hard to look at Keira directly. He could almost manage it and yet there was a spot on the wall a little over her shoulder at which he found it easier to look. She was there, right in front of him, the woman whose face he'd been picturing every day since she walked out. Since he thought they were done for the second time. Then the postcard with its simple message arrived and he didn't know what to think. Now they were in the same place again.

'How was Thailand?' he asked.

Her face lit up. 'Amazing – one of my charity contacts helped set me up to work on this project for desalinating water. It's going to change the lives of hundreds of people, perhaps thousands. Then I spent a bit of time teaching and working with these kids. It was exhausting – twelve hours a day or more. I didn't feel it at the time, though.'

She yawned and then giggled as she tried to wave it away.

'I needed the break,' she added.

A break from you, Andrew thought. He was glad she didn't say it.

Keira sipped her drink, nibbled at her cookie. This was what they'd become – coffee and cookies. An amiable afternoon thing to do with a friend, not exactly yanked heartstrings and the love of one's life.

She put down the cup very deliberately and then looked up, waiting for Andrew to catch her gaze. 'I'll never forgive you,' Keira said softly but firmly. 'I'm sorry – I want to. I thought about it a lot while I was away. I wanted to be able to come back and tell you everything was fine, that I can forgive and forget. But I can't.'

Andrew felt something sharp stabbing his chest. This was a heart attack, wasn't it? He tried to remember the first signs. Wasn't it something like shortness of breath? It was – and he could breathe fine. No heart attack – just the stabbing, vicious blow of the woman he loved saying she'd never forgive him. He wasn't sure which was worse.

'I don't blame you,' Andrew heard himself saying. The words plopped out from nowhere.

'I understand why you took my father's money,' Keira added, still sounding firm. She'd clearly rehearsed. 'He never wanted us to marry in the first place and when we started talking about children, he wanted to do anything he could to break us up. When he told you it was leave me with his money or have him destroy us – and you – I know what you must've been feeling. I grew up with him. I know he's overbearing...' She stopped, coughed, gulped. 'He's a bully – always has been – and he's used to getting what he wants. I know how powerful he can seem and I really do get why you chose the money. What I can't forgive you for is not talking to me. Not giving me the option of choosing *you* over my parents. You dumped me and that was it.'

She stopped as her voice cracked. Andrew was desperately trying to swallow the enlarging lump in his throat, though he had no idea how to reply. She was right.

Keira took a long breath and then continued. 'I've been home and told my father that my relationship with him is done. I'll never forgive either of you for what you've cost me over the past nine years.'

This was not what Andrew had expected. Whether or not her father was a bully, Keira had always been a Daddy's girl. Rebelling against him by marrying Andrew was just about the only thing she'd ever done to defy her father. Andrew could barely get the words out as the lump in his throat was now some sort of bowling ball.

'Does this mean we're done?' he asked.

There was a pause. A really long pause. Andrew watched his former wife's nostrils flare and unflare as she breathed.

There was a loose eyelash clinging to the top of her cheek, bobbing up and down as she inhaled.

Eventually, she spoke – though her lips didn't move. The single word was so quiet that Andrew nearly missed it.

'No.'

The pain in Andrew's chest returned with a stabby vengeance and he found himself gasping, realising he'd been holding his breath for however long he'd waited for the reply.

Keira quickly continued: 'I'm going to get a flat in the city. I'd been thinking about it for a while and I'm bored of being in the country. It's not really me. It's good in the summer, but I don't think I could take another icy winter stuck in the middle of nowhere.' She sighed and then laughed. 'You don't know what it's like – farmers having to run tractors through the lanes to clear the frost, people freaking out because their kids can't get to school – and then panic-buying bread and milk from the corner shop. Everyone thinks Britain's this cosy little island – but they wouldn't think that if they saw what goes on with parish politics. There was this whole thing last year over a waiting list for an allotment plot. Anyway, it all...' She tailed off, smiling. '*Anyway*... I'm moving back to the city.'

'That's good.'

Keira nodded a small acknowledgement. 'I left my job working for Daddy...' She coughed. '...Working for the charitable division of *my father's* business. I'm going to set up my own foundation and he's paying. I didn't give him a choice. I told him that I'm not ready to talk to him anytime soon – but if he wants any sort of relationship in the future, then he'll leave me be – and stay well away from you, too. I talked it through with Mum last week. She says she didn't know what he'd done. He's now put a lump sum in an account. I want to do something working with children, a bit like I was before. I'm looking for projects around the city. I want it to be self-funding in the end. I don't want his money. It's a means to an end.'

'Where does that leave us?'

Keira took another breath, perhaps playing with him, perhaps thinking it over. 'We're divorced,' she said.

'I know—'

'But, if you want, I would be happy to begin again from zero. We've not really known each other these past nine years, so it'll be like starting over anyway.'

She sat back, having apparently said everything she wanted. Andrew wasn't exactly unhappy – it was so much more than he deserved – and yet it was so matter-of-fact that he wondered what starting 'from zero' might actually mean.

As if reading his mind, Keira leaned forward. 'I want to go back to the beginning,' she repeated. 'That means living apart, having separate lives away from each other. It means the odd date once or twice a week. Taking it slowly. Dinner and a movie. Perhaps a walk up in the hills if it's a nice Sunday. The sort of thing that we used to do when we were kids.' She stared directly at him. 'You can have a day or two if you want – but it's that or nothing. You have to let me know if you're in.'

Andrew again found himself speaking before he'd thought about the words. 'I'm in,' he said.

Keira nodded but didn't smile. 'This time our first date will not be at a launderette.'

21

Andrew walked at Keira's side along the pavement that led back to her student halls. It was in the opposite direction to his, but he hadn't told her yet for fear that she'd say something about making her own way. He wondered if he should offer her his hand to hold. It had been a good night... Well, he thought it had been anyway. Their first date – according to Keira anyway – had been at the launderette. In Andrew's mind, when she'd asked 'are you up to anything tonight?' and he'd replied 'I was going to wash all my clothes', that hadn't counted as an invitation to a date. For Keira, it apparently had – and so their 'first date' (for her) was at the launderette. Tonight's date – his first, her second – had been more traditional. They'd gone for a meal at the Italian just off Oxford Road, close to Cornerhouse. He didn't have much money and had panicked when she ordered scallops for starter, but Keira had insisted on paying her share anyway, refusing to let Andrew put anything down on her behalf. After that, they'd had a couple of drinks in a nearby pub, one of the quieter ones, and now he was walking her home.

It was all rather pleasant, rather normal.

Discounting the launderette, this was the first proper date Andrew had been on. There'd been group trips to the bowling alley as a young teenager, a cinema visit for three lads and three girls at about the same age – but none could properly count as a date.

This was the type of thing people talked about, made movies about. Somehow, five hours had passed with just him and some beautiful girl, and he'd not even noticed. Funny how those hour-long lectures seemed to drone on until the end of eternity, and yet his evening with Keira had lasted five times that and had blinked by.

'I'm here.'

Andrew realised he'd been daydreaming. It was dark but still warm enough to be comfortable without a jacket. The sound of partying students was booming from a nearby building, with multicoloured strobing lights blinking onto the darkened street. He'd continued on for a couple of steps, even though Keira had stopped.

He turned to see her pointing at a red-brick square block on the opposite side of the road from the party. '*Here*,' she added for emphasis.

'Oh, right.'

'Where are you living?'

Andrew pointed in the vague direction of his halls, trying not to make it too obvious they'd already gone past.

Keira nodded at her flat again. Her head remained tilted as she looked at him and he felt as if there was a spotlight on him. That some over-enthused game-show host was about to ask a question to which he didn't know the answer.

'Do you want to come in for coffee?' she asked.

Andrew glanced to the flats, then back to her. 'I don't really drink caffeine this late,' he replied. 'I avoid Coke as well. It messes up my sleep.'

She smiled a little more, twirling a strand of loose hair.

'How about a drink of anything then? We've got beer, water, all sorts of spirits. I think there might even be a bottle of orange squash somewhere. It's not mine, but no one will mind. If you're *really* lucky, there's still a bottle of full-sugar cherryade in the fridge. We were making cocktails at the weekend.'

Andrew didn't get to reply as the door to the party flat across the road banged open, sending a stream of thumping music barrelling out into the night. A lad stumbled onto the pavement, almost colliding with a lamp-post before catching himself. The door slammed closed behind him, dimming the music but only adding to his confusion. He straightened his clothes, turning in a full circle before realising Andrew and Keira were watching him. At that, he gave a crisp military salute and then stumbled off into the shadows without a word.

'That was weird,' Andrew said.

'Kinda normal at this end of town.' Keira took a step towards her flat. 'So, are you coming in then?'

'I don't drink that much at night – not unless I'm *out* out. Generally, I try not to drink at all after eight. I always need to wee during the night, then I can't get back to sleep...' He tailed off, realising Keira was staring at him.

'You've never had a girlfriend, have you?' she said.

'Um...'

Before he could say any more, Keira reached out and grabbed his hand, dragging him onto the path that led to her flat. 'Come on. Coffee or no coffee, cherryade or no cherryade, let's go inside anyway.'

22

When Andrew got back to the office after his coffee with Keira, he was met by a loud 'ta-da!' as he opened the door. Jenny jumped up from her desk, pointing towards a stack of boxes in the corner that contained printer paper.

'What am I looking at?' Andrew asked.

'I built a fort. Don't worry, I got a bunch of other stuff done, too.'

'You built a *fort?*'

Jenny slumped back into her chair, chocolate digestive in hand. 'I'd kinda finished everything you wanted doing, then you'd put forts in my mind, so... ta-da.' She pointed at the boxes again. 'I was going to build a crossbow with a ruler and some rubber bands but you got back too quickly.'

Andrew eyed the fort once more and then took his seat. He wasn't sure if he should be annoyed, impressed or bemused. He was a mix of all three.

'Brew?' she asked.

'I'm all brewed out for one day.'

Jenny was fidgeting in her seat restlessly. 'Everything all right with—'

'It's fine.'

There was an awkward silence, with Jenny leaving a gap for Andrew to fill with details. He didn't take it.

'Any phone calls?' he asked instead.

Jenny winced slightly, which was unusual for her.

'How many?' Andrew added.

'Three – as soon as I said hello, there was just breathing at the other end of the line. The number's showing as a mobile – but it's nobody I know and no one picks up if I call back.'

'Is it the same number that called when we were at Darren Wiley's house?'

'Same number all day.'

'Hmmm...'

Andrew glanced at the filing cabinet, thinking about the cases with which he'd recently dealt and the ones that were ongoing. Nobody jumped out as an obvious nutter. Persistent hang-ups were often the work of dodgy call centres trying to dial too many people at the same time. This was more than that, yet crank phone calls – for the most part – were a thing of the past. Caller ID and better systems for tracing those responsible had made it easier to prosecute. Not only that, in the age of website hacks, viruses, trojans, denial-of-service attacks – or even plain abuse via anonymous social media accounts – it wasn't a very twenty-first century way of targeting someone.

'Jack Marsh?' Andrew mused out loud. 'He could've easily found out the company's phone number?'

Jenny shrugged. 'Doesn't really seem like his thing, does it? Nor his mother.'

Andrew turned away from Jenny, not wanting her to look directly at him. 'Did Ollie take your break-up badly...?'

'He wasn't happy, but this isn't his style. He's more likely to get high and try to write a song.' She paused. 'Braithwaite?'

Andrew shook his head. 'Not his style, either. He's got Iwan to send any messages.' He drummed his fingers on the table and then picked up the phone. It wasn't so much the hang-ups or the heavy breathing about which he was concerned – it was the fact that when he'd answered the first time, the caller had asked for Jenny. He asked Jenny to read the number and then dialled it. One ring, two rings... six rings. Andrew was getting impatient, ready to leave an angry voice-mail, but after ten rings, there was a long beep and then the line went dead.

'This is going to be a burner phone,' Andrew said.

He started hunting through his own list of contacts anyway, looking for someone at the mobile company with whom he'd not been in touch for a while.

Twenty minutes and a fifty-quid promise later and he had the details he wanted. The number that had been calling his office came from a pay-and-go SIM. Andrew got the network name – not that it made much difference – plus the fact it had been topped up with a voucher that morning. The owner had made six calls – all to Andrew's office. The only way to trace any further – at least according to Andrew's contact – was with a warrant. The source had been nervous at passing over the little information he had, saying Leveson and the *News of the World* had changed things. 'You can to go to prison for this sort of thing nowadays,' he added.

Andrew hung up and passed the news onto Jenny, though neither of them was surprised.

'Do you want some good news?' she asked.

'You're planning a bigger fort?'

'Oooh, yes. But, first, I've found a girl who used to waitress in the restaurant part of the Radisson last autumn. I reckon she might have been working on the night Jack Marsh and his teammates were staying there.'

'How did you find her?'

'Twitter. Her name's Mia Church. Three weeks ago, she

wrote that it was her final day at the Radisson. She's a student, so she was giving up the job to concentrate on her exams.'

'She doesn't work there any more?'

'No – so she might talk. I went back through her profile. There's all sorts of stuff about music, films, nights out, lectures – the usual stuff. Anyway, on the night Michelle Applegate went missing last September, she wrote that she was off to work. After that, she didn't post again for a month.' Jenny peered up, dimples on display. She might be hard to read sometimes, but everyone liked a good pat on the head when they'd done well.

'Good work,' Andrew said, writing 'Mia Church' on the pad on his desk.

Jenny wasn't done. 'I've also got Darren Wiley's criminal record. He—'

'Hang on a minute. Who did you get that from?'

Jenny batted him away with a dismissive wave of the hand. No big deal, don't worry about it. 'Someone I know,' she said coyly.

'It's just...' Andrew bit his lip, not wanting to shut her down, but still...

'I was careful,' Jenny added. 'The person won't get in trouble. No call logs, no computer trails – just an exchange of information between two mutual acquaintances. Anyway, I don't think Darren has learned his lesson. Despite all that stuff at his house, he's been done twice for handling stolen goods. Once for nicking car stereos back in the day when they weren't so modern and built-in. He was eighteen at the time, so over a decade ago. He got unpaid work.' Jenny typed away on her keyboard, muttering something under her breath and then she looked up again. 'Two years later, he was on a joint charge with someone named Finn Renton.'

She spelt it and Andrew wrote that name down as well.

'Sounds like a fish tank cleaner,' Andrew said. '"Want your tank cleaner than clean? Try our new formula Finn Renton".'

Jenny smiled, humouring him. 'Renton's got a much longer charge sheet. He—'

'You've got his as well?'

Another bat of the hand. 'Stop worrying! Renton's on bail, awaiting trial for theft from a shop. He doesn't seem to know what belongs to him and what doesn't. He's a terrible criminal, too – always getting caught. He lives in Longsight and I've got an address.'

'Any violence on his record?'

'Just thieving, plus drunk and disorderly and a cannabis possession.'

'Any photos?'

She turned her monitor, allowing Andrew to see a pasty, pointy-faced, snub-nosed rat of a man. 'Quite the catch,' she said. 'I reckon—'

Jenny didn't get a chance to say what she reckoned as the phone started to ring. Andrew and Jenny looked at each other, both thinking the same thing.

'I'll get it,' Andrew said.

And he did.

23

By eight o'clock the following morning, Andrew was in the car waiting across from Finn Renton's house. He was about to knock on his door when Finn emerged, picking his nose and fumbling in his baggy grey trackie bottoms. The pants were so loose that they almost fell down as he searched through his various pockets until he eventually found the door key, which he promptly dropped.

After picking it back up and locking the house, he headed along the street, one hand in his pocket, the other scratching his arse. Not knowing if he was going to be back anytime soon, Andrew set off after him. Considering his thin, runty physique, Finn kept quite a pace and Andrew had to jog in order to catch him at a pedestrian crossing.

He filed in a little behind Finn, largely anonymous among the bevy of uniform-wearing schoolkids and adults heading for the bus stop. Andrew followed him along Stockport Road, past the sports hall until Finn headed into the Nisa Local. He waited outside, leaning on the barrier next to the pelican crossing, enjoying the trickle of morning sun.

When Finn re-emerged, he was struggling with the plastic

wrapper of a cigarette packet. He first tried digging in his fingernails, then used his teeth, spitting the remains of the wrapper onto the ground.

'There's a bin there,' Andrew said, making Finn jump with surprise.

'Y'what?' Finn replied.

Andrew nodded at the transparent wrapper that was wedged in the gutter, barely a metre from the bin. 'There's a bin there. You missed.'

Close up, Finn Renton was even weedier than he seemed from a distance. It was hard to tell for sure because of his baggy clothes – but his shoulders were like a malnourished child's, the collarbone jutting out near the V of his top. Andrew suspected he was the taller person from the CCTV footage of the music shop robbery. He was pretty sure Finn was still wearing the same tracksuit. There were at least three bristled reddy-brown stains on the top, likely a remnant of dinner from any night in the past few days.

It suddenly dawned on Andrew that it was one thing to be a smart-arse – but a person could end up looking a hell of a lot less smart-arsey if some rodent-faced thug had a knife on them.

Luckily, Finn seemed more confused than aggressive, his nose twitching as if he knew trouble was ahead. 'Who are you?' he asked, stepping away from Andrew.

'Was there any particular reason you chose to rob that music store the other week?'

Finn goggled at Andrew, eyes widening so that thin veiny strands of red were nibbling around the edges. For a moment, Andrew thought he might actually pop with surprised bemusement, but then Finn ducked his head, flipping his hood up and hurrying past Andrew.

'Dunno what you're on about, mate.'

Andrew must've woken up on some magical side of the

bed because he was feeling surprisingly fit as he strode along-side the younger man, keeping pace and not losing his breath.

'I know you burgled the place,' Andrew continued.

'Not me, pal.'

'You busted in with two of your mates, nicked some instru-ments, some music books. You're on CCTV wearing the exact hoody you've got on now.'

There was the briefest of pauses, before: 'No way.'

'The music books were a bit weird – but I wonder if you know whose violin you took.'

Finn ignored him, upping his pace even more and charging across the road without waiting for the blinky green man. Andrew lost a few steps as he stepped onto the road and then had to jump back as an angry driver honked her horn and gave him the fingers for good measure. Presumably, it wasn't the Churchillian V for victory. After the car zoomed around the corner, Andrew set off again.

'Ignoring me isn't going to make this go away,' Andrew called after him.

Finn continued to say nothing, walking so quickly that he was practically jogging. He got to his front door a moment before Andrew, but as he fumbled for his keys, Andrew got in front, blocking the way. Finn's teeth were gritted as he reared back, as if about to strike, but Andrew could see in his eyes that he didn't have it in him. He wasn't ready to fight – he was ready to sprint.

'Seriously,' Andrew said firmly. 'Do you know whose violin you stole?'

Finn motioned to run but then stopped, torn between his escape and what Andrew was actually saying.

'Whose?' he growled.

'Why would you care if you didn't take it?'

Finn was caught between ignorance and wanting to know

if he'd annoyed the wrong person. 'I dunno what you're on about,' he said unconvincingly.

This time, Andrew stepped past him, away from the front door, leaving it clear. 'It's no skin off my nose, Finn. You can either invite me in for a brew, or I can go and tell the owner of that violin who took it. It's your choice – but if I were you, I'd open the door and stick the kettle on.'

It was risky, more of a Jenny scheme than something Andrew would come up with, but after a few seconds of posturing and pocket-groping, Finn wrestled his front door open, disappearing into the darkness without closing it behind him.

Andrew took that as an invitation, following inside, closing the door and then turning to find himself in a dimly lit bedsit. The carpet was manky cream-brown, covered in muddy footprints and smelled of a mouldy old PE kit. Everything seemed to be in one room, with a sofa and TV close to the door where Andrew was. Aside from a stack of CDs on the floor, there was little else to see, except for a small kitchen at the opposite end of the room.

Finn was struggling to connect his kettle to the wall, the plug scraping around the plastic casing. He growled and swore under his breath before reaching into the drawer under the sink and pulling out a knife. He was about to jab it into the socket when Andrew got to him.

'Don't do that,' Andrew said.

'What?'

'Stick a knife in the socket. You'll electrocute yourself.'

Finn pushed him aside and jammed the knife into the socket anyway, giving it a jerk until there was a fizzing crack. Andrew winced but nothing happened. Finn pushed the kettle's plug into the wall and flicked it on.

'You Old Bill?' he asked, not looking at Andrew.

'My name's Andrew. I'm a private investigator.'

Finn turned, leaning against the sink as the kettle started to hiss. 'What's that?'

'Basically, I find stuff out – like I found out you were one of the blokes who broke into the music shop.'

'Weren't me.' Finn shook his head with the conviction of someone saying they'd love a plateful of sprouts.

'I'm giving you a chance here, Finn. I'm not an idiot.'

'Who do you work for?'

'No one... not really. But the man who that violin belongs to isn't happy about it going missing. He's...' Andrew struggled for the right words. 'Let's just say he's not the forgiving type.'

Finn wrinkled his nose and then started to scratch his arms so hard that Andrew thought he might draw blood. There was a thin, blade-shaped scar from his ear to his neck and he'd clearly seen the rougher side of Manchester. This time, he didn't even bother to give it the hardman act.

'Look, man, I've done stupid things. I can't even nick stuff without getting caught. They've done me with DNA, finger-prints, a footprint. One time, I even left my coat behind.' He sighed, close to tears. Not at all what Andrew had been expecting. He crumpled against the cabinet like a soggy slipper.

'Finn...'

'My dad was a rum 'un. Used to be all sorts of nicked stuff around the house. Like a bloody Argos catalogue at times. No surprise I turned out like I did. What did people expect? He weren't interested in me doing my schoolwork, he was more bovvered about whether I could fit through the neighbour's cat flap to get the door open.'

'Finn...'

The man wasn't listening. He flung a hand towards the room in general and then looked Andrew dead in the eye. This time there were tears. 'Look, Mr Private Investigator. Mr Clever Dick. I have a lad who's really got something. I dunno where he gets it from 'cos it ain't me and it definitely ain't his mum – but he's amazing at music. His teacher reckons he's the bee's bollocks. She's talking 'bout seeing if she can get him into that music school in the centre. Reckons she knows someone who can pay for it.'

'Chetham's—'

'He ain't cheating nobody, mate.'

'No, Chetham's School of Music.'

Finn flapped another hand, talking over Andrew. 'Whatever. There's this piano at his school and he can just play it. Christ knows how. He don't need music books. You name it, he can play it. I bet he's even a genius on the triangle.'

Andrew couldn't stop himself – the triangle remark brought a smile and then Finn finally relaxed, grinning proudly to himself, too. The kettle clicked off, but they both ignored it.

Finn tugged on his baggy top. 'When you come from a place like me, people assume you're scum.' He shrugged, accepting it. 'But my lad's different. He don't have to be like me. His teacher's got him an audition at that Cheat-em place you were on about. But he needs an instrument. His school can't move the piano and it ain't as if I've got a pile of trumpets lying about. I had to do something.'

Andrew had expected denials, perhaps aggression, definitely stupidity. What he hadn't expected was tears from someone who, if nothing else, unequivocally loved his son and wanted to provide a better life.

'Where's the violin?' Andrew asked.

Finn shook his head. 'You can't take it, man. It's my kid's. His name's Nathan.'

'Things will be much worse if the owner finds out you've got it.'

Finn tried to stand taller and puff out his chest. It didn't work. 'You reckon? I'll get me mates together and take on whoever it is. They want it? They'll have to take it.'

Andrew said nothing at first, waiting for Finn to realise how ridiculous he sounded. 'All that for a violin?' he asked.

Finn shook his head again, more softly this time. 'All that for my kid.'

Andrew stared at him and then couldn't take it any longer. He sighed and moved back out of the kitchen. 'Tell you what. Let me borrow it...'

24

When Andrew let himself into the office, a higgledy-piggledy pile of mail was scattered across the concrete entranceway. He scooped it up, holding it under his armpit and cradling the violin case, before heading up the stairs.

Jenny was at her desk, tapping away on her keyboard. She turned, gasping an 'oh' of surprise.

'What?' Andrew asked.

'Is that... *the* violin?'

'Yep.'

'Finn Renton nicked it?'

Andrew didn't answer properly, slipping the case under his desk instead. He didn't want to talk about it. Next, he dropped the mail by his keyboard and then started to pick through it.

'Bin, bin, bin, bin, mine, bin, yours, bin, bin, mine, mine...' He paused, holding a large brown envelope up. It was slim and bendy, a single word written in capital letters on the front: JENNY. There was no address, no stamp. It had been hand-delivered. Andrew held it up for her to see.

Jenny first removed her glasses to squint away from the screen and then leaned across to take it from him.

'Recognise the handwriting?' Andrew asked.

'No...' She turned it over, looking at the back, which was equally devoid of clues. 'Should I open it?'

It was strange to hear her so reticent. Usually she'd go storming into situations and think about the consequences afterwards.

'I suppose...'

Jenny carefully pulled apart the corner of the envelope, peeping inside and then sniffing it for some reason. Seemingly satisfied, she ripped along the rest of the top and pulled out a card that immediately dispatched a coating of glitter onto her desk.

'This is a first,' she said, holding it up for Andrew to see.

She was holding a large Valentine's Day card, with a bright red heart on the front alongside some cutesy teddy bears that were either cuddling or dry-humping. Probably cuddling.

'It's about two months late,' Andrew said. 'Does it say anything inside?'

Jenny opened the card and turned it for Andrew to see. The single-word message was loud and clear: BITCH.

'It must be someone who knows me,' Jenny said with a smile, although there was little humour behind it. She put the card on her desk and then swept the glitter into the bin with the side of her hand.

'Jen...'

Jenny ignored Andrew, turning back to her screen and typing something. Andrew tried again and she replied 'What?' without looking up.

'The calls and now the letter... I think we should tell someone.'

'Who?'

'I have a friend in the police. She'll at least be able to get onto the phone companies so we can find out where the calls are coming from.'

'It's fine.'

'Do you know who it might be?'

Jenny didn't reply at first, flipping her glasses back onto the end of her nose and focusing on her screen. Once again, Andrew couldn't read her. She didn't seem scared. Perhaps it was embarrassment or self-consciousness because he was witnessing what was going on.

'Jen?' he repeated.

'I don't know. It's fine – don't worry about it.'

'Could it be Ollie?'

She made a low popping sound as she puckered her lips. 'I doubt it.'

'How upset was he when you broke up?'

Jenny stopped typing, digging into her bottom drawer and emerging with a Hobnob. It was like she had a mini bakery on the go. She didn't take a bite, instead holding it in front of her lips as if it was a small shield. 'Quite upset, I guess. I didn't really notice. I was just, "It's over," and he was all "Why?" and that. I wanted to get out of there, he wanted a conversation.'

'What happened then?'

'I got out of there.'

'Out of where?'

'We were in a pub just off Oxford Road. It was busy.'

'You broke up with him in a busy pub?'

'Yeah...' She spoke with no comprehension of why that might be awkward.

'It's just...' Andrew stopped, wanting to get the words right. Occasionally he felt like Jenny's teacher, which was always unnerving. 'Were you frightened of him?' he asked.

'Why would I be?'

'If you weren't scared of being around him, then breaking up in a public place is quite a brutal thing to do. Other people would've seen, perhaps overheard. If he didn't see it coming, it means he could have been doubly humiliated. Doubly hurt, perhaps? I don't know him, but, if someone was breaking up with me, I'd rather it was in a quiet, private place.'

Jenny removed her glasses and then put them on again, before finally biting into the biscuit. She seemed to be considering what he'd said. 'Yeah...' she replied, 'that probably would have been a better idea.'

Andrew nodded at the card. 'What do you want to do with it?'

She took a breath. 'Nowt... for now.' Her grin was back. 'What do you want to do with the violin?'

Andrew returned her smile. 'Nowt... for now.'

She snorted and it was as if everything was back to normal.

'Right,' Andrew declared, wanting to move on. 'Mia Church worked at the Radisson on the night Michelle Applegate went missing. She left three weeks ago. What else do we know about her?'

Jenny scoffed the rest of her biscuit and bashed away on her keyboard. 'She's a final-year student at MMU, so she'll either be doing exams now or very soon. According to her LinkedIn account, she's studying ornithology.'

'Birds?' Andrew asked, unsure.

'Birds. I didn't even know you *could* study ornithology as a degree.'

'Any idea how to get in contact with her?'

Jenny grinned. 'As a matter of fact she was complaining about her postman on Twitter a month or so ago. I have the road she lives on, but I'm not sure which number. She's not on the electoral roll up here, but that's not unusual for students. She lives with a couple of other girls, which might be a clue. I might be able to get a phone number from one of my sources...'

Andrew thought for a moment and then reached for his

jacket. 'Let's go for a wander instead.' He picked up the violin case and tapped it. 'First, I have a shop to visit.'

Mia Church lived on a street not far from the pleasant green of Gartside Gardens, a short walk from the main university campus – and only five minutes from where Jenny lived. There was a collection of relatively new semi-detached houses in the shadow of a monster pair of cranes that were busy erecting something that was likely going to end up being new student flats. There was always something being built in the area, with the general Peter Street and Oxford Road parts of the city a perpetual building site.

It only took a quick stroll along the street for Andrew to spot the RSPB sticker in the upstairs window of one of the houses. Considering how close it was to the centre of the city, the street was wonderfully quiet and was empty aside from a few cars parked half on the pavement. The house they assumed was Mia's had a neat lawn, but the one next to it was a total contrast. It was bin day, with rows of wheelies lined up along the pavement. Piles of pizza boxes were stacked next to the wall, with empty cans and bottles spilling out from a recycling box.

Andrew held the gate open for Jenny, motioning for her to go first. When looking to get information from young women, it really helped to have another young woman there to do the talking.

After Jenny knocked, the door was answered by a girl with long red hair and thick-framed dark glasses. She was wearing a dressing gown with enormous Elmo slippers. 'All right?' she said.

'Are you Mia?' Jenny asked.

The girl shook her head and muttered something that

sounded like 'hang on'. She disappeared inside and moments later there was a loud cry of 'Mia!'

Mia was next to the door, a short girl with a dark mob of hair and even thicker-rimmed glasses.

'Er... hello?' Mia said, eyeing Jenny and then Andrew, wondering if she knew them.

'Hi, I'm Jenny. I was wondering if you're free for a bit of a chat...?'

'Who are you?'

'Private investigators...' Jenny nodded at Andrew. 'Well, he is. We were hired by the mother of Michelle Applegate and—' Mia started to edge the door closed, but Jenny moved quicker, wedging herself into the gap while still managing a friendly smile. She didn't even break the rhythm of her sentence: 'We only need ten minutes.'

Mia stopped pushing at the door, frowning. 'I'm not sure what you think I can tell you about anything.'

'You worked at the Radisson, right?'

'Yeah... how—'

'And you were there on the night Jack Marsh and the rest of his team stayed there. Jack's girlfriend ended up in the canal at some point that evening. The police probably spoke to you at some point...'

Mia stepped backwards, allowing the door to open slightly. 'Well, yes... they talked to everyone who worked there. We all had to give statements, but then I never heard anything after that.'

Jenny sounded as firm but friendly as before. 'We just want ten minutes.'

'Why?'

'Because Michelle's mother *really* wants to know what happened to her daughter.' Jenny shrugged, her smile slipping into something sadder. 'Look, we're roughly the same age.

Michelle was the same when she ended up in the water. Imagine if your best mate or sister died and you didn't know why? You'd really want to get to the bottom of it, wouldn't you?'

Mia stared at Jenny and then reached for the door and tugged it open with a stifled yawn and a sigh. 'I guess you better come in.'

25

The inside of the house was a lot tidier than anything Andrew remembered from his student days. Classical music was drifting from upstairs, but Mia led Andrew and Jenny through a set of swing doors into a living room that had a television at one end and a sofa at the other. On the wall was a large poster of the periodic table next to an even larger poster that had drawings of various birds, along with the species names underneath. Mia sat at the dining table, which acted as some sort of barrier between the two ends of the room, waiting for Jenny and Andrew to sit opposite.

'Sorry for the mess,' she said, indicating the room that was devoid of anything Andrew would ever define as 'mess'.

Jenny turned in a circle. 'You should see *my* place if you think this is a mess.'

Mia peered around, yawning and wafting a hand to stop herself. 'Tess must've cleaned up. I didn't even notice. She's a bit of a clean freak. That suits the rest of us, though.' She looked from Jenny to Andrew and back again. 'So...'

Jenny didn't hesitate. 'Is it true you were working on the night Michelle Applegate ended up in the canal?'

She nodded. 'Right. Did someone at the hotel tell you?'

Jenny nodded, which was a little naughty. Andrew didn't correct her. 'How well do you remember it?' she asked.

Another yawn – and another apology. 'We had football teams stay every now and then, so it wasn't unusual. I wasn't on shift the next day, but when it all came out about what happened to Jack Marsh's girlfriend, everyone was talking and texting. The police interviewed everyone who worked that night.'

'Did you know any of the footballers?'

'Only because I'd seen some of their photos – and then because they'd stay over every couple of weeks. Some of the lads at uni were jealous. You got used to seeing the same faces, but that's not just footballers. We'd have business people and others stay every weekend. They'd nod at you and you'd nod back.'

'What are the footballers like?'

'How'd you mean?'

'I suppose some sportspeople have bad reputations.'

Mia stifled another yawn and said something about late-night revision. Her eyes were bleary. 'I never had a problem with anyone,' she said. 'Most of them kept to themselves. Some didn't really speak English. They were all polite when they were asking for stuff. I think one of the cleaners complained once that someone had left a mess – but I don't really know. Nothing major.'

'What about Jack Marsh specifically?'

'What about him?'

'Did you know him?'

Mia shrank slightly, leaning back in the chair and picking her knees up so that she was cross-legged. Suddenly, she couldn't meet Jenny's gaze. 'Sort of.'

'What does that mean?'

'Well...'

Jenny scrabbled into her bag and pulled out her phone, tapping the screen and spinning it for Mia to see. 'He gave me his number.'

Mia broke into a smile and the two young women laughed at the shared moment. 'Did he take your phone and type the number in?'

'Yep.'

They both winced. 'Ugh,' Mia said. 'I didn't know if it was just me. I suppose some girls must go for it.'

'Imagine that, though. What would you say when you called back? "Hi, remember me? You typed your number into my phone." Then he'd have to ask which girl you were because he'd given his number to so many people.'

Mia laughed again, nodding in agreement. 'I kept it for a few days, mainly to show the lads at uni. I deleted it after that.'

'Did you tell the police he gave you his number?'

The smile disappeared from Mia's face. 'I didn't think it was relevant.'

Jenny nodded along. 'You're probably right.'

Mia examined her before nodding slightly. She seemed a little embarrassed and had probably been wondering whether she should have told the police ever since it had happened. This would have been the first time someone had reassured her that it was okay.

'So what was he like?' Jenny added.

Mia was staring at her bird poster, not quite able to meet Jenny's gaze again. 'I didn't...'

Jenny said nothing, leaving a perfect silence that Mia couldn't stop herself from filling.

'I did think about it,' she said quietly.

Neither Jenny nor Andrew filled the gap. Mia took a breath. 'It was a few weeks before everything happened. I was on room service duty and had taken something up to a room where Jack Marsh was staying. He was with another bloke – one of his teammates. Danny something. I took their food in and he was telling me about what position he plays, that sort of thing. I wasn't interested, but then Jack said he had to pop next door. I assume he meant someone else's room. Anyway, me and Danny, well...' she shrugged, 'we had a bit of fun.' She peered at the table, apparently regretting it.

'There's nothing wrong with that,' Jenny said.

'I didn't tell the police that, either. Danny and Jack were staying in the same room together on the night they were asking about, too.'

'So...'

Mia shook her head slowly. 'It was a one-time thing with Danny. Then, a couple of weeks later, Jack gave me his phone number.'

'Did anything happen with Jack?'

A shake of the head. 'Not *that*.'

'But something did...?'

Mia gulped, still fixed on the table. 'Can I get in trouble for talking to you? I didn't do anything bad, but, well... you hear about withholding evidence and all that. I didn't think it was a big deal, plus I didn't want my bosses finding out that I'd... *y'know*... with one of the players. They'd have sacked me and I needed the money.'

'If you've not done anything wrong, then you can't get in trouble,' Jenny said. 'We're not taking notes, we're not recording anything. If you have something to say, nobody aside from us needs to know where it came from.'

Mia blew out a long breath. 'I didn't see either Danny or Jack on the night that girl ended up in the canal,' she said, before finally looking up to catch Jenny's stare. 'I was wait-ressing downstairs. I don't think I saw any of the players.'

'But something happened, didn't it?'

'I don't know – I really don't. It's just...' She gulped. 'On the night I was in the room with Danny, we got talking. I don't know how we got onto it, but he told me he was gasping for a smoke. He said some of the players smoke quite a lot and one of the reasons the club book them into a hotel is because it makes it really hard for them to get away with having a fag.'

Andrew felt a prickling at the back of his neck as Mia told her story. This was it.

'He was being really nice and I suppose I was a bit flattered. Anyway, there's a back exit at the hotel. You have to go through this staff-only door to get there and then there's another one marked as a fire exit.'

Andrew and Jenny already knew that from their jaunt around the hotel.

'Isn't it alarmed?' Andrew asked. It was the first thing he'd said since entering the living room and Mia turned to look at him. She seemed surprised, as if she'd forgotten he was there.

'Anyone can push through the fire exit,' she said. 'There's a sign to say it's alarmed, but I don't think it's ever worked. All the kitchen lads use it to nip out for a fag. Not all the staff know about it, I guess, but I was friends with one of the cooks and we used to use it. It opens into this alley that's in the shadow of the hotel.'

Andrew was surprised Jenny managed to hold onto a smirk of knowing she was right after all.

'Are there any cameras?' Jenny asked.

'Not that I've seen. Certainly not inside the hotel.'

'And can you get out onto the main road from there?'

'If you wanted to.'

'So Jack Marsh *could* have got out of the hotel without going through the front where the security cameras are?' Jenny spoke quickly, but it was the biggest question of them all. The hairs on Andrew's arms were standing.

Slowly, very slowly, Mia nodded. 'If Danny had told him

about the door. He'd have had to use the stairs, go through the staff door, then get along the corridor and out the fire exit without being seen, but that's possible.'

'I'm sorry to ask this,' Jenny said, 'but to be absolutely certain: did you tell the police any of this?'

An even slower shake of the head. 'I didn't want to mess up my course by losing my job. It was only a part-time thing for a bit of money on the side.' From nowhere she grasped Jenny's hand and squeezed, blurting out a flurry of words. 'It wouldn't have been him, though, would it? They say she was drunk and fell in the canal. It's not like he got her drunk, is it? She'd already been drinking. I read about it.'

Jenny didn't remove her hand. 'You're probably right,' she said.

Mia carefully released her grip and then leaned back. 'Do you think he did it?'

Jenny couldn't resist a quick sideways glance towards Andrew. 'That's what we're hoping to find out.'

Mia had little else to say, though she repeated herself to make clear that she'd definitely not seen Jack Marsh on the evening Michelle Applegate had ended up in the canal. She'd told them more than enough anyway. The issue would have been whether Jack knew about it. Without Mia's testimony, there was nothing to say he had any knowledge of another way to exit the hotel. There was nothing concrete, but for the first time, they knew that Jack *could* have exited and perhaps re-entered the hotel without being seen.

Jenny thanked Mia for her help and then she and Andrew headed outside. The front door was closed and they were at the end of the path when Jenny stopped. Andrew did too, following her gaze to his car, where there was a splintered circle in the centre of the shattered rear window. As he moved closer, Andrew could see the reason. Sitting on his back seat was a half-brick surrounded by a glittering pile of jagged glass.

26

Andrew might have complained about how annoying the radio advert was with its catchy, mind-drilling jingle about fixing windscreens – but he was ultimately glad the rhyming series of numbers had forever etched itself into his brain.

After returning to the office, Jenny was uncharacteristically quiet, though she still said she doubted it was her ex-boyfriend who was responsible. Andrew's car wasn't exactly distinctive – a dark blue Toyota – and yet, if someone knew he drove it, it would be easy enough to follow.

The afternoon had passed and they'd both gone home for the day – but Andrew couldn't sit around doing nothing. Somebody was targeting Jenny and he had a decent idea of who.

He was in a pub, trying to block out the warblings of the frontwoman whose band was currently offending his ears. The singer had green, spiky hair with a studded leather collar connected to a dog lead that was dragging behind her as she made various lunges with the microphone. Andrew couldn't make out many of the lyrics, though he did catch that she had rhymed 'depression' with 'oppression', which seemed about right. The longer she went on, the more he felt a victim of both.

He was by himself, wedged into a small booth close to a bar on the edge of Manchester's Northern Quarter. It was a mixed crowd of student types along with those he generally assumed to be hippie sorts. That would no doubt have him labelled a snob by Jenny. There was also a handful of suited beardy-weirdy pseudo-hipsters, with ludicrous amounts of hair wax.

It wasn't Andrew's scene. Despite the flat pint of bitter he was cradling, he quite fancied a cup of tea somewhere warm where he could put his feet up.

Oliver Raphael had been easy to find. His social media pages were largely concealed to people who didn't know him – but, with such a distinctive name, there was still a drip-drip of information about him online. Andrew had looked him up when Jenny was out of the office, noting the address and saving a photo to his phone. After leaving work, Andrew headed to the shop where Ollie worked and then followed him. With the rush-hour crush, it had been easy enough to go unseen.

Andrew had expected to trail him towards a house or flat, waiting until Ollie was alone and away from the crowds for them to have a chat. Instead, Ollie had headed through the throng of people past the Arndale Centre and then cut along Oldham Street, ducking into a pub. Andrew had followed... waiting for the right moment.

Two and a half hours later and it hadn't happened.

Andrew was on his second pint, not particularly wanting another and hoping the bar staff didn't notice how slowly he was drinking.

He wasn't sure what he expected of Jenny's boyfriend, given he'd only found out the lad's name a short time before. Ollie was a cross between the hipster lot and the slightly younger sportier crowd. His hair was ridiculous, some sort of whippy ice cream quiff thing that likely took hours every day to perfect. He had the sort of designer stubble that could only be sculpted with a precision razor, even though it was supposed to be casual, with a 'couldn't-be-bothered-shaving' look.

Ollie was wearing a Manchester United football shirt. He was mid-twenties, surrounded by his mates and crowded around a pool table. They were the usual gel, T-shirt and too much Lynx crowd. Even though the singer was doing her best to shatter eardrums in a quarter-mile radius, the lads were largely ignoring her, concentrating instead on beating each other at pool. Between them, there was around forty quid's worth of pound coins on the side of the table. They'd been playing for most of the time Andrew had been there and showed no sign of stopping.

Finally, Andrew spotted his moment. Ollie separated from his friends, whispering something to one of them and then plonking his empty pint glass on the bar before edging through the crowd towards the toilet. Andrew left his pint by his chair and followed, apologising his way through the packed pub until he reached the far side.

It only dawned on Andrew after he'd entered the toilet that, to an untrained eye – or even a trained one – he had just followed a younger lad into the bathroom having sat surreptitiously watching him for more than two hours.

This had 'grooming' written all over it.

Luckily the toilet was empty. Andrew crouched, spotting a single pair of bright white trainers in the end booth. He waited next to the hand-dryer, fiddling with his phone in case anyone entered. He'd rarely heard a sweeter sound than the flushing of the toilet. Ollie emerged and headed for the sinks, which at least meant he wasn't a complete psycho. He washed his hands and then moved towards the hand-dryers, wringing his hands and then noticing Andrew for the first time.

'Oh,' he said.

'Hi, Ollie.'

Ollie stopped where he was, eyes narrowing. 'Do I know you?'

Andrew moved quickly, striding forward and shoving his forearm hard into Ollie's breastbone, forcing him back into the wall. Ollie struggled, but he was skinny and, though Andrew wasn't exactly athletic, he had what could kindly be described as a 'bit of padding'. More importantly, he had momentum. Ollie struggled but had missed his chance to skip away.

'What are you doing to Jenny?' Andrew demanded.

Ollie coughed from the winding. He was trying to force Andrew backwards but only half-heartedly, not wanting a fight. 'What?' he gasped.

'Jenny. She broke up with you, so what's the problem?'

Ollie pushed again and this time Andrew stepped backwards and released him. They eyed each other for a moment. Andrew could feel his pulse racing in a way it rarely did. He was full of adrenalin, trying to contain his anger. Ollie was bemused.

'*Jenny?*' he said.

'You know what I'm talking about – the phone calls, the card.'

Ollie shook his head. 'I don't know what you're on about. I don't even know who you are.' He wrung his hands again and then his eyes widened. 'Hang about, you're *him*, aren't you?'

'Who?'

Ollie clicked his fingers. 'You're Andrew.'

Andrew suddenly felt self-conscious. It was no surprise that Jenny's former boyfriend knew the name of who she worked for – and yet he felt at a disadvantage, wondering what Jenny had been saying about him.

Ollie was suddenly on the offensive, lunging forward and making Andrew stumble towards the cubicles. 'You reckon *I'm* stalking *her*? She's the crazy one.'

'What?'

Ollie whirled a finger close to his ear. 'She's nuts, mate. Snooker-loopy – and she's got one hell of a thing for you.'

'What are you on about?'

'She's always saying things like, "Andrew wouldn't do it like that". She goes on about you *all* the time. I knew Jen was never that into me, but since she shacked up with you, she's totally lost it.'

Andrew stared at him, struggling to take it all in. 'Shacked up?'

'Whatever. Seriously, pal. She's a mentalist. If you're getting dodgy phone calls or whatever, it wouldn't surprise me if it was her.'

Ollie pushed past him, leaving Andrew stunned and staring at himself in the mirror. He had no idea what to think. 'Hey!' he called, just before Ollie got to the door.

'What?'

'I'm, um... sorry, I suppose.'

Ollie looked him up and down. 'Mate – she does this to people. You must know that.' He rocked back and then seemed to stand slightly taller. It was like someone had hit the jackpot on a fruit machine when he stepped forward again. As if he'd just realised something that should have been obvious. 'You don't know, do you?'

'Know what?' Andrew replied.

There was an awkward moment where Ollie pushed the toilet door fully closed, blocking out a little more of the singer. There was a hint of a smirk on his face. 'I thought you'd know. I guessed she was shagging you. Don't matter to me – but she gets night terrors. Screaming, shouting, waking up and clawing at the air.' He held his arm up, showing red crescent moons on his wrist.

'Jenny did that?' Andrew asked, unsure what to make of it.

'Middle of the night. Scared the hell out of me. Not her fault, I suppose – it's not like she was awake.' Ollie took another step forward. He scratched his head, confused. 'Hang on a minute, you don't know *any* of it, do you?'

'Know what?'

Ollie laughed humourlessly. 'About her brother.'

As Ollie pushed his way out of the toilet, Andrew stood and stared. He couldn't find the words to query that Jenny had always told him she was an only child.

27

Andrew couldn't sleep.

The clock next to his bed read 12:34, its block-like red digits taunting him through the darkness. He'd not bothered trying to close his eyes. He had lain and then sat in bed, thinking. When he got bored of that, he opened the curtains and watched the city below. Long lines of street lights stretched far into the distance, but there was a dwindling number of headlights zipping back and forth. It was the early hours of Wednesday morning and, though Manchester was busier than many places, it was far from a city that never slept. It was a city that dozed a bit when it was dark.

When Andrew had hired Jenny, he'd spoken to her references – both university lecturers – and then checked her name against old school records. In terms of that, everything checked out. She had a national insurance number in her name and a bank account. He'd seen her driving licence. For all intents, she was Jenny Mays.

Jenny had told him she was an only child whose parents lived abroad. He'd never pushed too much, not really needing to know, but figured there was money somewhere along the line. She hadn't bothered haggling over her initial pay, nor subsequent pay rises.

Within a few days of her starting, he'd forgotten what life was like working without her. She took things over with a natural flair and they'd become friends. He certainly saw her more than anybody else.

Deep down, he'd always known there was something more to her than he wanted to acknowledge. She threw herself recklessly into situations with seemingly little – if any – concern for herself. At times, she could be fearless, so much so that it became something more. She'd had a man hold a knife to her throat and not flinched; she'd attacked Iwan, who was twice her size and could crush her while barely breaking a sweat.

If he was honest with himself – *really* honest – there was a part of him that was scared of her. Scared of what he feared she was capable of.

Months previously, when Andrew had been trying to find out who shot a pair of teenagers in broad daylight, Thomas Braithwaite had taken a sinister interest in what Andrew did. He said Jenny had an 'interesting' past. He had purred it, delighted with what he knew. Andrew could have followed it up then and yet he hadn't. He'd continued turning up to work as if nothing had happened, as if nothing had been said. He'd pushed it to the back of his mind, pretending he didn't want to know.

Now he'd heard something similar from Ollie.

Jenny apparently had a brother. It wasn't simply that she'd never mentioned him, she had specifically told Andrew on more than one occasion that she was an only child.

Why lie?

If Jenny had a brother, why not say – even if they weren't in contact? Even if they'd not seen each other in a long time? It was a big jump from omitting him to denying he'd ever existed. What did that mean for the rest of what Jenny had told him about her life? Did her parents *really* live abroad?

Andrew had done the basic checks but there were so many more he could do. Police contacts could find out certain things and he knew someone in the births, marriages and deaths department at the register office. It would take a lot of work, but he could find the truth one way or the other.

The problem was that, by doing so, Andrew knew he would be crossing a line from which he couldn't retreat. He liked Jenny. He respected her. It was close to the point that it was hard to imagine doing the job without her.

Which left him with one lingering question he couldn't answer.

Did he *really* want to know the truth?

The clock now read 01:38. Another hour passed in which he'd done nothing but stare out the window and wonder.

Andrew thought about going back to bed but instead he padded through the flat, heading for the kitchen. He dumped a spoonful of espresso powder into the machine and then thumbed the button to start it whirring. He'd catch up on the sleep at another time.

He leaned against one of the stools and closed his eyes, breathing in the bitter aroma of the coffee as the machine continued to pop.

It took Andrew a few moments to realise that the muffled jangling was his phone ringing in the other room. He raced through the flat, skidding on the smooth bedroom floor and reaching the phone next to his bed a moment before it rang off: Jenny.

It was as if some sort of psychic connection had been made because he'd been thinking about her so much. Now here she was.

'Jen?' he said.

'Sorry to wake you,' Jenny replied, her voice croaky, tired.

'What's up?'

'Can you come over? It's really important.'

'Are you safe?'

'I... yeah. Just come.'

Andrew didn't hesitate. He grabbed the previous day's clothes from the floor and pocketed his phone. The coffee machine had just finished bubbling as he snatched his keys from the counter and then flew out of the flat, charging for the lifts.

The roads were as empty as Andrew had ever seen them as he drove along Deansgate. He reached a red traffic light but edged through anyway when nothing came from the other direction. He was soon on Oxford Road, cruising past the railway station, Palace Hotel and the row of shops and restaurants before he hit the university.

As he passed under the Mancunian Way bridge, a gaggle of student sorts were staggering across the road, giggling into the night and then nearly tripping over the kerb on the far side before bursting into more laughter. Andrew slowed and then sped up again, zipping past the Aquatics Centre and the Academy before finding Jenny's street close to the hospital.

All was still, with a murky orange glow from the nearby street lights, leaving everything in shadow. Andrew parked and then hurried across the road towards Jenny's small house, instantly seeing why she'd called. There were two downstairs windows, one on either side of the front door. The one to the left had a large sheet of cardboard wedged into the space where there was now a circular hole surrounded by spiky, dangerous-looking glass.

Jenny had the front door open before he'd knocked. She was smiling, one hand on her hip, wearing a pair of red and white pyjamas, as if nothing had happened and she hadn't given him an SOS call in the middle of the night.

'You took your time,' she teased.

Andrew stopped to look at the hole in the window. 'When did this happen?'

'A little before I called you. I was sleeping upstairs.'

Andrew stepped towards the window but couldn't see much in the gloom. He followed Jenny inside and she closed the door behind him, then he trailed her towards a small kitchen. A brick was in the centre of the room, surrounded by hundreds, thousands of glittering shards. The sink was full of dishes, but there was a sprinkling of glass on top, with even more sharp splinters littering the edge of the floor.

Andrew didn't dare risk stepping further inside. He turned back to Jenny, who was standing in the hallway. 'Did you call the police?' he asked.

'Too much hassle. They'll come out, take photos, ask the neighbours and all that – but no one will have been up at this time. It'll drag on and on, then nothing will happen. I'd rather it was just done with.'

Andrew took one last look in the kitchen and then switched off the light. Jenny led him through to her living room, which was beautifully cosy. There was a television in the corner, with two armchairs facing it and an array of beanbags underneath the window. There were no posters, movies or CDs. Nothing to show the things in which she might be interested.

'If I knew how to fix a window, I'd do it myself,' Jenny said. 'I'll have to call a glazier in the morning. I'll have to google it.'

Andrew watched her tap away on her phone for a moment, trying to figure out if there had been any tremor to her voice. It didn't sound like it.

'Jen...'

'What?'

'Aren't you bothered about who might have thrown it?'

'Kids, innit? You get loads of it round here. Either that or someone drunk on their way home when the pubs shut. Some bloke down the road had his car windows put through a couple of months ago. The glass-fitters must love this area.' She sniggered and it sounded genuine.

Andrew continued to watch her for a little longer until she bounced up, showing him her phone.

'Right, I've got a number for a glazier. I'll call him in the morning. He reckons he's twenty-four hours, but it's a bit tight to call him out at this time.' She was smiling as if they were on another adventure.

'I'm not complaining, Jen – but why did you call me if you're all sorted?'

'I can't really stay here now. I was wondering if I can kip at yours? I'll sleep on the sofa. I can sleep anywhere, me. Planes, trains, buses, boats, benches. You name it and I've probably slept there.'

On any other day, Andrew would've said it was fine in an instant. Of course it was – what else was he going to say?

Except that Ollie's stinging words were jabbing at the back of his mind – 'she's got one hell of a thing for you' and then 'She's a mentalist. If you're getting dodgy phone calls or whatever, it wouldn't surprise me if it was her'.

There were things Jenny *couldn't* have done – the brick through his car window for one; the heavy breathing phone calls for another... or most of them. Jenny had been upstairs when Andrew got the call at Darren's house.

But, if Ollie was right, could it be true that Jenny had put the brick through her own window?

Andrew was sweating and had to gulp away his guilt-riddled suspicion, trying to act as if everything was perfectly fine. He stood, speaking too quickly.

'Course you can,' he said. 'I'll take the sofa and you can have the bed. Before that, let's get a board in the window. I don't think the cardboard will last long.'

28

After an uncomfortable night on his sofa, during which Andrew hardly got any sleep at all, it was a busy morning. First they returned to Jenny's, where the glazier duly fitted a new window while Andrew helped her clean up the inside. He again asked her about contacting the police, but Jenny insisted she didn't want to.

In the afternoon, he dropped her at the office, saying he had a few errands to run, and then set off towards Liverpool.

As he drove, Andrew was aware that he felt protective of Jenny – probably some sort of father–daughter thing, though he didn't have a daughter to confirm those feelings. He was wary, too. It was hard to forget what Ollie had told him. He hadn't entirely discounted Ollie as the person who was harassing her and perhaps messing with Andrew's mind was part of his plan. Although Andrew knew that might be the case, he hadn't felt that when he'd been with Ollie in the toilets of that pub. Ollie seemed genuine.

But if it wasn't him, then who? Andrew struggled to believe Jenny had sent the Valentine's Day card to herself, let alone broken her own window. And, even if she had, what about the calls? In the first, a man's voice had asked for Jenny. She'd need an accomplice.

More to the point, if it *was* Jenny, if she had somehow set all this up, then why?

Before he knew it, Andrew was outside Thomas Braithwaite's expansive house. Steepling iron gates were attached to a thick wall that stretched far into the distance in both directions. There were cameras at regular intervals along the top, pointing outwards towards the street. Andrew parked the car and headed across the road. He didn't need to buzz because, as he neared, there was a 'ping' and the gates hummed inwards.

It was a long, imposing driveway that led towards the house. Perhaps as a reflection of the compared wealth, Braithwaite's house was significantly more extravagant than Jack Marsh's. It was like a smaller stately home, with three floors that each had seven windows. The lawns that surrounded the drive were perfect emerald green, with long straight mow lines stretching into the distance.

Andrew had visited a couple of times before and it never ceased to amaze him how breathtaking the house was.

Iwan was standing in the front door, arms crossed, waiting. He said nothing as Andrew passed, ducking into the massive, echoing tiled hallway. A staircase was in front, looping up to the second floor, and there was an enormous canvas painting of someone in a red coat riding into battle.

Still silent, Iwan led Andrew through more hallways until they emerged into a room lined with books. Cases climbed high towards the ceilings, all stacked with various tomes. There was a drinks cabinet in the corner, while one wall was entirely given over to a huge map of the UK. It was at least twice Andrew's height, with his head roughly in line with Manchester.

Braithwaite was in an armchair with a newspaper on his lap. As Andrew entered, he folded it over and dropped it into a rack next to the seat. He uncrossed his legs and stood, offering his hand for Andrew to shake, which he did. After that, Braithwaite nodded at Iwan, who took the hint and disappeared out of the room, closing the door behind him.

Braithwaite seemed slimmer than he had at the football, possibly more tired as well. 'Mr Hunter,' he said as the door closed. 'Wonderful to see you again.' He motioned towards the violin case in Andrew's hand. 'And am I to understand that you have something for me?'

Andrew passed across the case and Braithwaite took it, smoothing the hard outer shell. He didn't open it.

'Did you enjoy the football?' he asked.

'I suppose.'

'And what about your interest in Mr Marsh? How's that coming along?'

'Fine.'

Andrew was well aware that Braithwaite was trying to be charmingly intimidating, letting Andrew know he saw what was going on in his life. He stood, hands at his side, watching as Braithwaite continued to stroke the violin case.

'How are the women in your life?' Braithwaite asked smoothly. An afternoon DJ with a calming voice that made middle-aged divorcees go weak at the knees. Andrew found it chilling. 'The pretty one in your office,' Braithwaite added. 'Are you watching your back when she's around?'

'Why would I be?'

Braithwaite smirked and suddenly Andrew was full of fury. He clenched his fists, hiding them behind his back so that Braithwaite couldn't see.

'How are *your* kids?' Andrew snapped. 'Alexander's at university in Lancaster, isn't he? What about Ruby? Isn't she at boarding school in Hampshire?'

Andrew stopped himself from saying any more by digging

his nails into the fleshy part of his thumb and pinching as hard as he could. The room was like a fridge.

Braithwaite was still like a statue and then he sat, putting the violin next to the newspaper rack and picking up a china teacup that was on a small side table. He sipped the liquid and swallowed. Sipped and swallowed.

Silence.

Andrew felt like every hair on his body was standing up, as if he'd been electrified. He'd been so angry that he'd blurted out the first thing that came into his head, the one thing he knew with no question would infuriate Braithwaite. He wanted to hurt him, to let the other man know that two could play the game. The problem was that Braithwaite would *always* be able to play it better than Andrew.

Braithwaite eventually put the teacup down, smacking his lips as he picked up the violin case. He unclipped it and removed the instrument, running his fingers across the grain of the wood. He put it to his nose and then inhaled deeply, before tracing the LK in the bottom corner with a single finger.

'Thank you,' he said softly.

Andrew nodded, not trusting himself to reply properly.

Braithwaite fitted the violin under his chin, resting the bow on the strings. He rattled it back and forth, wincing as the instrument squeaked like a rusty door. He twiddled the tuning pegs, trying again with the bow and then making another half-dozen adjustments until he was happy.

When he did play, it was beautiful. Andrew had no idea what the piece of music was called, but he had a vague memory of hearing it before. Incomplete memories of a large music hall crept into his mind, though Andrew didn't know when he'd ever visited anywhere like that. Certainly not recently. Braithwaite's hand with the bow flitted back and forth delicately but forcefully, while the other darted across the fingerboard.

Andrew didn't know how long had passed, but Braithwaite finished with a frenzied flourish. He lowered the violin and gave Andrew a gentle nod, before returning the instrument to the case.

He took another sip of his tea and then licked his lips. 'Where did it come from?' he asked.

'I asked a few people I know, followed a couple of leads and it led me to this. You said you didn't need names.'

Braithwaite nodded to acknowledge the point. 'Fair enough, Mr Hunter.'

'Does this mean we're even?'

There was another long pause in which Braithwaite once again licked his lips. He stared off towards the large map pensively. 'That's a hard question to answer – but I do appreciate the work you've done.'

From nowhere the door behind him pinged open, with Iwan standing tall and wide, blocking the light from beyond. Andrew didn't know if he was psychic, had impeccable timing, or if he himself had missed some sort of secret signal.

Braithwaite offered a watery smile but didn't stand and didn't offer his hand to shake. 'Stay safe, Mr Hunter.'

29

Jenny emerged from the hotel bathroom and twirled on the tips of her toes, ballerina-style. 'Ta-da!' she sang, before stopping and curtsying. 'So, what do you think?'

Massively inappropriate, Andrew thought. He was alone in the room of a hotel with a woman who was a decade and more younger than him and also his work colleague. It was dark outside and, though the hotel was four-star, it all felt decidedly seedy. He was one step away from becoming a Tory MP at this rate.

Jenny was wearing a figure-hugging short black dress with what could only be described as stripper heels. He hadn't asked her to wear anything specific; she had brought along the outfit in her bag and then disappeared off into the bathroom.

'Well?' she asked again.

'Different,' Andrew replied. 'Very different.'

'Pfft, you're such a *man* sometimes.' She turned in a circle, looking for a clock. 'What's the time?'

Andrew checked his phone. 'Two minutes past nine.'

'Hmm... he's late.'

As if on cue, there was a loud rap on the door. Jenny grinned – she was in her element of danger and surprise.

Andrew darted out of sight, sliding across the king-size bed and wedging himself behind the floor-to-ceiling wardrobe. He pressed his back to the wood and muttered 'okay', listening to his heart race.

Moments later, he heard the snap of the door latch and then Jenny saying, 'Well, hell-ooooh there.' She sounded flirty and playful.

The next voice was male – Jack Marsh's: 'Wow, you look different from the last time.'

The door closed and then Andrew heard Jenny's heels clacking across the floor. 'Amazing what a bit of Polyfilla can do,' she said.

Jack laughed half-heartedly and then Andrew heard a soft squeak of springs. He stepped out from behind the wardrobe to see Jack sitting on the bed, legs splayed wide. He was relaxed in jeans and a tight T-shirt, with a baseball cap and pair of sunglasses next to him. Jenny was leaning on the writing desk, knees together, looking in Andrew's direction. Jack soon got the hint, turning and jumping at the sight of the other man in the room.

'Whoa,' he said, leaping to his feet.

Jenny shuffled around until she was blocking the way out. 'We needed to talk to you,' she said, 'but the only way I knew we could definitely get you to see us was if I phoned you.'

Jack turned between them, face falling as he realised the prospect of a filth-filled hotel tryst had been denied.

'Do you know what I went through to get here?' he said, raising his voice. 'I had to get past that lot outside my gates, drive across the city, park in the shadows at the back end of the car park and then take the stairs up here. I think the bloke on reception might've clocked who I was.'

'I once read about this woman in Ethiopia,' Jenny said.

'She walked eleven miles each day to get water for her family. The moaning cow doesn't know she's born.'

Jack smirked, at least showing he wasn't entirely self-centred. 'Fair enough,' he said, flopping back onto the bed. 'What do you want then? I've got to get back to the house by half-ten, else Mum will be on one.'

'Will she ground you?' Jenny replied.

Jack smiled even wider. 'It's not that, I just can't be done with her moaning. Ever since Michelle, she's always going on about not putting myself in situations and all that.'

'That's probably good advice,' Andrew said.

'Whatever, mate. What do you want?'

'We know you sneaked out of the hotel on the night Michelle ended up in the canal,' Andrew said. 'You went down the stairs near the lifts until you got to the ground floor, then you went through the door marked "staff only". You followed the corridor to the fire exit and, though it says it's alarmed, it isn't. You dropped the catch and there you were – outside. Your mate Danny McMichael told you about it. I'm guessing he's covered for you ever since.'

Jack's mouth hung open. A human flycatcher. No longer was he relaxed flop-on-the-bed Jack, he was shoulders-tensed coiled-spring Jack. He stood and then sat, then stood again. He twisted from Andrew to Jenny and then lunged towards the door. Jenny was in front of him, refusing to budge. It was through her or retreat and, for a moment, Andrew thought the footballer was going to barrel straight through her.

'You gonna hit me, too?' Jenny said. In her heels, she was as tall as Jack. She didn't flinch, her brown eyes staring into his, daring him. Andrew felt frozen across the room, too far away to do anything.

After a moment of stand-off, Jack stepped away, holding both his hands up and then backing away further until he was standing next to the office chair that was wedged under the desk. He tugged it out and spun it, then stopped it and leaned on the back.

'This is bollocks, bruv.'

'What is?' Andrew said.

'*This*. This is all wrong. I don't know what you're talking about.'

'Yes you do. That's the door that some of the staff use when they want to go outside for a smoke. Your mate Danny was craving a fag a few weeks before it all happened and he found out about it. You were in a room with him on the night Michelle died. She'd been texting you all night and you told Danny you wanted to go and meet her – if only to tell her to stop bothering you. The problem was that if you'd gone out the front, people would've noticed. It would have got back to your manager, or whoever was looking after you. Luckily – or *un*luckily – Danny had the solution. He told you about a way to get out where it was unlikely anyone would notice. If one of the kitchen staff happened to be hanging around, you'd apologise – "sorry, mate, I was just after a crafty ciggie". Most of the lads were star-struck by you anyway. As it was, I'm guessing nobody saw you leaving. All you had to do is make sure Danny kept his mouth shut and that was that.'

Jack stared at Andrew, eyebrow twitching as he wondered if there was more. 'You don't know what you're talking about.'

'Don't I?'

'Can you prove it?'

'Do I have to?'

Jack stepped towards Andrew, pushing himself up tall and shoving a finger in his face. 'I *knew* you were out to get me. *Knew* it. Told me ma so. This is a stitch-up.'

'So tell me it's not true. You've said it's "all wrong", you said I don't know what I'm talking about. What you absolutely *haven't* done is deny it.'

They glared at one another, but Jack broke first, spinning

away and then kicking the bin across the room. It clattered into a tall lamp in the corner, which clanged into the wall, flickered, but remained on. Jack and Andrew both stared at the bin as it twirled on the floor next to the lamp and then tumbled over. There was nothing in it anyway.

'I'm going,' Jack said. He grabbed his cap and glasses and then stormed across the room, going face to face with Jenny once more. 'Move!' he shouted.

Jenny glanced over Jack's shoulder to Andrew, who nodded slightly. She stepped out of his way, giving him a free route to the door.

Jack stepped around her and then swivelled to face Andrew again. 'I know your sort, mate: bitter and jealous. You wanted to be a policeman but you weren't good enough to pass the exams. If you reckon you've got something, then go to the police and prove it. If not, you can do one.'

With that, he trampled out of the room, slamming the door with as much force as he could manage – which ended up not being much because of the hinge at the top that ensured it closed softly and quietly.

Jenny slipped her heels off, shrinking half a foot in the process. She turned to Andrew. 'Well,' she said with a shrug, 'that went well.'

30

By half past ten, Andrew and Jenny were back at his flat. It struck Andrew far too late that, given he'd already paid for the hotel room, Jenny could have stayed there for the night. He'd not thought of it and she'd not suggested it.

Her flat was still out of bounds because of 'the wrong sealant' for the window, or something like that. Who knew? It sounded like one of those builder-type things that only burly men with dirty fingernails could get away with saying. 'Yeah, mate, there's not enough super grease in that. You've only got the normal stuff.' Still, that was nowhere near as bad as some privately educated prat in a suit sitting in some London skyscraper playing silly beggars with other people's money. At least the builder could spin a yarn to a person's face.

Jenny was still wearing the dress from the hotel room, her bare legs curled up underneath herself as she watched the local news. Some poor woman had been snatched outside a pub in Rusholme, bundled into a car and then raped in a car park somewhere on the back end of an industrial estate on the edge of the city. The police had photofits and good descriptions of the men and their car, but, even if they were caught, the woman's life would never go back to being the same.

Jenny watched transfixed and Andrew watched her. He wanted to ask what was in *her* past. Was it something bad? He almost hoped it was – at least that was a reason to lie. If she had simply pretended to not have a brother with no reason, wasn't that much worse? Lying for the sake of it, because it was possible... well, that was psychotic, wasn't it? He didn't know the terms, wasn't sure he wanted to know them.

Andrew was washing up a pair of plates when he remembered one more thing. A few months ago, Jenny had spent a couple of days with his Aunt Gem while Andrew had been away. It had felt strange – yet Gem was charmed by her. Gem told him that Jenny had spoke about her mum and dad. They'd had entire conversations about Jenny's parents living abroad. Could she *really* have made all that up?

Andrew put the plates away and then flashed a smile towards Jenny. She returned it, but then started to yawn and rubbed at her eyes.

'Long day,' she said.

'Long day,' he echoed.

She stretched her arms high, showing off far more flesh than Andrew was comfortable seeing.

'I don't mind sleeping on the sofa tonight,' she said. 'I can sleep anywhere. I'm like a sloth.'

She gets night terrors. Screaming, shouting, waking up and clawing at the air...

'You take the bed,' Andrew replied. 'I'm fine out here. I've fallen asleep on the sofa on more nights than I care to remember.'

Jenny patted the spot close to her and Andrew crossed the room and sat. The news had ended and it was onto the weather. There was another sunny day due, with a strong chance it would carry through to the weekend. That would mean the city's streets would be packed with people wanting to enjoy the warmth while they could. It was hard for Manchester to seem welcoming when everyone had their heads down, fighting against gales and squally rain. The city was always a different place with the sun out. There'd be entertainers in Piccadilly Gardens, probably pop-up food stalls around the various public squares as well. There were always more young people around on the warmer days, too; shopping, mooching or generally just hanging around. Andrew always felt as if the city came into its own on the days when the skies were blue.

'Are you worried about something?'

Andrew had been drifting but Jenny brought him back into the room. 'Sorry?' he said.

'Is something on your mind... other than Jack Marsh, I mean. You seem distracted.'

Andrew continued watching the television, not taking the risk of looking at Jenny. 'Just busy,' he replied. 'I'm off on holiday with Gem soon enough. I think I need a break from it all.'

'You've never really told me what you want me to do while you're away. Should I still go into the office?'

'You're fine doing any bits of due diligence or CV checking by yourself. I'll have to sign anything off, but we won't take on any work that's urgent. If you end up running out of things to do, it's not a problem. You don't have to go in for the sake of going in. You've been working for me for, what, nine months? Ten? You've not had any time off. Not only that, you've done extra hours all over the shop. Lates – like tonight – weekends, like when we visited Jack Marsh's house on Sunday. It's my fault—'

'I choose to do those things.'

'Yes, but I should be making sure you have a break, too. It's only us, it's not like I've got an HR department to keep on top of this, so it's down to me.'

'Pfft, it's fine.'

'It's not, Jen. I'm probably breaching employment laws over hours and breaks. I've taken advantage and things are going to have to change.'

Jenny went quiet at that, folding her arms and focusing on the television. A few minutes passed and then she said, 'I *am* allowed to make my own decisions, you know.'

'What?'

'It's not like you force me to do anything, or make me work when I don't want to. Half the time it's my idea anyway.'

As well as the multitude of new questions Andrew had fizzing around his mind, there was the oldest one he'd wanted to ask since she first started to work for him. Finally, he asked it: 'Why do you do this, Jen?'

'Do what?'

'Work for me. You have an IT degree and, though there's a bit of crossover, there's not much. Lots of people study one thing, then go off to work doing another but you're capable of so much more than this. You could get more money elsewhere, definitely better hours. You could probably set up your own business if you wanted. I'm not complaining – I'm really not – but I don't know why you'd want to spend every day sitting around the office.'

'It's fun.' Jenny made it sound as if it was the most obvious thing going.

'*What's* fun? The paperwork? The typing?'

'All of it. I like the people. Not knowing who's going to knock on the door. Not knowing the answer – like today. All the official stories say Jack Marsh couldn't have left that hotel, then we go and find out that he might have done. It's exciting.'

'Lots of things are exciting, Jen.'

'But this is me and you versus the world, isn't it?'

Andrew didn't know how to reply. In some ways, he felt like that, too. His reason for working, even though he could retire to his flat, was that he liked the variety of people who came into his life. He could be picky enough to turn away the cases that didn't interest him and work on those that would keep his mind whirring.

A knock on the door interrupted anything with which he could have replied. Jenny looked to Andrew, who could only return a blank stare. He lived so high up that he wasn't used to visitors at all, let alone when it was closing in on eleven at night. His flat's buzzer hadn't sounded, either.

Andrew jumped up and crossed to the door, unlatching the bolt and opening it, then stepping back. Keira walked into the flat without a word. She was dressed modestly in skinny jeans and a floaty top. Her short hair was poking out from underneath a beret that was at such a gravity-defying angle that Andrew couldn't quite figure out how it was remaining on her head. She had a bottle of wine in her hand and closed the door without looking around.

'Hi,' she said.

'Hi.'

'I thought I'd surprise you. I've been looking at flats today, then I didn't fancy driving back down south, so I got a room at the Travelodge on Piccadilly. It was all a bit... lonely – plus I think they've got a hen party in. Bit early in the week but who knows nowadays. There was someone crying in the room next to me and I couldn't take listening to it any longer. I was going to call, then I figured I may as well walk here. Some bloke downstairs was on his way up, so I tailgated him into the lift and here I am.' She did a small leg-bob curtsy. 'Honestly, you should see some of the places I've been around earlier. There was this two-bedroom flat just over the river and the *walls*—' She stopped, turning and noticing Jenny for the first time. 'Oh,' Keira said.

Jenny gave a small wave. 'Hi again.'

Andrew felt his worlds colliding horribly. 'Someone put a brick through Jenny's window,' he said quickly. 'She would have been back at her place tonight, but there was some issue with... I don't know.'

'Sealant,' Jenny piped up. 'Something to do with sealant. Don't ask me.' She grinned, but it was the wrong thing to do.

Keira turned between Jenny and Andrew, almost over-balancing.

'No need to explain.' She stumbled over her words and then brushed Andrew's arm with her free hand, offering him the bottle with the other. 'Here, you take this. I've got nowhere to store it and it was only a fiver at the Tesco Express anyway.'

'Keira—'

'No, no, I understand. I should have called. I know I'm ambushing you and it's late.'

She pushed the wine towards him and Andrew had no option other than to take it. Keira turned quickly but tried to open the door with the lock part at the top, rather than the handle at the bottom. She pulled it inwards, but it didn't open, then she tried twisting the catch, even though it wasn't locked. Andrew opened the door for her, then Keira was somehow past him like a ninja before he could get out of the way. He followed her into the hall, trying to keep pace as she rushed back to the lift.

'Hey,' he called. 'Can we talk?'

Keira thumped the ground-floor button and then took a half step back, tapping her foot in anxious anticipation of the lift arriving. 'I should have called.'

'It's nice to see you. I'm glad you came over.'

'Another time, yeah?'

The lift pinged, the doors sliding open, its timing appallingly impeccable. 'I'll call you,' Andrew said.

Keira smiled in a not-smiling kind of way. 'Yep. See you.'

With that, the doors clinked shut and she was gone again. Andrew found himself staring at the illuminated buttons as the lift zoomed downwards floor by floor. It stopped on the ground, with the G remaining lit up, taunting him.

Eventually, Andrew turned and went back to his flat. He locked the door and then realised he was still holding the bottle of wine.

Jenny hadn't moved from the sofa. She had twisted to peer over the back towards him. 'Sorry about that,' she said.

'Not your fault.'

'If it's any consolation, I *really* don't mind sleeping on the sofa. I've got myself comfy now.'

31

Much of the awkwardness had been forgotten by the next morning. Andrew drove his car to the office, while Jenny walked. She was there before him, kettle already boiling, as if the previous evening hadn't happened.

'No messages,' she said. 'All seems quiet. The general email box is only spam, too – though you might be in line to inherit half a million dollars from some bloke in Africa.'

'Again? What am I going to do with all this money?'

'I've sent him ten grand via Western Union to sort out the paperwork, so now you can sit back and wait for the money to roll in.' She paused. 'Is there anything you'd like me to do?'

'Danny McMichael – Jack's teammate and room-mate. Check him out the same way you did Jack. There's probably nothing but you never know. We're not going to get to talk to him either way, but he's worth looking at. If Jack snuck out, Danny must be covering.'

Jenny turned and started typing on her computer, already on it.

Andrew's desk phone started ringing and he scooped it up, cradling it to his neck while trying to put his laptop down.

'Is that Hunter?' a man's voice asked.

'This is Andrew Hunter, who's calling?'

'It's Jack Marsh.'

Andrew hadn't expected to hear from Jack again, let alone the morning after their hotel altercation. He tried to sound professional, polite. 'How can I help you, Jack?'

'You busy?'

'Not massively.'

'I've phoned in sick to training. There's a doctor coming over in a bit, but I've got an hour if you can get to the house.'

'Now?'

'Now – just you, though. Not the girl. She creeps me out.'

When Andrew got to Jack's house, there were no fans camped outside, but there was a mail van. A postman was standing next to the gates, wearing shorts and a red polo top. He nodded to acknowledge Andrew. 'Y'all right, mate?'

Andrew nodded at the sack of mail next to the postman's feet. 'Is that all for Jack?'

A shrug. 'It's the same most days. Oh to be popular, hey? I don't get it myself. What do people think they're going to get back from him? He gets thousands every week. If his full-time job was replying to mail, he'd not get through it all.'

The buzzer next to the gates sounded and then Jack's tinny voice sounded. 'On my way,' he said.

The postman raised his eyebrows to Andrew and then nodded up at the CCTV camera pinned to the post high above them.

'You don't carry that to his door every day, do you?' Andrew asked, pointing at the bag of mail.

'Most of the time it's his mum who answers. She opens the gates and we drive down.' He lowered his voice, though it was probably unnecessary, 'Can't see myself living with my mum if I had his money.'

Andrew didn't disagree. It was a bit odd.

The postman went quiet as Jack appeared on the other side of the gates. He was in jeans and a hoody, somehow still managing to look fit and athletic. He nudged the gate aside and offered an unconvincing smile to the postman before handing over a pair of empty mail sacks. He took the full one with a muttered 'thanks' and then held the gate open for Andrew.

The two of them headed along the drive in silence. When they got inside, Jack dropped the mail next to the door and then led the way into what turned out to be a kitchen. It was modern and sparkling, as if the counters and appliances had never been used. Like something out of a catalogue, as opposed to something in a person's house. Jack perched himself on a stool, leaving Andrew to shuffle onto another one nearby.

'Mum's not here,' Jack said. Andrew didn't reply, so he quickly added: 'How'd you know about the fire exit in the hotel?'

'Does it matter?' Andrew said.

'S'pose not.' He motioned to the kitchen. 'You want a drink or something? Coffee? Make whatever you want. I don't even know how half this stuff works.'

'I'm fine.'

Jack slumped, puffing out a long breath. 'You think I'm scum, don't you?' he said.

'I don't think anything,' Andrew replied. 'If anyone has a problem, it sounds like it's you. You always talk about other people judging you, looking down on you, or thinking badly of you. I've never said anything like that to you, never assumed anything, never tried to "stitch you up", as you said. All I wanted to do is ask questions about Michelle.'

Jack dipped his head slightly, acknowledging the point.

'You're right,' he said, leaving a long, long pause afterwards. When he continued, he was almost whispering. 'I did leave the hotel that night.'

Andrew felt something punching his chest. It was the exhilaration of being correct, or, as Jenny had said, the buzz of knowing something nobody else did. But there was danger, too – and that was something of which he'd seen quite enough in recent times.

'I didn't kill 'Chelle,' Jack added. He looked up. 'Honestly? It's horrible, but she didn't mean that much to me. I'm not trying to be mean or owt, but I wasn't in love with her. Never been in love with any girl really. At the time it all happened, I wasn't sure if we were going out with each other. I told her we were done, but she was still calling and texting. I went round her house a few days before and we ended up shagging. It's not like I planned it, it just happened.'

'That's probably why she thought you were still together.'

He shrugged. 'Right – but it's not like I knew this was going to happen. I know I've been a dick... a *lot* of dick when I was younger. Mum's always on about cleaning up my act. I can't handle the booze, so I've cut right down. And, yeah, I like girls – so what? I'm not the only one. It's not like I want to kill anyone and, even if I did, why would I go after someone everyone knows is connected to me?' He motioned towards the house in general. 'Why would I risk all this for someone I wasn't that bothered about?'

Andrew couldn't argue with any of those points. 'But you did leave the hotel that night...?' he said.

Jack nodded. 'It weren't a big deal – or it shouldn't have been. If 'Chelle had got home that night, no one would have known any different. When it all happened, it's not like I could tell the police I'd left the hotel. They'd have made their own minds up about why, then I'd have been in trouble at the club. The gaffer would've done his nut. Danny would've probably been in trouble as well, 'cos we're supposed to keep an eye on our room-mates.'

'If all that's true, if this is all one innocent mix-up and a coincidence around the timings, then why *did* you leave the hotel?'

Jack turned away again, running a hand through his hair. 'Aww, man... look is this between us?'

'If you want it to be.'

'No police?'

'That depends on what you have to say. If you actually did kill someone, I'm obliged to report it. Same with all serious crimes.'

'I didn't kill anyone.'

'So...'

Jack took a deep breath. 'I went to a different hotel,' he said. 'There's this one down the back of Bridgewater Hall about five minutes from the Radisson. You can get there along the alleys and there's hardly anyone else about.'

'What did you do there?'

He looked at the floor, voice a croaky murmur. 'I was with two girls.'

Andrew took a moment to think it over. If he was making it up, Jack was a damn good liar. 'Fans?' Andrew asked.

A gentle shake of the head. 'I paid cash. It wasn't the first time. I sort of knew them.' He corrected himself: '*Know* them.'

Andrew wasn't entirely surprised. From what he knew about Jack, there was only ever likely to be one reason why he left the hotel that night.

'How did you get back into the Radisson?' Andrew asked.

'Danny let me in through the fire exit. When everything came out about 'Chelle over the next couple of days, he kept quiet for me.'

'And the girls...?'

Jack took an enormous breath and started scratching his cheek as if there was a spot of which he couldn't rid himself.

'They want money,' he said, more firmly this time. 'You're the only one who knows. At first it was a few hundred quid. One of them said her car had broken down and she couldn't afford the MOT, then the other said Christmas was coming up and she needed some spare cash for presents. I probably gave them two or three grand each and then I didn't hear from them for a little bit. Then it was new year and one of them wanted a dress. Then they both turned up outside the house. Mum was in – but she thought they were fans like all the others. I ended up taking them for a drive out towards the training ground. They said that they knew enough to bring me down. Unless I pay them five grand each a week, they'll go to the papers. One of them reckons she's got pictures of me on her phone.'

'Does she?'

Jack shrugged. 'Maybe. I don't know. It's not just the papers, though. They say they'll tell the police about me sneaking out of the hotel, and who knows what'll happen then. I didn't kill 'Chelle – I really didn't – but I did lie and that's all the police will hear. The best that can happen is that I'll be in big trouble for saying I didn't sneak out, plus I'll be in the papers as that bloke who shags prostitutes. The worst is that they somehow pin everything on me.'

'How long have you been paying them?'

'Since January.'

Andrew made a low whistling sound. It was a comfortable six-figures he'd already paid out. 'How do you get that much cash without anyone asking questions?' Andrew asked.

'People *are* asking questions,' Jack said, agitated. 'My accountant wants to know what I'm spending it on. I tell him clothes, shoes and stuff – but it's not like I've got the receipts. I can't keep holding him off. Sooner or later Mum's going to find out – and then it'll all hit the fan.'

Andrew had a moment to take it all in. The situation was quite the mess.

'How long were you out of the hotel for?' Andrew asked.

'Dunno, bruv – it's not like I had the clock running. Probably an hour, something like that.'

'What time?'

'Maybe one in the morning? Something like that.'

It was Andrew's turn for a deep breath. No wonder Jack had been so wary of talking. Michelle and her friend Chloe had said goodbye to each other at half past twelve. Give or take a few minutes, it was roughly the time Jack had sneaked out.

'Are you asking me what you should do?' Andrew asked.

A shrug. 'I dunno... I just thought you'd want to know.'

As Jack slumped, Andrew knew that he believed him. It was an extravagant story but entirely conceivable. The problem was that Andrew didn't know where that left him. Did Michelle *really* die through a drunken accident? Her mother was never going to believe that.

Andrew stood and straightened his top. 'You know what you've got to do,' he said.

'What?'

'You know, Jack. You're not a stupid lad – I know that from talking to you. Your mum might be a bit protective, but she'd know, too.'

Jack dipped his head and offered a resigned: 'Tell the police?'

'What's the alternative? Hand over ten grand a week for the rest of time? Sooner or later, one of those women will tell a friend anyway. Perhaps they'll get drunk, perhaps they'll get a boyfriend. Maybe they'll just get bored – but one way or another, it'll come out. At least if you go to the police then you're in control to a degree. If the papers get it first, you're done for.'

'Yeah...'

Andrew stepped around him, moving towards the door. 'Have you got anything else to say?'

A shake of the head. 'I think I've probably said enough.'

Andrew was almost through the door when he stopped himself, one foot in the kitchen, one foot out. 'Can I ask you one more thing?' he said.

'Whatever you want.'

'You told me not to bring Jenny. You said she creeped you out. Why?'

Jack spun on the stool to face him. 'Last night, bruv, the way she looked at me when she was standing in front of the door. She weren't moving and she didn't care if I was going to go through her. It's not like I was going to kick off, but she didn't know that. There was a moment – just a moment – where I thought she was going to go for me. She had this look in her in eye...' He tailed off. 'I dunno, bruv... you've got a volcano ready to blow there. I've been with a few girls, but I ain't never seen a look like that.'

32

Andrew had a lot to think about as he drove back to the office, not least the fact that he believed everything Jack Marsh had told him. There was still the possibility that if Jack had left the hotel via the fire exit, Danny McMichael could have done as well. There was no room-mate to keep an eye on him – though he would have had to be back in time to let Jack into the hotel. Even with that, there was no chance of Andrew being able to speak to one of the other players. He'd gone through enough hoops to get to Jack.

And then there was Jenny.

People were lining up to tell him there was something not quite right about her – Braithwaite, Ollie, Jack – but what did any of it mean?

He parked in the office space and then headed up the stone stairs, emerging onto street level and a narrow cobbled alley. The buildings were tall, their shadows making everything a few degrees cooler than it was elsewhere. The shadow stretched across the entire passage, with only the faint hint of blue visible when he looked directly up.

Andrew tucked his hands in his pockets and hurried along,

taking the turn that led to the glass-fronted office where Tina was no doubt doing half a dozen things at the same time.

He was just thinking about how much he fancied a cup of tea when there was a squeal behind. Andrew turned to see a white van barrelling towards him. The alley was only wide enough for a vehicle with a little clearance on either side, so Andrew pressed himself to the wall, as much out of the way as he could manage.

It didn't matter where he was, there was always some idiot driving too fast. Always some prat in a hurry to get to the next set of traffic lights.

Andrew felt the rush of the wind as the van drew level with him, the head-height mirrors only a few centimetres from colliding with his skull. The rush only lasted a second and then the van was past him... except that it wasn't. The brakes shrieked and then the rear doors clanged open.

Two balaclava-wearing ogres jumped down from the tail-gate and lunged for Andrew. He tried to race backwards but realised what was happening far too late. There was nowhere to go anyway. Andrew had his back turned, wanting to run, but the bigger of the men grabbed his shoulder, squeezing so hard that Andrew yelped in pain. He flung an elbow back-wards, feeling it connect with flesh that was so solid he cried out a second time.

A fist connected with his lower back and his vision swarmed a kaleidoscope of colours. He flung another elbow but connected with thin air as another blow thundered into him, this time booming into his ear. Andrew stumbled side-ways, collapsing to one knee before being hauled roughly to his feet by the collar of his shirt.

Then it was just black as something was thrust over his head. He tried to grab at whatever it was – a sack or a bag – but his arms were being wrenched backwards with such force that his shoulders felt like they were going to pop from their sockets. Something hard clamped around his wrists, keeping his hands firmly behind his back. He tried to scream for help, but there was nothing except a squeal of agony.

Andrew felt himself being lifted, outnumbered and outmuscled, and then he was dumped on the cold, hard metal inside the back of the van. Before he could move, the doors clanged closed, the echo resounding through his already sore ear and sending Andrew spinning and tumbling, until he collapsed on his side. With his hands locked behind, he struggled to right himself and had no opportunity to regain his balance because the wheels screeched once more, sending him head-first into the solid metal wall.

33

Andrew felt helpless. He couldn't see a thing and was left trying to anticipate the movements of the van based on the revs of the engine. Even sitting down didn't help much. He found what he assumed was a corner, feeling the metal against his sides, but every time the vehicle hit a pothole, he was thrown into the air, landing painfully on a combination of his arse, thighs, arms and back.

There was little respite even when the van was idling at junctions or traffic lights. Whatever had been used to secure his wrists was so tight that it was digging brutally into his skin. His breath was short and tight, but thinking about it only made it worse because of the sack over his head.

Andrew could still feel his phone in his pocket, but there was little he could do except try not to land on it when the van took one of its regular lurches to the left or right. He thought about shouting for help when the van rolled to a stop but could barely hear anything over the roar of the engine. It was doubtful anyone outside would hear him and, even if they did, he was helpless enough as he was. What did he think a passerby might do? Rip the doors off their hinges? Even if someone called the police, it could be too late by then.

Aside from the engine, the only thing he occasionally heard when the engine revs softened was the muffled sound of the radio. Perhaps he was hearing things, but it sounded like Radio Three or Classic FM, the gentle tones of an orchestra seeping into his empty cabin, providing a bizarre melancholy considering the situation in which he found himself.

After a while, the van slowed and then bumped over what felt like a pair of speed humps. Andrew had almost become used to steadying himself and managed to remain upright as the vehicle slowed even further and then – finally – rolled to a stop.

Andrew heard a set of doors open and then clunk shut. He braced himself, feeling tense at what might be to come. Was it worth crying out for help now?

Silence.

He'd expected the back doors to be yanked open, but there was nothing. Should he bang on the sides?

Andrew shuffled along the wall of the van, listening.

Nothing.

Was this why he'd been snatched – to be left to rot in the back of a van? He could make a noise but had no idea where he was. Surely it wouldn't be a public place? If it was somewhere more private, drawing attention to himself could make his predicament worse by annoying his captors.

Andrew sat and waited. He twisted his fingers as best he could, thumbing the harsh plastic that was digging into him. It felt like the type of cord that came attached to extension leads. He tried to wedge his fingers into any slack loops, but it had been yanked so tightly that he couldn't find any.

More waiting. More nothing.

It might have been a few minutes but it could have been a lot longer. Andrew wasn't sure, but he jumped as the doors were pulled open with a metallic squeak. There was no warning before the hands were on him again, heaving him up and shunting him forward. He felt weightless for a moment, only realising he was being lifted when he was already back on the ground – this time out of the van.

Andrew was poked in the sides and back, forcing him to move ahead. There were multiple sets of footsteps echoing around what felt like pure concrete. Wherever they were felt cold. He didn't fight because there was no point. His wrists were still secure and he couldn't see anything.

'Stop.'

The single word was the first Andrew had heard since being snatched. He did as he was told and then there was a scratching as something was dragged across the ground. An object creased into the back of his knees, forcing him into a sitting position, where, surprisingly, he found a chair waiting for him. Somebody grabbed his wrists and, momentarily, he was free – except that he wasn't because his arms were pulled back further and then he realised he'd been untied and then retied to the chair.

More footsteps, more echoes and then silence.

He waited but nobody spoke. As far as he could tell, nobody was moving.

'Hello...?'

Andrew's voice echoed around a room that felt much larger than wherever he'd been walking.

'Hello...?'

The final 'O' reverberated around, bouncing back and forth, making him shiver. Then, without warning, the sack that had been over his head was gone. There was a blinding white and Andrew screwed his eyes closed, fighting against the pain of the light. Even with his eyelids clamped closed, it still hurt, the brightness of the room battling against his senses.

It took him a short while, but Andrew slowly began to

open his eyes until the sizzling array of multicoloured stars slowly morphed into a room so white it felt like he was in an operating theatre. Bright light poured from above and, aside from the blank wall ahead of him, Andrew could only see two things: a dark silhouette in the shape of a man all too familiar and a single wooden chair.

'Hello, Mr Hunter,' Thomas Braithwaite said. He was wearing a smart suit, with black shiny shoes. Dressed for a day in a boardroom or court, not for this blank room.

With the bag removed and his eyes uncovered, Andrew began to feel his other senses return. He could smell bleach, almost taste it. He twisted sideways but could see nothing other than blank walls. No windows, not even a door – though he was unable to look directly behind.

'Where am I?' Andrew gasped.

'I borrowed this room from a friend,' Braithwaite said. 'It's for special occasions only. You're underneath something very noisy. You can shout if you want, but no one will hear you.'

Andrew sensed movement behind but still couldn't twist enough to see what – or who – was there. He suspected Iwan had been one of those who'd snatched him – Braithwaite's burly henchman certainly had the physique. Andrew had no idea who the other man might have been, not that it mattered. Iwan had been waiting to have a crack at Andrew for months, this time with no tyre irons. Well, this time when *Andrew* didn't have a tyre iron.

When nobody emerged from behind, Andrew focused back ahead. Braithwaite was removing his jacket carefully, folding it delicately and then placing it over the back of the empty chair at his side. He unclipped his cufflinks, pocketing them, and then rolled his sleeves up slowly and deliberately.

He stood, staring at Andrew, face free from emotion, and then strode purposefully forward. Andrew winced as Braithwaite neared, expecting a blow that never came. Instead,

Braithwaite leaned over him, so close that Andrew could smell the aftershave on the other man's neck. Braithwaite reached past him and then stood up, clutching the violin case. He stepped back and presented it with one hand, even though Andrew was still tied to the chair.

'Where did you get this?' Braithwaite asked. He sounded calm, in control.

'I can't say.'

Whump.

The case whistled through the air, thumping into the ear on which Andrew had already been struck. He reeled to the side, the chair rocking and then bouncing back into position. Andrew's ears were ringing as he tried to blink away the pain. It took him a few seconds to recover and then he blinked his eyes open to see Braithwaite still standing in front of him, the case in his hand. Andrew hadn't seen him move.

'This might be a simple violin to you, Mr Hunter, but it is a symbol of respect to me. I don't allow myself to be scammed and people do *not* fail me. So, with that in mind, I have one very simple question for you: are you a failure or a scam artist?'

Andrew shook his head, croaking, 'Neither.'

This time he saw Braithwaite coming, not that he could do anything. The case fizzed through the air once more, cannoning into the same ear. The chair screeched sideways, again rocking but not overbalancing. The sound was muffled, as if he was underwater and Andrew realised his ear was probably bleeding.

Braithwaite waited for Andrew to open his eyes and compose himself once more. Braithwaite's calm was evaporating, knuckles shaking as he thrust the violin case into the air. His voice was a growled fury.

'This is *not* the instrument I asked you to retrieve – and yet it comes in the correct case.' He straightened his shirt, calming his tone once more. 'Where is the real violin, Mr Hunter?'

Andrew shook his head, readying himself for a blow that didn't come.

'Do you have it?' Braithwaite continued.

'No.'

'Did you think you'd sell it yourself, knowing what it might be worth, or are you incompetent?'

Andrew shook his head. He didn't know why, but he'd felt sorry for Finn Renton. The thieving, scrote of a man who'd mucked up his own life but had a kid who was actually talented. Andrew had taken the genuine violin and the one he'd bought from the car boot to a different music shop a little out of the city and asked them to copy the engraving. He'd put the one from the boot sale in the genuine case and returned Braithwaite's to Finn. He knew he was playing with fire when he'd handed Braithwaite the forgery, but once he'd heard Braithwaite play the instrument, he convinced himself all would be okay.

He could have done it the other way around – given Finn the forgery. Why not? It seemed the obvious thing to do, and yet Andrew suspected that, deep down, he wanted to get one over on Braithwaite. He thought Jenny could be reckless and perhaps he'd learned from her?

He knew Iwan would continue to visit. Braithwaite would keep coming for him. There would *always* be one more job. He could give up Finn Renton, but so what if he did? All he'd be doing was condemning one more person in the way he had by following Max Grayson and handing over details of his drug-dealing. It would never end.

'Do you have an answer?' Braithwaite demanded.

Andrew shook his head.

Braithwaite turned and threw the case into the wall. As it struck, the catches sprang open, sending the instrument from inside crashing to the floor. Braithwaite stomped across to it and then put his foot through the back of the violin. There was a solid crack as the wood wrapped itself around his foot, which only seemed to enrage him further. Braithwaite stamped up and down and then kicked the splinters away.

He turned and headed back to Andrew, standing over him, out of breath. 'You know what you've done, don't you?'

'What?'

'You've put those around you in danger. Your girlfriend – that blonde with the short hair, not to mention your bit of stuff in the office.'

'Leave them out of this.'

Braithwaite smirked a vile snarl. He leaned forward, eye-to-eye with Andrew. 'What are you going to do about it?'

Andrew tried to meet the gaze, but there was no way he could match the ferocity. He craned his neck backwards, trying to get away.

'Come on,' Braithwaite taunted. 'What are you going to do?'

Andrew didn't reply.

'Exactly,' Braithwaite spat. 'You're going to do nothing. You're in no position to make demands. A click of my fingers and you'll never leave this room.' He took a step backwards, walking behind Andrew and then leaning in to whisper in his ear, 'Not alive anyway.'

Andrew fidgeted but still couldn't escape. The words had brushed his ears, tickling, hissing. Braithwaite continued to walk around him.

'Did you hear about that poor girl in Rusholme? Snatched from the street, driven to a car park and raped repeatedly. Awful crime. Terrible. Imagine if that were to happen to one of the women in your life...?'

Andrew dived forward but only succeeded in falling flat on his face. His hands were still bound to the chair and he ended up rolling around, trying to get to his feet but only managing to entangle his limbs with the chair's. Braithwaite's foot connected with Andrew's back, but compared to the rest of the pain he was in, he barely felt it.

'Leave them alone,' Andrew shouted.

Another blow rattled into his back and then Braithwaite was in his face again. Any trace of calm was long gone, saliva dripping from his lips. 'What did you say?'

'Don't you *ever* threaten them,' Andrew hissed back. 'This is nothing to do with anyone else. This is you and me.'

Braithwaite dragged Andrew up until the chair was standing again. Despite his trim physique, Braithwaite was sweating, panting for breath.

'Is this really the way you want to play it?' Braithwaite said.

Andrew said nothing.

Braithwaite continued to eye him and then stepped away, nodding to whomever was out of sight behind Andrew. He heard the footsteps but he could see nothing.

Then there was only black.

34

Andrew woke in a heap next to his car. He assumed it was Iwan who had been behind him in the white room. Iwan must have whacked him in the head and then... Andrew didn't know. His hands were unbound and, considering the circumstances, he didn't feel too bad. That was apart from the storm of a headache pounding behind his eyes. The drumming was so loud, there were stars speckling the rim of his vision.

He pushed himself to his feet, using the back of the car to support himself. The car park only had room for a dozen vehicles and each of the spaces was occupied. There was nobody else around. No white van. No Braithwaite or Iwan. Andrew checked his phone, which was somehow still working, and realised that he'd lost two hours. If it wasn't for that – and the pain – the entire incident could have been a dream. There were a couple of missed calls from the office – Jenny – but that was it.

Andrew took a step towards the exit, but his knees were jelly and he stumbled into the vehicle adjacent to his. He put his palms on the bonnet, trying to clear the disorientation.

Everything was spinning, the walls and cars flying towards him and then zooming away again.

Slowly, Andrew clawed his way to the exit. He pulled himself up the stairs, crawling the first few and then finally managing to get to his feet. When he reached the outside, the fresh air hit him in the same way as Braithwaite's violin case. He pressed himself against the wall, *squeezing* his eyes closed.

'C'mon...' he muttered to himself.

Miraculously, the preposterousness of his pep talk seemed to do the trick. When Andrew opened his eyes, he could see the cobbles ahead of him with clarity. He kept one hand on the wall, tracing his way forward until he was opposite the glass office. Tina spotted him, offering a trademark wave while still managing to type with the ferocity of a whirring Tasmanian devil. Andrew managed something close to a wave in return, but the speed of her work was making him dizzy.

He let himself into his own office and then headed up the stairs, bundling through the door into the smell of instant coffee and Crunchy Nut Cornflakes. Jenny spun in her seat.

'You're back,' she said.

'Excuse me,' Andrew replied, before moving as quickly as he could across the office into the bathroom.

The mirror told a harsh story.

There was a cut just hidden by his hairline and blood had oozed into his right ear. It had pooled and then scabbed, leaving a near-black trail that looped around his cheek. Andrew turned the warm tap on full, letting it run until the liquid was steaming. He wadded a handful of toilet roll and then dabbed away as much blood as he could. The wound itself stung, but the rest of the marks on him seemed to be superficial. With his top off, he twisted as best he could, trying to see if there were any more bruises on his back from where Braithwaite had kicked. It looked clear.

Andrew washed the rest of his face and then turned off the

taps, staring at his reflection and running through the events of the day once more. He'd almost forgotten everything Jack Marsh had told him.

He dressed himself again and then tidied up the bathroom before heading back into the office. He popped a pair of aspirin from his top drawer and then clicked the kettle on.

'Brew?' he asked.

Jenny was staring at him. 'Are you sure you're all right?'

'Fine. Why?'

'Well... you've been gone for around four hours. I tried calling but there was no answer. I didn't know if you were still at Jack's, or if there was something else going on.'

'Everything's fine.'

She tilted her head. 'You look like you've fallen down a set of stairs.'

Andrew turned back to the kettle. 'Huh?'

'Your eye's a bit black.'

'I hit my head while getting out of the car earlier. Nothing major.' He could feel Jenny's gaze burning into his back but ignored what she'd said. 'Do you want a tea?' he asked.

Jenny said no and Andrew settled for the gooiest of black coffees for himself. It was so thick, he thought about taking a spoon back to his desk.

'Any cards in the mail today?' he said as he finally sat down.

'Junk, mainly. Nothing else.'

'Phone calls?'

'A couple but nothing dodgy.'

That was one thing. Andrew slurped his coffee and rubbed his head. He wondered if perhaps Ollie *was* responsible. There hadn't been any incidents since Andrew had confronted him. Hang-ups and Valentine's Day cards certainly weren't Thomas Braithwaite's style for intimidation.

'How was Jack?' Jenny asked.

'He had quite the story to tell...'

Andrew told Jenny everything about the first part of his morning, stopping at the part where Jack had explained why he was creeped out by her. He said he'd had a few errands to run after that and omitted to mention anything about his encounter with Braithwaite.

Jenny was excited. 'So he's finally admitted he sneaked out of the hotel?' she said.

'Right.'

'Do you believe him about the escorts?'

'If he was going to make up something, he could have come up with anything that painted him in a better light, but he didn't.'

'If he didn't kill Michelle, did she just fall in the canal?'

'I don't know.'

Jenny reached into her bottom drawer and held up a packet of Hobnobs. 'Biscuit?'

'No.'

A packet of chocolate digestives. '*Choccie* biscuit?'

'No.'

'Mini Roll?'

'I'm fine, Jen.'

She nodded, returning the packets to her drawer, and then held up a chocolate bar. 'KitKat?'

'Jen – I'm fine. How much have you got in there? It's like you're running a corner shop.'

She grinned. 'I'd *love* to run a corner shop. Imagine having a cash and carry card. I'd go crazy in a place like that.'

Andrew was going to mention that his business was eligible for a cash and carry card but couldn't take the potential excitement.

'Do you think we'll ever know what happened to Michelle?' Jenny asked, tucking into her KitKat.

Andrew clucked his tongue, thinking. 'I'm not sure where to go from here. We've walked her route. The CCTV is online, showing her heading through the city, but I don't see how we can ever know for sure what happened when she turned off Portland Street. There's no cameras, no witnesses to talk to – certainly no one the police wouldn't have already been in contact with. We could get down to Canal Street and ask some of the bar owners if they were working that night. The worst that can happen is they'll tell us to get lost, or say they didn't see anything.'

'The police will have done that, though, wouldn't they?'

'Yes – and they'll have been able to find potential witnesses who were out drinking that night.' Andrew accidentally touched his ear and then winced away. 'Did you find out anything about Danny McMichael?' he added.

'Only really football stuff. It doesn't look like he's ever been in trouble and the papers don't seem that bothered by him. He's married with a couple of kids. I know that doesn't necessarily mean much, but unless we can talk to him—'

'We can't.'

'In that case, I'm not sure what else we can do.'

Andrew agreed. Danny McMichael was a dead end – as were most of his other ideas of how to go about things. Jack Marsh had a murky past, but Andrew didn't believe he was a killer. He hated being defeated, but it felt like the end of the line.

He leaned back in his chair, drumming his fingers. 'I'm going to let it sit for a day or two,' he said. 'Maybe one of us will come up with someone else to talk to, or there'll be something we've missed. I'll take the file home later and read it all through.'

Andrew realised Jenny was watching him. It felt like she wanted to say something.

'What?' he asked.

'My flat's sorted, but I was wondering if I could stay at yours another night. It's just that—'

'It's fine. Don't worry about it.'

Andrew didn't know what her motivations were, his opinion had been warped enough over the preceding days. Beyond anything Jenny might have to say, it didn't matter. Braithwaite's threat to Jenny and Keira was still fresh in his mind and the closer he had them to him, the safer he hoped they'd be. At least his flat was relatively secure. Many floors up, security cameras on the ground floor – and so on. If someone was determined, it wouldn't stop them getting to him, but his flat was more secure than Jenny's house.

'I'm not going to be in this evening,' Andrew added. 'You can still stay there, but you'll have the flat to yourself. There's food in the fridge, so eat what you want.' He paused, then added: 'That's not a challenge, by the way.'

Jenny laughed but sounded surprised. 'You up to anything fun?'

'I'm meeting Keira for tea. I'll walk you back and give you my spare key, then I was going to go straight out.'

'You don't have to walk me. If you're going out, just go. It's only five or ten minutes.'

Andrew thought about it, wanting to tell Jenny about Braithwaite's threat but desperate not to worry her. Deep down, he didn't believe Braithwaite was being serious when talking about either Jenny or Keira. It was a tactic to get to Andrew. Sooner or later, he'd be back, wanting another job doing, and then Andrew would have to make a decision.

'Fine,' he said. He crossed the room and unlocked the filing cabinet, rifling through the bottom drawer. He tossed one of his spare keys across to Jenny, who caught it one-handed. 'Please don't lose that.'

'When have I ever lost stuff?'

'Good point.'

She pocketed the key and then looked up. 'Is there anything I can help with?'

'Where's the Braithwaite file?'

'Under B. Surprisingly.'

Andrew flipped through the files until he found the Braithwaite one. Considering the nature of the man, the brutality of what Andrew had been through a short time ago, it seemed ridiculous that the details they had on him were kept alongside those of the other cases they'd had.

After locking the cabinet, Andrew returned to his desk and started to read. One way or another, he had to bring all this to an end.

35

Andrew had not eaten out in the Curry Mile area of Rusholme for years. It stretched along Wilmslow Road to the south of Manchester, one long row of brightly coloured Indian, Pakistani and Bangladeshi restaurants, all competing with one another for customers and space. That was only the start, with dozens more takeaways from all cuisines and then a host of new shisha places that toed the line of operating within anti-smoking laws. Considering the length of time Andrew had called the city his home – plus the fact he'd been a student there – his lack of time in the area was something of a disgrace. Some people came from miles around to sample the south Asian cuisine and yet he'd not bothered to get off his arse and travel down the road since he'd been a younger twenty-something.

After a text that morning, it was Keira's suggestion to change that.

Andrew parked close to Platt Fields Park and then walked up the road as if he were heading back to the city centre. The air smelled of exotic spices, though there was an undercurrent of cheap kebab meat as well.

It was still early, not long after seven, and the sun was clipping the tops of the buildings. The area sat roughly halfway between the Fallowfield and Oxford Road university campuses, but the tight Moss Side terraces bordered it as well and the streets were teeming with people.

Andrew checked the text from Keira with the name of the restaurant. There were far too many vowels in it for his liking, but that at least made it easy to find.

Crossing the road was an altogether trickier proposition.

The tarmac was a bewildering jumble of bike lanes, bus lanes, bus stops, and other criss-crossing white lines. It was like whomever was in charge of line painting had suffered a seizure but had carried on regardless.

Andrew stood opposite the restaurant waiting, waiting, waiting... and then he darted across when there was something vaguely resembling a gap in the traffic. He remembered too late that much of him still ached from the van abduction, though he made it across in one piece.

The restaurant was impressive, in a Vegas-Blackpool tacky sort of way. There were pink and green flashing bulbs strobing needlessly given it was still light outside – and some sort of rotating globe above the door. As he got inside, an Asian man in a suit shook Andrew's hand and welcomed him while simultaneously helping him to slip off his jacket like a particularly creative pickpocket.

Further inside and the restaurant was at least twice the size Andrew would have guessed from the outside. Long rows of tables stretched deep into the darkness, with everything immaculately laid out and the type of low-level lighting more usually associated, or so he presumed, with 'genting'.

Andrew pointed towards Keira, muttering that he was with her and – perhaps politely – not getting a raised eyebrow of 'she's-out-of-your-league' confusion from the waiter.

Keira was sipping from a wine glass and toasted Andrew with it as he sat. 'Found it then?' she said.

Andrew's first thought of a reply was a sarcastic 'well, duh'. In the old days, he'd have blurted it out, but now, with things the way they were between them, he wasn't sure if they had that sort of relationship.

'Not too bad,' he replied, wishy-washily, sickening himself. It was small talk for idiots. Like the month after Christmas, where everyone's first question was, 'Have a good Christmas?'

Andrew *hated* those people. What was the reply ever going to be? 'No, pretty bad, actually. Nan died, the dog got ill, I put on half a stone and then, to top it all, I ran over a homeless man and didn't stop'? People only ever offered the same mundane 'yeah, not too bad' and then started to talk about the weather.

'Nice day, isn't it?' Keira added.

Andrew mumbled something about the weekend's forecast, but, inside, a tiny part of him was dying. Once, they'd talk about everything and anything. They'd watch passers-by and take the piss, they'd discuss places they wanted to go, things they wanted to see. They had friends to gossip about, books to dissect, movies to go over. Now they were talking about directions and weather.

There was some respite as Keira started to list the things she fancied on the menu. Above and beyond small talk, food was one thing in which Andrew *could* get interested. There was some curry laced with pineapple that she pointed out, strongly hinting that he should order that because she was going to go for something with coconut. In the end, he let her choose for them both and then they were back to awkward silences and the type of conversation more usually associated with two people who didn't speak the same language.

The biggest problem was where did they go from here? Andrew had spent years dreaming of moments like this, of being back with his ex-wife and doing the normal things he so missed. But it was all an illusion, because things could never be as they were. They were older and their lives had taken different paths. Besides, he was hardly going to tell her that someone had thrown him in a van that day and then threatened her.

They spent the wait for the courses talking in a not talking kind of way. So many words, so little meaning.

It was likely because of the barely there lighting, but it took Keira a little while until she noticed the mark around Andrew's hairline. She leaned forward, dabbing it with her finger like a mother poking an injured child's knee. 'What did you do here?' she asked.

'One of those spring-back doors,' Andrew replied. 'I opened it and then forgot the whole "spring-back"-thing. Caught me in the ear.'

She nodded and then looked back to the table.

'How was Thailand?' Andrew asked.

'Hot. Everyone's gearing up for Buddhist new year at the moment, so it was exciting.'

'How long's the flight?'

'Twelve hours.'

'Non-stop?'

'That's how I went. You can get a layover but...'

Another dead end of conversation, which was thankfully overshadowed by a tray of poppadums and pickles arriving. Andrew didn't know why he'd even asked. What was next? How's the airport? What food did you get on the plane?

'How's Jenny?' Keira asked, not looking up from her plate.

'She's fine.'

'What happened with her window?'

'I'm not too sure. Someone put a brick through it, but she didn't want to go to the police. She says it's probably just kids.'

Keira crunched into a poppadum. 'She's pretty.'

Andrew finished his mouthful but couldn't bring himself to look properly at his ex-wife. 'You've said that before.'

At that moment, the waiter chose the worst possible time to float by and ask if everything was okay. He checked if they wanted more to drink and then drifted away, the damage done. The silence lingered, broken only by the snapping of poppadums.

'All she does is work for me,' Andrew eventually said.

'And live with you.'

'She's not living with me!' Andrew snapped the reply before realising he'd done it. He quickly lowered his voice. 'She's staying at mine for a couple of nights while her window is fixed. She's, what, ten, twelve years younger than me? This isn't an issue.'

Keira swiped a dribble of mango chutney up from her plate with her finger and licked it clean. She wiped her mouth with a napkin and then sat back. Her lips were pursed as if she wanted to say something.

'What?' Andrew said.

Keira leaned in, her voice low. 'I don't want to sound like a bitch, but there's something about her that...' She puffed an exasperated breath. 'I don't know. Something not quite right.'

Andrew looked up to her. 'What do you mean?'

'I can't put my finger on it. We've only met a few times and even then it's only been for odd moments. We've never had a proper conversation, never been together when you're not there. I can't explain what it is. I just...' Another breath. 'Sorry – I just don't like her.'

Andrew felt lost, sinking. Was it only him with whom Jenny had some sort of rapport? He had people queuing up to tell him all wasn't right, but nobody could give a proper reason.

'Sorry,' Keira added. 'You know I'm not normally like this about people. I don't know why I said it.' She touched his arm, forcing a smile. 'Look, your business is literally your business. I'm being stupid. Take no notice.'

'She's really good at her job,' Andrew said. '*Really* good to the point that I'm not sure how I'd get by without her. I've never entirely got my head round the computer system, but she's helped with all sorts. She's really smart. She comes up with ideas I'd have never thought of.'

Keira shrugged. 'You don't have to defend her to me. You're the one who works with her. I'm not sure I even understand what you do – and I'm not trying to be a cow when I say that, just honest. I'd be annoyed if you started criticising the people I work with. I shouldn't have said anything. I'm sorry. Forget it.'

Andrew nodded, indicating he would – except there was no way he could. Was he the only one who got Jenny, or was he the only one blind to whatever her true nature entailed? Right now, he felt like he was the only sane one in an institution. He was screaming at the world that *he* was fine and it was everyone else with the problem.

36

After the meal, Andrew walked Keira back to her car. The Curry Mile was a very different place after dark, with a glittering wash of dappled lights blinking from both sides of the road. It was underwhelmingly spectacular: long rows of fruit machines next to each other, battling for attention. Andrew both liked and disliked it.

When they got to her vehicle, Andrew told Keira to 'stay safe', thinking of Braithwaite's threat, although she – obviously – took it as a more general piece of well-wishing. He'd already made the decision not to tell her about Braithwaite, largely because he didn't want to worry her and also because he didn't think Braithwaite would go that far. It was Andrew he wanted.

There was a moment in which they looked at each other and he wondered if he should take the lead by making some sort of grand romantic gesture of sweeping her into his arms.

It wasn't him. He'd probably end up losing his footing and drop her on her head, or something like that. Nothing said 'I love you' better than a trip to A&E with a fractured skull.

In the end, knowing him too well, Keira grinned and leaned in, hugging him. Andrew held her back, cheek pressed into her hair. She wanted to go back to the beginning, to take it slowly, and here they were doing just that.

She kissed him on the cheek – nothing more – and then they said goodbye.

'We should do this again,' she said.

Andrew agreed and then watched her go. It had been awkward at times, but their second first date hadn't been a total disaster, which, considering his record with women since his divorce, wasn't bad at all.

Andrew drove back to his flat and parked. He waited for a moment, overly aware of potential white vans and terrors within, then he headed up the lift to his floor. He fully expected Jenny to be curled up on the sofa watching television while eating ice cream, cereal, chocolate or whatever else she'd found. Instead, when he pushed the door open, the lights were off. Andrew switched them on, though all it revealed was an empty living room. The duvet under which Jenny had slept the night before was still folded at the end of the sofa, seemingly untouched in the hours since they'd left.

'Jen...?'

Andrew's voice echoed around the flat, unanswered. He went to his bedroom, though the bed was still unmade and the blinds down, the way he'd left everything that morning. He checked the bathroom, but that was empty, too. Andrew did one more lap of the flat – Jenny's overnight bag was next to the sofa where she'd left it and the sink still contained a bowl and a plate from their breakfast. As far as he could see, all was as it had been from the morning.

If Jenny *had* been back, why would she have left her bag?

Andrew's chest tightened. He slipped his phone from his pocket and dialled her number. It rang and continued to ring until: 'Hi, it's Jenny. Leave a message after the beep... *beeeeeeeep!*' Andrew waited for the next bit. 'That wasn't the actual beep,' her voice added. 'There is no beep there's a sort of plip thing, so leave your message after that.' She sounded bright and happy. There was a pause and then a plip.

'Jen, just wondering where you are. Call me.'

Andrew hung up, stared at the screen and then dialled once more. He got voicemail again and hung up. An Arctic chill tingled at him, but he wasn't ready to admit he was wrong yet. It *wasn't* Braithwaite. Not yet, anyway. Jenny could have returned to her own house for some reason.

Andrew left his flat and knocked on the door opposite. It was soon opened by a black man with bushy stubble, who nodded a surprised 'hi'. Andrew didn't know the man's name, although they knew each other in the same way Andrew knew everyone else on his floor. For the most part, he and his neighbours kept to themselves. They were polite enough to nod at one another when they passed in the corridor, got into the lift at the same time, or lobbed bags of rubbish down the trash chute – but that was about it.

'Hi,' Andrew replied. 'I was wondering if you've heard anything from across the corridor? I've got a friend staying for a few days and I wanted to make sure the noise was fine.'

The man shrugged. 'It's fine, mate.'

'Cheers.'

The door closed and Andrew knocked on the doors of the flat either side of his, asking the same question. Nobody had seen or heard anything that day, which wasn't a surprise but hardly reassuring either. They might have heard nothing because nothing had happened, or because their music or the television was turned up.

Andrew locked his flat and returned to his car. Before he set off, he called Jenny once more, but still only got her voicemail. The upbeat sound of her voice grated as he willed her to actually answer.

The roads around the university were busy as Andrew drove to her house. A group of lads in fancy dress were doing the conga close to All Saints Park on their way into one of the nearby pubs, while other students filmed the spectacle on their phones. Every traffic light seemed to be red as Andrew stopped and started his way towards Jenny's place, trying to assure himself that all was fine.

When he arrived at her house, the lights were off. There were a few sawdust shavings underneath the newly replaced window, but the blinds were down and he couldn't see inside. Andrew knocked and waited, pressing his ear to the door, though he couldn't hear anything. He tried phoning once more but got voicemail again – and there was no sign that her phone could be in the house.

A young woman roughly Jenny's age turned out to be her next-door neighbour. She was in fleecy pyjama bottoms and a dressing gown when she answered and left the door on the chain.

'Sorry,' Andrew said, 'I'm looking for my friend who lives next door. Jenny. Do you know her?'

The woman shook her head.

'I've sort of... lost her,' Andrew added. 'I've tried her phone, but she's not answering.'

'Long dark hair?' she said.

'That's right.'

'I've seen her around, but I wouldn't know her name.'

'Do you know if she's friends with anyone around here?'

Another shake of the head. 'Sorry.'

The woman clearly wanted to go, so Andrew apologised again and stepped away. He started to pace the street, phoning Jenny twice more. The result was the same as before. Fighting back a rising panic, Andrew continued to the end of the road and then followed the lane that flanked the back of the houses. He counted them down until he was pretty sure he was at the back of Jenny's. He looked both ways and then jumped the gate.

The yard was small and empty, except for a bicycle concealed by a rain cover underneath the back window. Andrew pressed against the glass, trying to angle himself in a way that would allow him to peep through the small gap in the curtains. Even when he managed it, all he could see was a bare patch of wall in her living room, certainly nothing that could help him find Jenny. He tried the back door just in case, though it was locked. Out of ideas, he headed back to his car.

Two more calls to Jenny's mobile went unanswered, so Andrew scrolled through his contacts list, thumb hovering over Thomas Braithwaite's name.

Should he call?

Was Andrew's attention what Braithwaite wanted? If so, had he wasted the past hour by knocking on doors and trying to find Jenny when he already knew what had happened to her? He'd last seen her four hours before. In that time, so many things could have happened. If she'd been snatched in the way he had, she could be on a ferry at Liverpool docks by now, or hidden away at the other end of the country. Braithwaite could have done anything to her.

Andrew pressed the button to call Braithwaite and then instantly thumbed the end call button before it connected. He paused over the redial button and then dropped his phone on the passenger seat. If she wasn't at her home and she wasn't at his, there was one other place Jenny might be.

Andrew parked in his office space and hurried along the cobbled alley, fighting the sense of fear as he passed the spot from which he'd been grabbed. There were no street lights and the only illumination came from the steady haze of orange of the main throughway at the end. He got to his office unscathed, though his heart was a hammer thumping away at his chest.

The door was locked, the lights off – exactly as Andrew had left it when he and Jenny had finished earlier on. He'd gone to the car park, while she'd set off through the tight mangle of alleys towards the spot where she would eventually emerge onto Cross Street.

Andrew walked the route just in case, but, for much of it, there was not enough light to see anything anyway. The backs of the offices doused the tight roads in shadow and, aside from scattered rubbish and the odd person using the lanes as a cut-through, there was nothing. Certainly no signs of a struggle.

Back at the office, Andrew let himself in. He locked the door and left the lights off as he headed upstairs.

'Jen?'

The upper lights were darkened, too – as he'd left them – and there was no sign anyone had been around their desks. Andrew shone the torchlight from his phone around the room, finding the pair of upside-down mugs on the draining board. As far as he could see, nothing was out of place. The only other light was the red LED blinking underneath his monitor, telling him the computer was off.

Andrew sat at Jenny's desk, almost falling over as he misjudged how low her seat was. He looked underneath her keyboard and mouse mat, but there was nothing. Her drawers were locked, but he undid them with the spare keys they had concealed underneath the cactus that lived on the window sill. The top drawer was full of paperclips, pens, Post-its and the usual array of stationery. The second contained envelopes and a file relating to another case they'd been looking into. Nothing unusual.

The bottom drawer was three times the size of the others and was packed with the types of thing more usually associated with a shopping trolley packed by an eight-year-old. There was a box of Crunchy Nut Cornflakes and another of Coco Pops, plus half-eaten packets of Hobnobs, chocolate

Hobnobs, chocolate digestives, rich teas, chocolate rich teas, Bourbons, shortbread fingers and Fox's Creams. There were also two large bars of untouched Cadbury's Fruit & Nut.

Andrew marvelled at the amount of sugar she'd packed into one drawer and was about to close it when he noticed the large red envelope wedged between the two boxes of cereal. There were two words on the front: *Emergency only*. The handwriting was Jenny's – neat and efficient. It was sealed, but Andrew figured this was as much of an emergency as it was going to get. He ripped open the envelope and then picked a second, slightly smaller one, out from the first.

No, really. This is only for an emergency – Jenny's handwriting again. She drew a circle over the letter 'i' instead of a dot.

Andrew couldn't help but smile. He opened the second envelope, but that only revealed a third.

Seriously, if this isn't an emergency, don't open this.

He could almost hear Jenny's voice saying the words she'd written on the envelopes. Andrew pulled apart the final one anyway and twice read the card inside. Even with the situation, he couldn't help but smile sadly.

Regardless of what anyone else thought of her, Jenny was something special.

Which was all the more reason why he needed to find her soon.

37

Andrew sat at his own desk, following the bullet point instructions from Jenny's card. When he loaded findjenny.com, he was taken to a black screen with three small white squares. He typed his day, month and year of birth into the gaps and then pressed enter.

For a panicky second nothing happened, and then the screen flashed bright with colour, displaying a map of the United Kingdom. Almost instantly it began to zoom in, first on the central part of the country, then more specifically on the north-west of England, then Manchester itself. The screen froze momentarily, the blue M60 motorway ringroad hooped around the edge of the city before it zoomed once more.

East Manchester.

The earrings Jenny had taken to wearing weren't a fashion statement at all – one of them contained a tracker that synced with a website she'd set up herself. She didn't want Andrew to spy on her as such – but she did want to him to be able to find her in an emergency.

He wondered if she was more observant than he'd given

her credit for. Things with Braithwaite had been building and perhaps she'd realised something like this could happen.

The map zoomed once more, showing the massive Clayton Vale park on the left of the screen and the far edges of the motorway on the right. Another flash and it was homing in on the Droylsden area of Manchester.

Two final flickers and there was a red dot hovering over a single house on a road that backed onto Ashton Canal.

Jenny – or at the very least, her earrings – were in a house five miles away.

Andrew's first instinct was to charge across the city, but he wanted to be prepared. He typed the address into the electoral roll and came up with a name that meant nothing to him: Tyler James.

He didn't think he'd ever met anyone named Tyler and the last name meant little. Andrew searched the name, looking to see if there was any further information, but a credit check revealed nothing important and there were no hits from the *Morning Herald*'s online news archive. Next, he tried searching for Tyler's name along with Braithwaite's – but there was no obvious link between the two. Andrew knew he could try one or two of his sources to get more information – a criminal record check, that sort of thing – but he'd already lost five minutes.

He didn't stop to think much more. It was a straight drive out of the city, albeit one punctuated by nonsensical traffic lights that were on red, even though there was hardly any traffic. Andrew drummed the steering wheel anxiously and called Jenny twice more, getting voicemail both times. The satnav got him through the final few streets until he emerged onto the street where Jenny's dot had been.

He wasn't sure what he'd been expecting, but it was a picture of suburban normality. There was a mix of neat semi-detached and detached new-builds, each with tidy white-rimmed double-glazing, small patches of green at the front and pristine driveways. It was as picket-fence-perfect as England got.

Andrew drove to the end of the cul-de-sac, turning around in the circle at the end and then heading back the way he'd come. He parked on a connecting street and then walked through the shadows of the pavement, surveying his surroundings. There was nobody on the street, not even any passing cars. Most of the curtains were pulled closed, but a few had the blueish light of a television spilling through the front windows. This didn't have the feel of something Braithwaite could have set up, but then Andrew had no idea what else might be going on.

Number thirty-six was close to the end of the cul-de-sac, detached with a small black rail fence surrounding a patch of grass at the front that wasn't even a metre wide. It could barely be called a garden. The downstairs lights were on, seeping through a gap at the top of the dark curtains. There was a small, unmarked white van on the driveway, but nothing unusual. Andrew stood directly underneath the street lamp, which, because of the angle at which the light was set, happened to be the darkest spot on the street. He turned in a circle, taking in the houses around him, looking for movement. There was no one around, nobody showing the slightest bit of interest in him.

Andrew headed to the front door and knocked sharply. He held his breath, waiting and wondering what might be inside. He heard a shuffling and then the door opened to reveal... a stranger.

The man was a few inches shorter than Andrew, nearly bald and thin, though not in an athletic way. He had youthful eyes and largely unwrinkled skin, making it difficult to judge his age. It was like he was a young man trapped in an old person's body – some sort of not very good Hollywood comedy caper. Probably involving Adam Sandler. The man blinked up at Andrew, eyes widening. 'Hello?'

Andrew had been expecting something more than this. A person he knew, or at least recognised – or some Iwan-like brute.

'Hi,' Andrew stammered, 'Um... sorry, I think I might have the wrong place. I was looking for my friend.'

The man – presumably Tyler James – continued to stare. Beyond him was a bright hallway, nothing untoward. 'Who's your friend?' he asked, rubbing at his eyes. It was only then that Andrew noticed the vague rounded outlines cut into the area above his cheekbones. Andrew tried to picture him with glasses and then wondered if, perhaps, he wasn't such a stranger after all.

'No one,' Andrew replied quickly. 'I think I've got the wrong address. Sorry to have bothered you.'

The man mumbled something Andrew didn't catch and then clicked the door closed.

Andrew stepped back onto the pavement, trudging slowly in the direction of his car, counting to ten and then turning to see a flicker of the downstairs curtain.

He sped up, making sure he was out of eyeline from the house and then tucking underneath another lamp-post to think.

The man's identity was a mystery and yet there was something niggling at the back of Andrew's mind that made him think they'd seen each other before. What's more, with the way the man's eyes had widened, it felt like *he* knew Andrew.

Above that, he trusted Jenny – and the tracker she'd set up said she was inside.

Andrew kept an eye on the window of number thirty-six while he hurried from lamp-post to lamp-post. He paused underneath each one, making sure nobody was watching, until he was back at the front of the house. Once there, he squeezed into the gap between the side wall and the parked van, side-stepping until he reached a wide garage door with a gate at the side. It was panelled wood, a little taller than he was. There was no light at the back of the house, leaving thick shadows that stretched from the neighbouring property. Andrew could barely see anything himself, but at least that meant the cover shrouded him. He tried twisting the gate handle, rattling it gently, though it was blocked.

After taking a breath, Andrew pushed himself onto tiptoes, reaching over the gate down to where the latch should be. It was a stretch, but the tips of his fingers scraped the top of the metal catch. He pushed up even higher, cheek grazing the wood as his back strained and his shoulder clicked so loudly that it actually echoed. Andrew clamped his lips together, forcing himself not to grunt in pain as – finally – his fingers reached the solid spherical catch. He popped it up and the gate creaked inwards.

Andrew held his breath, listening in case the sound had been heard. A few seconds later and he was in the back garden. It was small and tidy, a rockery lining the length of one fence with a puddle of grass surrounded by paving slabs. There was a barbecue underneath the window and a single gnome staring at him from the far corner, lit up by the white of the moon.

All ridiculously, unerringly normal.

Except for the gnome.

It had a sky-blue hat and scarf – and suddenly Andrew knew exactly where he'd seen Tyler James before. He'd been one of the crowd by the players' coach at the football stadium and also outside the gates of Jack Marsh's house. He'd been with the woman who had an enormous chest and wore shirts that were way too small. She'd told Andrew that

Jack was going nowhere in response to the newspaper rumours of him leaving and then goggled as Jenny said they'd been invited to the house. Andrew had barely registered them – two hardcore fans among a sea of slightly more normal supporters.

Andrew eyed the house, looking for curtain twitches or any other signs that he was being watched. When there was nothing, he crept to the back door and delicately tried the handle, which was locked. He ran his finger along the window frame, just in case they'd not been secured, but he wasn't that lucky.

What should he do?

He could call the police – but what could he realistically tell them? He could hardly explain about trackers in earrings. They'd think he was mad.

He could knock on the front door again and try to barge past Tyler. That was assuming he answered. The woman he'd been with at the football was bigger than he was, the sort of person who looked like she could give sumo wrestling a good go. Assuming she also lived here, Andrew didn't particularly fancy his chances against her.

It was now nearly five hours since he'd last seen Jenny and any number of awful things could have happened to her.

This was no time to be fannying about.

Andrew picked up the biggest stone he could see in the rockery and hurled it at the back door as hard as he could. He hoped for splintering glass, thousands of pieces, the satisfying crunch of something being shattered.

Instead, the rock bounced off the glass and dropped back to the ground with a pitiful dink. As far as Andrew could see, it hadn't left an indent.

He thought about picking it up to try once more, but there was suddenly light streaming through the thin blind of the room next to the back door. Andrew ducked behind the wall of the porch as the sound of a key turning clinked around the garden.

Everything happened in a flash.

The door was pulled inwards and Andrew heard someone stepping outside. He launched himself forward, thankfully shouldering into Tyler as opposed to the woman. The man's puny frame barrelled backwards, his head smashing into the wall as Andrew ran over him. Andrew didn't wait to look for the damage. The man groaned and that was that: Andrew was inside.

He found himself in a kitchen, the sink piled with dishes, a mop leaning against a tall freezer. Through the next door was a living room. The wall was filled with long rows of CDs and movie cases. The television was on, showing some sort of wildlife documentary, with a steaming cup of tea on a small table next to an armchair.

Everything was so normal, so unassuming. What if Jenny's website was wrong? Or if Tyler had been in Manchester that day and found a lost earring in the street? Andrew was starting to worry. This was breaking and entering, possibly attempted burglary. Definitely assault because of the way he'd walloped Tyler in the garden.

He raced back into the kitchen and then through the second door, finding himself in a hallway. Up the stairs onto a landing and there were four doors from which to choose.

'Jenny?'

Andrew's voice didn't sound like his own, cracking and panicked.

No answer.

The first door was the bathroom. Shampoo and shower gel bottles were in the corner, towels were hanging neatly.

The room next door housed a large, neatly made double bed, with a sky-blue teddy sitting at the end.

Andrew blasted through the next door, heart racing, adrenalin firing. He switched on the light but was moving so quickly that he had to do a double take to even begin to absorb what was in front of him. It was horrifyingly freakish. The stuff of nightmares. He was left staring at the walls open-mouthed as footsteps boomed on the stairs below.

38

The floorboards were bare, with errant strands of carpet attached to the skirting boards from where it had been pulled up. The walls were covered in photographs, colour and mono-chrome, long-lens and close-up. Jack Marsh was in many of them – but so was a disturbing array of women. Andrew recog-nised almost none of them, but there, towards the upper right-hand corner of the furthest wall, was Michelle Applegate. She was sitting on Jack's knee, one arm around the back of his neck as they smiled at one another. There were more, too: Michelle by herself outside her house; on an escalator; sitting with her friend, Chloe, at a bar somewhere.

Andrew barely had time to take it in before he heard the footsteps nearing. He turned to see Tyler approaching, kitchen knife in his hand. Blood was gushing from the side of his head, leaving a trail of red where he walked. He was gasping, gurgling, trying to run but struggling.

'*You,*' he said as he reached the landing.

Andrew backed into the room, having nowhere else to go. Aside from the photograph-lined walls, it was empty. Nothing to use as a weapon – unless he wanted to try jumping through the first-floor window. Given a rock hadn't cracked the double-glazing, he didn't fancy his chances of getting through the glass.

Tyler continued advancing, waving the knife in front of him.

'Where's Jenny?' Andrew said.

Tyler didn't reply. He stood where he was, catching his breath, and then Andrew saw the next hammer blow. Close to the light switch was a montage of photographs showing Jenny. She was outside her house; unlocking the office by herself; waving at Tina from the alley; in a supermarket with a basket full of biscuits. In the final photo, she was with Andrew and Eloise Marsh, heading up the driveway on the day they'd first visited Jack's house. He and Eloise were facing the house, but Jenny was side-on, in perfect profile. Tyler had been stalking her – or them – since the weekend.

'Did you put a brick through my car?' Andrew asked, suddenly getting it. 'And Jenny's window?'

Tyler shrugged. He seemed to be struggling with keeping himself upright.

'Where is she?' Andrew repeated.

Tyler stepped forward, head bobbing from side to side as he stretched the knife in front of himself. Andrew jinked to his left and it was like they were dancing as Tyler circled him. He lunged with the knife, the tip nicking Andrew's jacket but not catching as he darted away. Tyler tried again, this time the blade whistling past Andrew's cheek.

They'd shifted positions completely, with Andrew finding himself next to the door. He could turn and run but didn't fancy being chased by a lunatic with a knife. He'd seen too many Westerns in which some dead-eye dick could hurl a blade across a crowded bar and embed it in some bloke's back.

Tyler was grinning manically, but, from nowhere, Andrew had a moment of clarity. When Tyler leapt forward again,

Andrew flipped the light switch, dousing them in darkness. He ducked sideways and heard the clatter of Tyler colliding with the wall. Andrew could barely see himself, but it didn't matter because he was a step ahead. He flung his fist forward, connecting with Tyler's head and sending it thudding into the wall a second time. There was a clang of metal, a grunt of pain – and then silence.

Andrew moved carefully, leaning forward to turn the lights back on and then looking down to see the fallen man. There was blood pooling from both sides of Tyler's head and he'd landed on his wrist, leaving it bent at a near right angle. Andrew picked up the knife and then turned back to the wall.

As well as Jenny and Michelle, there were at least another twenty women who'd been photographed with Jack at various times. For most, there was only a single picture, but for others, there were dozens. Close up, Andrew could see the other photos of Jenny. There were two of her at the training ground when they'd visited to interview Jack – and another of Jack himself heading into the hotel where Andrew and Jenny had been waiting to ambush him days previously.

Pinned to the back of the door was a large poster of Jack Marsh, resplendent in his kit, running in full flow with a football.

For whatever reason, the nutjob at Andrew's feet was determined to protect his idol from any female attention. He'd likely done for Michelle and now he'd targeted Jenny. Andrew peered around the photo mosaic that covered the walls, wondering if there were any other missing girls among the pictures. Any more 'accidents' who didn't happen to have a persistent mother like Anna Applegate determined to discover the truth.

The lump in his throat made him hope he wasn't too late for Jenny.

Andrew nudged Tyler further into the room with his foot, switched off the light and then closed the door.

He tried the final room, but there was nothing except for a single bed.

Andrew headed back downstairs. He tried a door in the hallway, though it was only a cupboard. He had his phone in his hand, trying Jenny's mobile once more – hoping he'd hear the ringtone from somewhere in the house, but there was nothing. He thought about calling the police. He might end up in trouble – but the room above at least proved some of what Tyler had been up to. There'd be more, too. Phone trails, forensics around the house, probably in the van. The police might be able to make him talk, but, if Jenny had been dumped somewhere, it could be too late by then. That didn't explain why her earrings were apparently here.

Phone trails...

If it had been Tyler who'd put a brick through Jenny's window and the back of his car, then perhaps he was responsible for the hang-ups as well.

Andrew dialled the mobile number that had been calling his office and then breathing heavily. He stood still, listening to it ring at his end and then... It was very faint, barely a whisper on the breeze, but Andrew could hear the rhythmic beeping of an old-fashioned ringtone.

He hurried into the living room, but the tone was even fainter. Back to the kitchen and it was a little stronger, though still sounded floaty and distant.

The phone rang off, so he dialled again, standing by the sink and listening. The tone started to beep once more and Andrew followed it out the back door, across the yard, through the gate, to the garage. There was a smaller door next to the main car entrance. He expected it be locked but...

As soon as Andrew burst inside, there was a shriek of alarm. The woman who'd been with Tyler outside Jack

Marsh's gates was standing in the centre of the room, mobile phone in her hand. She was wearing the same tight football shirt he'd seen her in before, a squat beer-keg of a woman, with stubby arms and a dome head.

'What the—?' she exclaimed.

Jenny was in a chair on the other side of the woman, arms fastened behind her back, legs tied to the chair. Her eyes were closed, head flopped to the side.

Andrew didn't think. He charged at the woman, taking her by surprise and slamming his shoulder into her. His force sent them both catapulting to the floor in a heap of sprawling limbs. The woman landed with a thud and gasped, winded, as Andrew's elbow drove into her belly with his full weight. If nothing else, she provided wonderful padding.

Andrew bounced up, but the woman stayed down, gulping and groaning. He still had the knife in his hand and waved it in her direction, as if he was going to use it. She wouldn't know that he didn't have it in him.

'Jen,' Andrew said. He backed towards the chair, watching the downed woman as she crawled into a sitting position, eyeing him with fury. The garage smelled appallingly and it took Andrew a few moments to realise why. There was an empty vodka bottle at the feet of the chair and another half-filled nearby. Pooled underneath was a mushy pool of vomit.

Andrew crouched next to Jenny, trying to control his gag reflex. He spoke her name but got no response.

'Jen,' Andrew repeated, lightly touching her cheeks.

For a moment, nothing happened, but then her head lolled to the other side. Her eyes didn't open, but at least she was alive.

'Can you hear me, Jen?'

She mumbled something in reply, but it was a gurgle of words.

Andrew was standing in her vomit and the smell was

almost overpowering. With the knife, he sliced through the cable ties that were holding her to the chair and then picked her up, half-carrying, half-dragging her to the garage door. All the while, he growled threats to the other woman, who remained winded on the ground, clutching her stomach.

There was a second or two while he lowered Jenny to the floor in which Andrew momentarily had to turn away from the woman. When Jenny was down, he sprang back up, expecting an attack, but she hadn't moved since he'd landed on her. Every breath she took was a rasping wheeze.

Jenny was flat on the cold ground, moaning to herself, so Andrew crouched and turned her onto her side, whispering that she was safe now.

He went to stand, but her hand clasped his as she mumbled something under her breath. Andrew thought he heard his name, so he leaned closer.

'Hi gonvh you,' she said.

He asked he to repeat it, but it was no use, because she made even less sense the second time. The only word he could make out for sure was 'you'.

After assuring her the ordeal was over, Andrew did what he probably should have done in the first place. He called the police.

39

It was almost four in the morning when Andrew opened his front door and headed inside. He reached out to help Jenny, but she assured him she was fine to walk by herself. Her face was pale but, other than that, she looked relatively good given the circumstances.

Andrew switched on the light as Jenny headed to the sofa and yanked the duvet over herself. She'd slept through most of the journey from the police station, although she was looking more awake now.

'Do you want something to drink?' Andrew asked.

'I'd love a brew.'

Andrew headed to the kitchen and filled the kettle. 'Anything to eat?' he called across.

'What biscuits have you got in?'

Andrew searched through his cupboard but could only come up with half a Christmas cake his Aunt Gem had given him a few months before. He put it on a plate and gave Jenny the whole thing with a fork, which immediately cheered her up.

She was about to dive in when he suddenly realised something. 'Do you need to take it easy with food?' he asked.

Jenny shrugged. 'I'll live.'

She devoured a large corner piece, covered in thick marzipan and even thicker royal icing, then 'mmmed' in pleasure.

Andrew dunked a teabag into a mug, gave it a swirl and then put the tea down at her side. He sat at the far end of the sofa and she rested her feet on his lap.

'So...' he said. 'Earrings.'

Jenny smiled and just about managed a croaky laugh. 'I knew they'd come in handy sooner or later.'

'Your invention?'

'I ordered them from America. I registered the domain name for my site and then uploaded the software they provide. Not too hard, really. Didn't know when it all might come in handy.' Jenny swallowed another piece of cake, or, to be more precise, another chunk of icing. 'This is good,' she said.

'Gem made it. I think she generally goes for a fifty-fifty split of cake to icing.'

'That's a good ratio.'

'I'll tell her you said so.'

Jenny sipped her tea and had some more cake.

'Do you want to sleep?' Andrew asked.

She shook her head. 'Later. You?'

'This is like being at uni. Stay out till dawn, sleep for an hour, then go to lectures.'

'Did you do that often?'

'Once or twice. I think I've been an old man since I was about seventeen.'

Jenny smiled again. She yawned and then swallowed a second. 'Not tired,' she insisted.

'Why didn't the doctors keep you in?' Andrew asked.

'They said I'd thrown up most of the alcohol. I've always

been a lightweight with booze. They were talking about pumping my stomach, but then said they didn't need to bother. I've had worse nights out. What about you with the police?'

'I gave them a statement of sorts and I'm back there...' Andrew checked the clock, 'in about six hours. They want to talk to you as well.'

Jenny shrugged, consoling herself with more icing. She wasn't bothering with the fork any longer, instead picking the chunks of white from the cake.

'What do you remember?' Andrew asked.

Jenny closed her eyes in a long, tired blink. She looked like she needed to sleep but batted Andrew away when he suggested as much.

'I was nearly here,' Jenny said. 'I'd cut down the back of Great Northern where the arches are under the train line and this white van pulled up next to me. There was a woman in the front seat—'

'The police say her name is Zoe,' Andrew said.

Jenny nodded. 'Right, Zoe. She asked for directions to the Trafford Centre and I was by her window. I was laughing, saying she was way off, and then... I don't know. The next thing I know, I'm in the garage where you found me.'

'Did she hurt you?'

'Not really. What are those curved knife things?'

'A sickle?'

'She had one of those and told me that if I shouted for help, she'd cut my throat. She had a bottle of vodka and she'd tip some into my mouth and tell me to swallow. It's quite hard to do that when you're tied to a chair!' Jenny laughed as if it was a joke but Andrew couldn't match her.

'How much did you drink?' he asked.

'I dunno – I'd swallow some but managed to dribble little bits out. That annoyed her, so she tried to tip it into my throat, but that only made me sick, which annoyed her even more. In the end, she was pouring a capful, making me sip it and then pouring a little more.'

Andrew waited for Jenny to have something else to drink, then asked if Zoe had mentioned Michelle Applegate.

Jenny coughed slightly before replying. 'Not by name, but she was saying I was one of Jack's sluts, that if she couldn't have him nobody else would. That sort of thing. I didn't know there was somebody else involved.'

It was Andrew's turn to share information. 'Tyler James,' he said. 'Zoe's husband. I'm not sure why they were doing what they were. I'd guess it's a bit like Eloise told us – the men want to be him, the women want to be *with* him. Who knows?'

'She kept asking how many times I'd slept with Jack,' Jenny said. 'She wanted to know when we started sleeping together, what he was like, how big he was…' She winced. 'At first I was denying everything, but that only got her angrier. I started making stuff up because that was the only thing that calmed her down. I said we'd had an on-and-off relationship for two years, that I used to travel to away games to meet up with him, that sort of thing. If I answered all her questions, she gave me a break in between the drinks.'

Andrew ran a hand over his head. Suddenly, *he* needed a drink – then he resolved that he really didn't.

'What I don't get,' Jenny said, 'is why me? It's not like I've *actually* slept with Jack Marsh. I've only met him twice – both times with you.'

Andrew explained about the bizarre upstairs room that was wallpapered with photographs of various young women.

'I don't think it was specifically *you*,' he said, 'more, women in general. They either felt protective over Jack, or jealous of the women in his life. Perhaps both.'

'Does that mean…?' Jenny said, tailing off.

Andrew nodded. 'Probably. There were pictures of Michelle in there. The police will go through the garage, but it's been a long while since it all happened – and that's if Michelle ended up in there at all. After she disappeared from the CCTV, anything could have happened. The van was big enough for Tyler or Zoe to bundle Michelle inside and then her body wasn't found for another ten or twelve hours. The difference between her and you was that she was drunk to start with. At least you had the sense of mind to stall and buy yourself time – not to mention the earrings.'

Jenny was still picking at the icing and there was a thin white trail of crumbs on her chin. 'Were there any other girls?'

'I don't know – there were a lot of photographs in the bedroom. The police will be looking through them all, so I suppose we'll find out. It wouldn't surprise me. Lots of people go missing in this city.'

'Was it them with the bricks and the hang-ups?'

'Definitely the hang-ups. The reason I found you is because I dialled the number that had been bugging us. Probably the bricks, too.'

Jenny offered the plate back to Andrew. She'd eaten two-thirds of the icing and barely any of the cake.

'Don't you want any more?' he asked.

She rubbed her belly. 'Later.'

'This is a first. I didn't think I'd see the day when you were actually full, let alone turning away cake.'

'First time for everything,' she smiled gently.

After putting the cake back in the fridge, Andrew returned to the sofa, where Jenny was covering a yawn with her hand.

'You should get some sleep,' Andrew said.

Jenny waved him towards her and wrapped her hands around his neck pulling him close. 'Thank you,' she whispered.

Andrew had nowhere to put his hands, resting one on top of the sofa and patting her side with the other.

She released him with another yawn. 'What's next?' she asked.

'A day with the police. Official statements, informal chats, video tapes, things to sign. Meanwhile, they'll be searching Tyler and Zoe's house. It's going to be a long few months until it all gets to court.'

Jenny smiled weakly and closed her eyes, turning to face the backrest of the sofa. Andrew was going to offer her the bed, but she'd already turned it down once and was practically asleep anyway.

'Just one thing,' Andrew said.

Jenny's eyes fluttered open but were barely focused.

'What?' she said.

'When I got you out of the chair, I rolled you over and you said something to me. I couldn't really make it out, but I think the first word was "I" and the last word was "you". I didn't catch what you said in the middle.'

Jenny frowned but only for a moment. 'Drunk talk,' she said.

'Do you remember?'

'No... but sometimes drunk talk is true talk.'

She closed her eyes once more and this time Andrew let her sleep.

40

It was a few minutes after four in the afternoon when Andrew and Jenny finally got out of Bootle Street Police Station. Andrew had slept for around three hours in the past day and half – and six more hours of answering the same questions over and over had drained him to the point that he would do just about anything to curl up in his own bed underneath a cosy duvet. Jenny was coping better than he was, perhaps buoyed by the fact one of the PCs had specifically gone on a biscuit run for her at lunchtime. From what Andrew had heard, she'd chomped through two packets of Fox's Double Chocolate Crunch Creams in less than half an hour – before washing the lot down with enough tea to keep Indian farmers in work for a long time.

She was quite something.

A crowd of journalists, photographers and general rubber-neckers were hanging around the entrance to the station, having been tipped off that something big had happened involving Jack Marsh. Andrew doubted they knew the whole story, but it wouldn't be long now. Luckily, none of them knew who Andrew or Jenny were. The atmosphere on the street was a mix of tense anticipation for whenever the police announcement would come and party-time hip-hip-hooray because something interesting was going on. It had to be better than sitting around an office rewriting copy from other news websites.

Andrew and Jenny edged past the crowd, heading through the alley and emerging onto Peter Street, with the Radisson directly ahead. It was where they'd started and now – it was where they'd ended.

'Do you want to get something to eat?' Andrew asked. He was feeling slightly more awake now he was outside. 'We can go anywhere you want – even if it's some place that sells only toast.'

'I'd *love* a bit of toast right now,' Jenny said. 'Thin layer of Marmite on the bottom, raspberry jam on top—'

'That sounds like the most disgusting thing I've ever heard.'

'Have you tried it?'

'Of course not.'

'So how do you know?'

'Logic,' Andrew said, tapping his temple. 'That's how I know.'

'Pfft.'

Andrew was about to ask what – if anything – Jenny wanted to do next when a car beeped its horn from across the road. There was a sporty blue hatchback parked on double-yellow lines with a familiar face in the driver's seat. The din of the traffic meant Andrew couldn't make out what the driver was calling, but the sentiment was clear.

They waited for a gap and then dashed across the road, Jenny calling 'shotgun' when they were halfway across. Andrew wasn't one to argue – especially when it came to ludicrous American tropes – so he folded his legs into the back as

Jenny bounced into the passenger's seat. The car smelled of new leather and was spotless.

Eloise Marsh wasn't exactly smiling, though she wasn't scowling either – which was a large improvement on the last time either of them had seen her. She was wearing expensive-looking sunglasses but took them off to peer at Andrew in the back seat.

'I take it you want a lift,' she said.

'Jen?' Andrew added.

'There's this amazing little burger place out in Bury,' Jenny began, before listing the menu off the top of her head. There seemed to be a lot of cheese involved.

Eloise didn't argue, pulling away and heading in the requested direction.

'As you might be able to guess,' she said once Jenny had finished, 'the police have been in contact today. They brought round photos of two individuals both my son and myself recognised as people who hang around our gates. Apparently, they've taken stalking to a new level.'

'So we discovered,' Andrew replied.

'It sounds like I owe you an apology.' Eloise didn't exactly sound apologetic, more annoyed. She glanced away from the road towards Andrew, sunglasses at the end of her nose. 'My son told me that he'd spoken to you about... his other issue as well. That is also being dealt with by the police, so I thank you for the advice you gave him.'

Andrew mumbled 'it's fine' but was taken aback by Eloise's clipped politeness. She'd said 'my son' twice, both times managing to make it sound like a swear word. He guessed she hadn't taken the news of Jack's escapades too well.

She asked for details of what had happened the previous night, but Andrew fudged it as best he could, not wanting Jenny to have to relive it again. He said that they'd followed some leads that had taken them out to a house in Droylsden, one thing led to another, and here they were.

'Tyler and Zoe James,' Eloise said. 'I'd never heard those names and now I'll never forget them. We – and by "we", I mean "I" – spent most of the morning going through old sacks of mail. You saw yourself how hard it is to keep track of everything. Some weeks are better than others, but if my son scores or something, everything goes crazy again. We could employ someone for the mail, but then it's more money for this, more money for that. Where would it end? Ultimately, my son has an agent who does *his* best and I'm left trying to pick up the pieces of everything else.' She tailed off as she negotiated a roundabout and Andrew was left trying to figure out what she meant.

'Are you saying you got letters from Tyler and Zoe?' he asked.

'At least half a dozen – probably more because we had to throw a lot out. The police have them now. There was nothing weird in there – well, no weirder than anything else. The letters are largely derivative – wishing my son well for a weekend game, even though the letter came *after* it had been played. A lot of it went beyond football. They didn't know my son personally, but they come from the same estate we do. For whatever reason, they think that means there's a connection. Did you hear about the Save the Garages campaign?'

'Is that the place where Jack grew up playing football?' Jenny asked.

Eloise still didn't seem entirely happy about Jenny's presence and turned momentarily towards Andrew before answering, making it clear with whom she was having the conversation. 'My son used to play on this paved area across the road from where we lived. He'd kick the ball against the garage doors for hours, sometimes with his mates, sometimes by himself. Bloody noise drove the neighbours and me crazy.

They had environmental protection officers out, plus the police used to get called all the time. The kids would play football against the "no ball games" sign. The police would say that, technically, the sign wasn't an enforceable law because it was a council issue, then the council would come out and say the kids had to stop – but you know what lads are like. They'd tell these blokes in suits to piss off, so the police would get called and everything would go round in circles. A few years later, once my son was busy playing football for real, everyone forgets that. It's not "Oh, what a load of little oiks kicking a ball against the garages"; it's "Oh, I remember Jack Marsh. Used to play football against my house. Come on in for a cup of tea." Some of our old neighbours popped up in the papers like you wouldn't believe. Giving it The Big I Am, as if it was down to them my son did all right for himself. Hypocrites.'

Eloise had been on a roll, seemingly forgetting what she was talking about. She changed lanes to make a turn and then started again. 'Anyway, these two – Tyler and Zoe – according to the police, they used to live out the back of us. They were a couple of years above my son at school. When developers wanted to knock down the garages, they were the ones who started a petition against it. Christ knows why – the best thing that could happen to that area is a fleet of bulldozers going in. I suppose they wanted to be friends with my son but, well… I tend not to associate with crackpots. As for him, he'd have probably been more interested if this Zoe woman didn't have a face like a bleached arsehole.'

There wasn't much more to add than that.

Eloise drove in silence, heading for Bury and Jenny's burger place. A few minutes later, her voice had calmed again and she added: 'Do you know what will happen to them?'

Andrew had been almost asleep in the back seat but blinked himself awake. 'One of the officers I kind of know mentioned that Zoe's solicitor has already mentioned sectioning, but I don't know.'

There was another few minutes in which the only sounds were that of the traffic and then Eloise turned briefly to Andrew to get his attention. She spun back to the road before speaking, whispering a softer – genuine – 'Thank you.'

Andrew wasn't sure how to reply – it wasn't as if he'd been working for the Marshes and he'd not had a chance to properly contact Anna Applegate so far. The police said they wanted to talk to her first. He took the gratitude in the spirit he was sure it was meant, replying, 'No problem.'

'Do you want money?' Eloise asked.

'No...' Andrew paused, thinking it through and really not wanting to get an earful. 'Though perhaps you could donate something to Anna Applegate—'

'*Her?!* You know what she put on her website, don't you? The things she's been saying.'

'It's also down to her that this has been sorted out – and there's what happened to her daughter...'

Another pause and then a quieter, conciliatory: 'I'll sort something.' Eloise spun once more, peering over her sunglasses to Andrew and then looking back to the road. 'Can I trust you with something?'

'Of course.'

'*Both* of you? I don't want this ending up on the Internet later on. Things are bad enough as it is.'

Jenny answered positively and then Eloise caught Andrew's eye in the mirror.

'My son is moving to Spain,' she said. 'It won't be for a couple of months yet and the paperwork needs to be finalised, but it's being sorted out now. It'll probably end up in the news in the coming days, so everyone will know soon enough. We'd had enough before any of this came out. I'm already looking at villas.' Another glance in the mirror. 'Anyway, sorry for being such a bitch, but someone's got to keep an eye out for Jack and if it's not going to be me, then who? If either of you have kids, you'll know what I mean.'

It was only as they were pulling off the motorway that Andrew realised he'd not turned his phone back on since getting out of the police station. He held the button and then the screen lit up and debated whether to connect to the network, or spend a few minutes idling about like a stroppy teenager. It opted for the latter, before connecting in the end. As soon as it did, the phone started to buzz. Andrew had six missed calls from his aunt, the final one of which had been half an hour previously. He called her back, holding the phone close to the window as he figured he might get a better reception.

His aunt answered on the fifth ring but the connection was choppy and cut out almost immediately. Eloise must have sensed something was wrong because she turned and asked Andrew if he wanted her to pull over. When she did, Andrew called again. His aunt answered straight away and even the dodgy reception couldn't hide the quiver in her voice.

'Andrew?'

'What's wrong, Gem?'

'It's um... well, it's nothing. Sort of. It's... Do you think you can come over?'

'Are you safe?'

'Yes, I... Well I think so.'

So much had happened in the past day that Andrew had forgotten his first thoughts when Jenny had gone missing. The panic over who'd taken her. Hearing his aunt trembling with fear had his hands shaking with rage and pity. Whatever had happened to her was surely because of one person.

Braithwaite.

41

Eloise Marsh U-turned without complaint. She dropped off Andrew on the edge of the estate where his Aunt Gem lived and then said she'd get Jenny back to her house safely. Jenny had wanted to tag along but Andrew told her no. She had then decided she was going to get some sleep at her own place.

Andrew raced around the large green at the front of Gem's block, keeping to the pathway because – regardless of what had gone on – Gem wouldn't let him in her flat if he had muddy shoes. He charged up the concrete steps and headed along the exposed walkway until he reached her door, out of breath. He knocked gently on the window and then a little harder on the door, waiting for her quivering voice to sound from the other side.

'Who is it?'

'It's Andrew.'

The first bolt clunked, quickly followed by the other five and then Gem wrenched the door open. She seemed even smaller than usual. She claimed to be exactly five feet tall, but Andrew doubted that. He wasn't a giant by any stretch, but she wrapped her arms around him, head on his breastbone.

'Oh, Andrew...' It sounded like she was on the brink of tears.

He took off his shoes and then relocked the front door behind him. As he crouched for the bottom lock – the one he never quite understood how Gem reached – Andrew found himself gagging slightly. It was distinctively grim, the type of smell if was hard to forget. The hallway, or at least a small part of it, reeked of excrement.

There was no sign of her pug, Rory, but Andrew's first thought was that the poor little guy had had an accident. Gem's hips and knees meant she had days where she struggled with the stairs – heck, *he* struggled with the damned things – so Rory couldn't always get down to the green to a walk. Andrew had been so busy that he hadn't had time to come round in recent days.

After taking off his shoes, Andrew padded through to the living room, where Gem was on the sofa, Rory at her side. The little dog was dozing away but opened his eyes momentarily to make sure he approved of Andrew before seemingly deciding sleep was preferable.

The room was cluttered with trinkets and general clutter that she'd amassed over her lifetime. There was so much that Andrew found it oppressive. He didn't know where to look because the walls were covered by ceramic plates, clocks, snowglobes, postcards, sticks of rock and just about anything else that could be bought from a seaside tat shop. She liked it, though, so who was Andrew to say anything.

'You look tired,' Gem said. Since talking to her on the phone, Andrew had been in such a panic that he'd been running on the final dregs of adrenalin still left in his body. Now she mentioned how tired he looked, it was like it hit him. He sat in the armchair, leaning forward and rubbing his eyes.

'It's been a long day – a long couple of days.' Andrew

fought back a yawn and then added: 'What's been going on, Gem?'

'Just the kids again. You know what they're like round here. There's nowhere for them to play, so they end up egging each other on.'

'There are plenty of places for them to play.' Andrew pointed towards the front window. 'There's a massive green out there for a start. What have they been up to?'

Gem would usually argue, always finding a reason why the young people who lived around her were hard done by. Andrew sometimes wished he could share her optimism and belief in other people.

'They put... *mess* through my letter box,' she said.

That explained the smell.

'When?'

'It was there this morning. I cleaned it up, but then realised it was dirty outside, too. There were eggshells on the step and the door was covered in it. Took ages to scrub it away.'

'Oh, Gem...'

'Then they were out there with their music earlier. It was getting Rory in a right tizz. You know what he's like if he doesn't get his afternoon nap.'

'Out where? The balcony?'

She nodded and Andrew went for the window, pulling aside the curtain to look out on the spot where he'd just been. There were, of course, no teenagers hanging around any longer.

'I asked if they could turn it down, but they were so *rude*.' Gem shook at the final word and Andrew's blood boiled.

He sat back down, trying to think calm thoughts. 'What happened?' he asked.

'Dennis from a couple of doors down came out because he couldn't hear his TV. He said he'd call the police and they went away.'

Gem reached and stroked Rory's back and then the area around his eye that was a slightly different colour from the rest of him. A few years previously, she'd found him abandoned at the bottom of the stairs by her flat. He was covered in blood from where he'd been used as a football. Nobody had come forward to say the dog belonged to them, so Gem had nursed him back to health. Now the pudgy little so-and-so rarely left her side.

The moment of tenderness was interrupted by a loud knock at the door. Gem froze, her fingers resting on Rory's ear. When her eyes met Andrew's, all he could see was fear.

Andrew raced to the window but couldn't get a good enough angle to be able to see the door. He couldn't see anyone outside, so moved through the flat, undoing all the bolts and then opening the door.

There was nobody there.

Andrew stepped outside, peering both ways along the concrete balcony, but it was clear. Down below, the green was empty. He leaned over the rail, trying to get a glimpse of the row of flats below, though he couldn't see anyone there either.

Back inside, Andrew locked only the central bolt and then headed back to the living room.

'Have you had many of those recently?' he asked.

'One this morning, another just after lunch. I shouted "hang on" because it takes me a while to get to the door, but when I opened it, there was no one there.'

Gem might be in her seventies, but Andrew wouldn't have guessed if he didn't know. She kept as active as her body would allow her and her mind was still sharp when it needed to be. Now, though, she looked her age. Her skin greyer, eyes tired. She'd lived on the estate for a long, long time, watching it decay around her, though she didn't think like that. She was loyal to an area that showed no loyalty to her and it broke his heart. No matter how often Andrew tried to get her to move, or how much help he offered, she wouldn't have it.

Andrew could feel his hands shaking with rage that he was struggling to conceal. 'I'm going to pop out for a bit,' he said. 'Lock up behind me. When I get back, I'll tap the window so you know it's me. If anyone knocks on the door, ignore it.'

'Where are you going?'

'For a walk. I won't be long.'

Gem trailed Andrew to the front door, where he put on his shoes. When he got outside, he waited until he heard the final bolt slide into place and then moved quickly to the concrete steps at the end, heading down to the ground. He was on the edge of the green, with four sides of two-storey flats around him. There were a couple of hundred flats in total, plus the pair of tower blocks a short distance away.

Andrew walked quickly, sticking to the walkway underneath the balcony and looping around the green. He heard televisions that were too loud, music seeping through fragile front doors, a few kids crying, a couple having a row. Nothing unusual in an area where there were so many people living on top of one another.

He continued past the row directly opposite Gem's, circling around the back of the block to where there was a play park. There was a sorry-looking roundabout with much of the paint scratched off. One of the swings had been spun around the top of the frame, leaving it too high to reach. There was nobody in sight.

Andrew moved back to the quadrant, following the route he'd taken when he first arrived. It was only when he neared the stairs close to Gem's flat that he saw a flash of dark. It was hard to muffle footsteps on the harsh concrete, but Andrew did his best, jogging on tiptoes up to the balcony, where he found a kid in a black top edging along the walkway in the direction of his aunt's flat. The boy had short sandy hair and was moving slowly for seemingly no reason.

Making sure he didn't step on the assortment of rubbish that was outside the various flats, Andrew trailed the boy, gaining on him easily. The youngster was in line with Gem's window when Andrew snagged him, taking him by surprise and spinning him around until the boy was pressed backwards against the railing.

'What the—' the boy gasped in surprise, but Andrew was bigger and stronger.

'What are you doing?' Andrew demanded.

'Get off me, you paedo.'

Andrew pushed harder so that the boy was bent backward across the rail. His legs were kicking but nowhere near Andrew. 'Why are you harassing an old woman?' Andrew shouted.

'It's not me.'

'What's not you?'

The lad snarled up at Andrew, annoyed he'd even acknowledged anything untoward was going on.

'Who sent you?' Andrew said.

'You gay or summat? Get off me.'

Andrew had his forearm across the boy's chest and pressed a little harder, enough to lift him off the ground. Andrew was now the only thing stopping him from tumbling over the rail and the kid knew it. There was panic in his eyes.

'What makes you think you can make people's lives a misery?' Andrew growled.

'I'm not.'

'So what are you doing?'

'Nothing.'

Andrew released a little of the pressure, allowing the kid's feet to touch the ground. 'Do you even live here?' he asked.

'What's it to you?'

They glared at one another, but there was only anger in the youngster. What was he going to do next? Throw him over the railing? The kid was only fourteen or fifteen. Andrew released him and stepped away.

'Don't let me see you round here again,' he said, trying to sound as threatening as he could.

The boy edged around him, backing towards the stairs. When he was out of arm's reach, he called Andrew a sneering list of four-letter words and then ran for it. Andrew watched him go, leaning over the balcony to see the direction in which he headed – though it was away from the estate rather than towards it. It crossed Andrew's mind that perhaps there was some innocent reason for the youngster being there. Perhaps he wasn't going to knock on Gem's door at all and Andrew had misread the situation?

Bit late now.

Andrew stood with both hands on the rail, staring out towards the green and the flats beyond. Could the harassment of his aunt be a coincidence? It couldn't be Tyler or Zoe this time, so if not them, who?

Braithwaite?

Was this a way of getting to Andrew through his aunt?

He knocked on the window and heard his aunt unbolting lock after lock before she welcomed him back in with a smile.

'What do you want for tea?' Andrew asked. 'I'm cooking and I'm not debating it.'

Gem opened her mouth, all set to argue regardless. There was nothing she liked better than piling a plate with enough food for a small family and then watching Andrew struggle to eat it all. In the end, she smiled warmly.

'Mashed potato,' she said. 'Plus something meaty for Rory. He likes steak on a Friday. I got him some in especially. He likes it well done but not too well done. And make sure you cut it up into little pieces for him – you know what he's like.'

42

Andrew's pledge to cook tea became a promise to stay for the evening and then to stop for the night. Gem had fussed, saying she was fine, that Rory was fine, that everything was all right – but it clearly wasn't. She spent the evening nervously eyeing the window and any outside noises made her jump, even though nobody else knocked on her door.

She insisted that Andrew take her bed, but that was never going to happen and, in the end, she fell asleep halfway through the news anyway. Andrew gently shook her awake and then helped her to bed. After she'd changed, he tucked her in, although Rory seemed determined to take up as much of the bed as possible. For a little guy, with his limbs splayed, he was almost as big as Gem. She kissed Andrew on the forehead, whispered a 'thank you', and then rolled over.

Andrew grabbed a blanket and headed for her sofa, which was surprisingly comfortable. He slept in the clothes he'd been wearing all day, only managing to doze in short bursts before he was awoken by a noise from outside. Each time, he checked the window, though there was nobody there. As time passed, the number of lights dotted around the green dwindled until it seemed like everybody was asleep.

Everyone except Andrew.

At half past one in the morning, Andrew jumped awake, certain something awful was happening – only to realise that the asthmatic elephant that had woken him was a combination of Gem and Rory trying to outsnore each other. He stood in the bedroom doorway, watching their respective chests rise and fall in almost perfect symmetry. Rory had somehow contrived to take up even more space on the double bed, lying on his back, hind legs spread wide, leaving Gem with only the corner.

Not that she appeared to mind.

Back in the living room, Andrew switched on the television. Gem only had the basic channels, which wasn't a problem as he found a late-night repeat of some game show. He couldn't hear it over the snoring anyway, so turned on the subtitles and snuggled back under the blanket. As the contestants became stupider, Andrew's blinks became longer until...

Andrew sat up, kicking the blanket aside. He was sure he'd heard something. The snores of Rory and Gem were now silenced and the television was showing the rolling news channel. Andrew looked to the clock – half three.

He stood, stretching and yawning, then nudged the curtain slightly to the side. Through the slim gap, all he could see was the darkness of the green, lit by intermittent lamps around the edge. There was nobody on the balcony immediately in front of the flat.

Andrew returned to the sofa and sat, stretching once more. He turned off the television and then sat listening to the silence. Whatever had woken him – if it was anything other than a dream – was gone.

After yet another yawn, Andrew realised the pressure from his bladder was probably the reason he had woken up. He headed through the flat barefooted until he reached the toilet next to the front door. He left the light off, fumbling around until he'd found the bowl. He closed the door and then, moments later, it was like a tap had been turned on.

Life brought with it many pleasures. There was food, drink, travel, company, sex and much more – but very little touched the perfection of emptying a bladder in the early hours of the morning.

Andrew's head was drooped and he was half-asleep, ready to return to the sofa, when...

Footsteps: more than one pair. Voices, too: male and young-sounding.

Andrew strained to listen, willing his bladder to give it a rest. He hadn't drunk that much through the day. The voices continued and then there was a low metallic clang, quickly followed by the snap of a letter box.

Was it Gem's? Andrew couldn't tell.

More voices, urgency.

Andrew finally zipped himself up and opened the bathroom door. The smell hit him instantly. He'd filled up enough cars in his time to know the unmistakeable, throat-grating stench of petrol.

It was already too late.

The letter box was open, a puddle of liquid oozing across the welcome mat, more still dribbling along the inside of the door. A hurried voice from outside shouted 'now' and then Andrew saw everything as if it was happening in slow motion.

A match flicked inside, cartwheeling towards the ground. The letter box snapped shut with a deep clang as Andrew leapt away from the door a moment before the fire hit. There was a whoosh and then flecks of orange, red and yellow erupted from the mat, engulfing the front door in a frenzied blast of licking flames.

Time sped up again with a frenetic bang that made Andrew drop to his knees, covering his ears. He pulled himself up on the wall, the singeing flames prickling at his back.

'Low,' he shouted to himself, charging along the hall on all fours like a chimp. He blasted into Gem's bedroom, shouting her name. Rory was already up, huge brown eyes gazing at Andrew in confusion. Gem took longer to move, rolling over and moaning in sleep-deprived stupor. Andrew had no time to explain, so he grabbed her. She shrieked in alarm before realising it was him – but by then, they were already in the kitchen. Rory raced as best he could around Andrew's feet, though speed wasn't his greatest asset.

Andrew slammed the door to the hallway, though smoke immediately began to seep around the edges.

'We've got to go,' Andrew gasped. 'The flat's on fire.'

Gem immediately burst into tears, screaming with fear and confusion. Andrew was sweating from the heat.

'My bag,' she said.

'There's no time.'

'But Francis... it's my only picture.' She pointed towards the living room. Francis was her husband who had died such a long time ago that Andrew couldn't remember ever meeting him. There were more tears in her eyes as she stood and tried to push past him into the living room.

Andrew turned back to the hall door, where the paint was beginning to bubble. 'I'll get it – but only when you're outside,' he replied.

As she stood at the kitchen table listening to the flat she so loved crackle around her, Andrew leaned across the sink and opened the window. He pushed it as far as he could but it was one of those stupid security ones, which could only open wide enough to let flies in and nothing out. Andrew lifted himself onto the counter next to the sink, resting his back against the wall, and then he kicked the frame as hard as he could. His first blow barely registered, but the next bent the window back by a few more centimetres.

Behind him, there was a loud boom from the hallway, but Andrew didn't turn, kicking with all his might until the hinge finally buckled and the window swung outwards.

'The window, Gem,' Andrew said. He jumped down and lifted his aunt onto the counter, then helped her to spin so that her legs were hanging outside to where there was a rickety metal catwalk. Whoever had designed the building must have a degree in buffoonery because they'd installed a fire escape at the rear of a block of flats where there were no back doors.

'You're going to have to jump,' Andrew said. 'It's only a short drop. You'll be all right.'

Gem whimpered softly, not wanting to go. 'Rory,' she said.

'I'll pass him to you when you're out – then head to the far end of the walkway. Knock on everyone's back windows as you go.'

Gem breathed deeply, sobbing once more as another bang echoed from behind. Sweat was pouring from Andrew's back.

'You've got to—'

Andrew didn't need to finish his sentence because his aunt jumped. The drop was only the height of the window, minus the length of her legs, but she still disappeared out of sight for a few terrifying moments. Andrew jumped up, trying to see where she'd landed, but she reappeared almost immediately, tears streaming down her face as she called Rory's name. Andrew lifted the dog into the sink and then climbed onto the counter again, picking him up and handing him through the window to his aunt. He was so heavy that she almost dropped him, sinking herself as the pair of them landed on the metal.

'You okay?' Andrew shouted.

Gem didn't reply, but she set off along the walkway, shouting and banging her next-door neighbour's window.

Andrew turned to see things had deteriorated quickly. Thick, dark smoke now covered the entire ceiling and was wisping its way around the cupboards. The paint on the kitchen door was popping and snarling, leaving a crust of blue on the lino. Andrew ducked low, rushing into the living room. He grabbed his phone from the side table next to the sofa, pocketed it and then hunted around underneath until he found Gem's bag. It was ridiculously large, not far off the size of Rory and more like a holdall someone might take to a gym as opposed to a handbag. It was also as heavy as the weights someone might do in a gym. She must have biceps like a weightlifter.

He hoicked it over his shoulder and then dashed back towards the kitchen, where the smoke was spiralling down to the floor. He'd seen fire before, worked on a case in which someone seemed intent on burning things to the ground. In a moment of clarity, he paused momentarily in the living room, gulping down as big a breath of air as he could manage, and then he was off.

The smoke sizzled his eyes, tore at his skin. He could feel it clawing him, trying to tear him down, but Andrew moved with the frenzied fury of someone who'd just witnessed another person try to burn down his aunt's flat with her in it. The pain didn't matter. He leapt onto the counter, clearing the taps with his feet and then launched himself outside, somehow managing to land without even stumbling.

The unsteady metal groaned underneath him but held firm. Andrew ran one way, knocking on windows and shouting 'Fire,' then raced back the other, making as much noise as he could until he found Gem at the far end of the catwalk. The metal ladder was going to be hard work for her – not to mention poor, terrified Rory – but it would be manageable.

First Andrew gasped in the clean, cool air, savouring each wonderful breath – then he took out his phone and called 999.

43

It was late afternoon when Andrew knocked on Jenny's front door. She was in an apron, the front covered in a mix of crusty butter and sugar, a smear of chocolate on her cheek.

'You again!' she deadpanned, before realising that Andrew wasn't laughing. 'What's happened?' she added quickly.

She invited him in and Andrew told her about the fire, plus his second day in a row with the police. They were going to be on first-name terms before long. Jenny listened, her face a growing blur of confusion and horror. The story was interrupted by a ding from the kitchen. Jenny popped up, first grinning and then remembering what was happening.

'Cupcakes,' she said.

Andrew followed her into the kitchen, where the smell of cake seemed to be seeping from every corner.

Jenny opened the oven and took out two dozen cakes, placing them on the side. 'I was hungry,' she said, fighting back a small smile that Andrew didn't mind at all. Normality was good. 'Where's Gem now?'

'I've got her in a hotel that's pet-friendly. There's actually a pet spa on site, so she was going to have a bath, while Rory was toddling off for a shampoo of his own.'

Jenny giggled and Andrew couldn't resist joining in. 'The poor little guy,' she sniggered.

'I know. Considering everything that's happened, Gem's doing all right.'

'What about her flat?'

Andrew shook his head. 'The fire was contained – *just* – but there's no way she'll be back anytime soon. Actually, there's no way she'll be back at all. I should have put my foot down a long time ago and made her go somewhere else. I'll find her a bungalow or a flat somewhere that's nice, where there are neighbours she'll be able to chat and gossip to. That's all she wants, I think – community. She grew up in those flats when there used to be a society and didn't realise it had slowly disappeared.'

'Do you think she'll go?'

'She won't have an option. Even if the flat could be tidied up, it'll be months away. It's a crime scene at the moment anyway. The neighbours got out safely and the police are doing the usual door-to-doors. They were saying they're hopeful of getting something, but it's not the sort of area where people routinely talk to the police.'

Jenny stared at him, perhaps reading his mind. 'And...?'

Andrew didn't feel ready to say it... not yet. He nodded towards the cakes. 'Can I have one?'

'They're not cool enough to ice yet.'

'I'll manage.'

She picked one up and handed it over. 'Icing's the best bit,' she said.

'So why bother with the cake?'

She threw her hands up. 'Exactly! I've been saying that for ages.' Her face fell. 'Oh, you're joking.'

Andrew offered a small smile and then nibbled the corner. 'It's good,' he said.

'Of course it's good. How can anyone make bad cakes?'

She watched as Andrew ate, a role reversal from how things usually played out.

Andrew leaned against the sink, yawning and eating. He was so tired – not just physically but of everything that had been happening.

'Braithwaite,' he said quietly.

Jenny nodded. 'You sure?'

'Who else?' Andrew apologised for not telling her sooner and then told her how Braithwaite had been blackmailing him to do jobs; threatening that Andrew's DNA could be implicated with a previous house fire. He didn't know if it could happen, but the threat was enough. He told her about switching the violins because of some ridiculous loyalty he felt to Finn Renton's apparently talented kid, even though they'd never met. He told the story of how he'd been abducted from outside the office and that Braithwaite had threatened him, her and Keira.

He didn't know whether he should be surprised – but Jenny's reaction wasn't one of fear, or resentment that Andrew had kept things back, it was determination. 'What are we going to do?' she asked.

'I have an idea,' Andrew said.

'Let's do it then.' Jenny was already untying her apron as if they were about to head out the door and get cracking.

Andrew held an arm across her. 'Jen…'

'What?'

'I'm going to ask you to do something I have absolutely no right to do.'

She stared up at him with big, bright brown eyes. 'Sometimes, perhaps all the time, I think I'd do anything you asked me.'

Andrew couldn't meet her gaze. 'That's what I'm afraid of, Jen.'

'Why?'

The room felt as if it was closing in. Andrew could still feel the prickle of the fire on his back, hear the fizzing and cracking of the paint. He closed his eyes for a moment, trying to force himself to get the words out. He felt Jenny's hand taking his and opened his eyes again. She was half a step closer than she had been, all eyes and dimples.

'Hi,' she said softly.

'We're friends, aren't we?' Andrew asked.

'Of course.'

The words were stuck in Andrew's throat. He couldn't look at her. 'Braithwaite said something to me a while ago,' he said. 'He told me you had an interesting past, that I should beware of you and watch my back. Then Ollie said—'

'You talked to Ollie?'

Andrew nodded, wishing he'd told her before. 'Briefly. I thought he was the one harassing you – the phone calls, the brick through the window. I should have said. He told me you had a brother.'

He could feel Jenny staring at him. She said nothing, waiting... waiting... waiting until Andrew finally looked at her. There were tears clinging to her eyelashes. He'd never seen her cry before, wasn't sure if he'd ever seen her upset.

'Do you know?' she asked, voice bobbing with emotion of which he didn't know she was capable.

Andrew shook his head.

'You *could* know. You're a detective. You could've gone looking.'

'I didn't... I haven't.'

'Why? If you knew there was something there, why wouldn't you want to know?'

They stared at each other for a while. Andrew didn't know

how long. She wasn't crying, but the tears remained where they were, defying the gravity that wanted to drag them along her cheeks.

'Because we're friends,' Andrew managed. 'Because, if you want me to know, you'll tell me.'

Jenny's eyes were so large that she was on the brink of looking like a Japanese cartoon. She reached up and wiped away each of the tears individually, then took a deep breath. 'Do you want to know the truth?'

And there it was.

As simple as that.

All the worry he'd had over what might be in the past, the agonising over barely concealed hints from others. All that and she was willing to tell him anyway.

All he had to do was ask.

Slowly, Andrew shook his head. 'Not yet,' he said. 'Not today.'

Jenny beamed up at him. In wiping away the tear, she'd smeared the chocolate further across her cheek. 'Cake?' she asked, stepping away. 'Cake solves everything – even carrot cake and I don't count that as cake.'

'If carrot cake isn't cake, then what is it?'

'It's just sort of... there. An abomination. I'd ban it if it was me.'

'What about apple turnover cake?'

'Oooh,' Jenny gushed, 'I love a bit of apple turnover cake. And pineapple turnover. Slightly warm, bit of ice cream. It'd probably squeeze into my top-ten cakes of all time. Maybe. Well, perhaps not. It's up there though. Top twenty.' A pause. 'Top thirty.'

She stopped, the grin slipping. 'What do you need me to do?'

'I wouldn't ask if I could think of another way.'

She continued smiling, not needing to say anything.

Andrew gulped, took a deep breath, and then asked if she'd ever been to Lancaster.

44

DAYS LATER

Andrew waited at the gates to Thomas Braithwaite's house, feeling the pressure of the watching cameras. He didn't bother to look up at them, not wanting to give anyone the satisfaction of knowing how scared he was.

In a chart of monumentally stupid things he'd done in his life, this was a new entry, straight in at number one.

He pressed the buzzer a second time and waited, still not looking up at the cameras. Nothing happened and he continued to stand, counting to sixty in his head and then pressing the buzzer again. He did it eight times before the shape of Iwan finally appeared from the back of the house. He ambled along the driveway, taking his time and prolonging the wait. Once Andrew reached sixty, he leaned forward and pressed the buzzer again anyway.

It was too late to go back now.

When Iwan reached the gate, he stood on the other side, examining Andrew through the bars and scratching his chin. There was a crooked half-smile on his face. 'I can't figure out if you're the stupidest son of a bitch I've ever laid eyes on, or if you've got the biggest set of balls. If it were me, I'd have been running for the hills. I'd be on a plane, trying to get as far away from this area as possible. But here you are – not just running, but on Mr Braithwaite's doorstep as if you're here for a tea party.' He chuckled to himself and shook his head disbelievingly.

'Is he in?' Andrew asked.

'Is *who* in?'

'You know who.'

Iwan half turned towards the house. 'Are you sure you want to do this?' He nodded towards Andrew's car. 'You can drive away now and get back to whatever it is you do.'

'Is he in?'

Iwan sniggered again. 'Suit yourself,' he said, removing a small box from his pocket and pressing a button to open the gate.

Andrew stepped inside, waiting politely until it was closed behind him and then trailing Iwan up the driveway. He tried to keep his pace level, ignoring Iwan's 'how's the head?' remark, and generally trying to pretend he wasn't terrified out of his wits.

They continued around the side of the house into the spectacular rear garden. There was a pristine, perfect lawn, with a stable in the far corner and a set of jumps in front. Andrew had been before and knew the way, following the path towards the enormous conservatory that was attached to the back of the house. It was bigger than Gem's flat, probably bigger than many of the shoebox new-build houses.

The door was unlocked and Iwan headed inside, holding it open and allowing Andrew to pass. Braithwaite was sitting at a small black metal table, wearing a suit even though it was breakfast, and there was a gourmet feast in front of him. Andrew spotted croissants, jam, toast, marmalade and a large espresso pot. It was like a hotel's breakfast buffet.

Braithwaite smiled up at Andrew, ensnaring him in the

water-blue gaze from which it was so hard to escape. Andrew found himself sitting on the other side of the table without being invited, though nobody objected.

'Thank you, Iwan,' Braithwaite said, nodding slightly towards the other man, who bobbed his head back and then disappeared into the house. Braithwaite picked up a knife and started to butter some toast. 'Good morning, Mr Hunter. To what do I owe this very great pleasure?'

'Do you have email on your phone?' Andrew asked.

It wasn't what Braithwaite had expected. He stopped what he was doing, butter poised. 'Sorry?'

'Your phone. Does it have email?'

'Why?'

'Because I'm going to send you a Tesco voucher. Why do you think?'

Braithwaite's eyes narrowed. 'Of course it has email.'

'What's your email address?'

There was no reply for a moment and then Braithwaite finished buttering his toast before putting down the knife. He bit off a small corner, chewing thoughtfully. When he was done, he read out an address.

Andrew took out his own phone, tapped an email as quickly as he could and pressed send. Then he sat back and waited.

It was probably only thirty seconds or so, but it felt like a lot longer than that. Sweat was trickling along Andrew's back and the collar of his shirt was suddenly so itchy, he wanted to rip off his own skin. Andrew did his best to ignore it all. Sitting impassively. Waiting.

Braithwaite had two more small bites of his toast, chewing with his mouth closed, before reaching into an inner pocket of his suit and taking out his phone. He pressed a couple of buttons and then stopped, staring intently at the screen.

Andrew tried to read him. Fury? Surprise? Fire of a thousand suns? The other man didn't even twitch. Andrew thought he must be an incredible poker player.

Braithwaite eventually tapped a couple more buttons and then returned the phone to his pocket. He had one more bite of his toast and then looked up.

Andrew fought not to shrink under the gaze. He had to sit tall, to be confident, even though he wanted to do exactly what Iwan had suggested – run for the hills.

'So...' Braithwaite said, his lips barely moving. 'What is this?'

Andrew leaned in. He'd gone through the words so many times in his head and now here they were, actually coming out of his mouth.

'This is the end of whatever it is that's going on between us,' he said, voice holding steady. 'We have *no* feud, *no* alliance, no anything. I don't know you and you don't know me. This is what used to be called Mutually Assured Destruction. If anything happens to me, my ex-wife, anyone who works for me, my friends or my family – hey, if anything happens to someone I say hello to on the street – those photographs will be sent to every newspaper in the country. They will go to every business rival you have, not to mention the police. Everything I have is with two separate solicitors – one of whom isn't in the UK. They know what they have to do if they don't hear from me regularly. I didn't start this – I didn't *want* this – but I'm finishing it.'

Braithwaite leaned back in his seat, smiling with so little humour, he could have been drowning a small animal. 'You're the big man now, are you? Taking pictures of my son at university?'

'You gave me the idea,' Andrew said. He even managed a wink.

'You got a couple of shots of my son snorting what appears to be drugs, so what?'

'Not just *taking* drugs, *dealing* drugs. Like father, like son, hey? I've sent you the tiniest selection of what I have. There are far more incriminating ones. It's one thing to blackmail a councillor because of his kids, not so fun when it comes back to you, is it?'

Braithwaite's smile widened. He sucked on his teeth, pinching his lips together into a pensive pout. 'You know this is a Pandora's box you're opening. Once you've done that, there's no going back.'

'It's not,' Andrew replied firmly. 'This is me closing that box. Nothing – and I really do mean *nothing* – will happen to me or anyone I know because of those photos. You continue doing whatever it is you do and I'll continue to run my business and live my life. That's it.'

Braithwaite nodded, his grin like a viper's. Broad and thin, ready to strike. 'That's how you think this goes?'

Andrew stood. His leg wobbled slightly, but he disguised it by stepping around the chair and using it as a shield. He glanced towards the inner house, but Iwan was nowhere to be seen. He gripped the back of the chair to keep level, telling himself not to lose it now.

'It's how I know it goes,' he said. 'You kidnapped me and then tried to burn down my aunt's house. She could have died – and for what? Your ego? Your satisfaction? She'd done nothing to you. She's the type of woman who takes in a battered dog and spends all her money looking after him. She feeds him better than she does herself. She asks after the local kids, even though they're the same lot who go knocking on her door. She's pined after her husband for twenty-odd years and, aside from a night or two out at the bingo or the legion, she lives in her tiny little flat and causes nobody any harm.'

Andrew had blown it. There were tears pouring down his face and his voice that he'd somehow managed to keep level for so long was now a cracked mess of tear-streaked words. He stepped around the chair, towering over the seated Braith-waite, pushing a finger into his face.

'...And you, like the chicken you are, hide away in your massive house using creatures like him' – Andrew jabbed a hand towards the house – 'and kids, estate kids, to set fire to her house?!'

Andrew used his sleeve to wipe away the mix of tears and snot. Braithwaite was trying to push himself backwards, though there was nowhere to go.

'We. Are. *Done*,' Andrew said. 'You're too scared to do your own dirty work, but I will promise – *promise* – you this. If you want to go man-to-man, one-on-one, whatever you want to call it, you know where I am. No one to hide behind, no games. If you want to do that, then I'll meet you anywhere you want. Otherwise, I never want to see you again.'

Andrew finally stepped away, almost tripping over the chair in which he'd been sitting but not caring. He kicked it away, sending it crashing into the glass with a thunderous thwack that boomed around the enclosed space as if lightning had struck. Andrew wiped his face once more, just as Iwan rushed through the doorway to the house. He saw the chair, saw Andrew and lunged for him in a growl of spitting fury.

'No!' Braithwaite shouted. He was on his feet, too, straightening his suit as Iwan did as he was told and stepped away.

Iwan was left standing between the two men, unsure where to look.

'Thank you, Iwan,' Braithwaite growled. When Iwan didn't move, Braithwaite darted across the room, pushing the larger man in the chest. 'I said: *Thank. You. Iwan.*'

He spoke with such wrath that it was impossible to miss the meaning. Iwan turned, eyes not leaving Andrew as he headed back into the house. Andrew and Braithwaite stood apart from each other, both apparently out of breath.

'Fine,' Braithwaite hissed. 'We'll do it your way.'

Andrew didn't know if he was being genuine or simply saying that. Only time would tell. He spun and headed for the door, only stopped by Braithwaite's loud cough. He turned to see the other man's hand outstretched, ready to be shaken.

Andrew eyed it, then looked up into the deep blue eyes of the man who was offering the apparent olive branch. Then he turned and walked away.

THE GIRL WHO CAME BACK

Thirteen years ago Olivia Adams went missing. Now she's back... or is she?

When six-year-old **Olivia Adams** disappeared from her back garden, the small community of Stoneridge was thrown into turmoil. How could a child vanish in the middle of a cosy English village?

Thirteen years on and Olivia is back. Her mother is convinced it's her but not everyone is sure. If this is the missing girl, then where has she been - and what happened to her on that sunny afternoon?

If she's an imposter, then who would be bold enough to try to fool a child's own mother – and why?

Then there are those who would rather Olivia stayed missing. The past is the past and some secrets *must* remain buried.

THE WIFE'S SECRET

Charley Willis was thirteen years old when her parents were killed in their family home and she was found hiding in a cupboard upstairs.

Fifteen years later, Charley is marrying Seth Chambers. It should be the happiest day of their lives, a chance for Charley to put her past behind her, but just hours after the ceremony, she is missing.

No one saw her leave. No one knows where she is.

One thing is for certain... Seth is about to discover he doesn't really know the woman he just married. And his nightmare is only just beginning.

LAST NIGHT

It's the early hours of the morning and Rose Denton wakes up behind the steering wheel of her car. She's off the road, through a hedge and in a field.

There's blood on the windscreen and bonnet – but it's not hers and there's no sign of anything or anyone she might have hit. The last thing she remembers is being in a hotel on a business trip but now she's miles away.

Back home and her daughter's boyfriend is missing. The last thing he did was argue with Rose over money. He left no note, no text, no clue as to his whereabouts.

The police have questions – and so does Rose's family. But those are little compared to the ones she has for herself.

What happened last night? And, perhaps more importantly, does she really want to know the answer?

TWO SISTERS

They told us he had been missing for nearly two days, that he probably drowned. They told us a lie.

Megan was ten years old when her older brother, **Zac**, went missing among the cliffs, caves and beaches that surround the small seaside town of Whitecliff.

A decade on and a car crash has claimed her parents' lives.

Megan and her younger sister **Chloe** return to Whitecliff one summer for the first time since their brother's disappearance. Megan says it's to get her parents' affairs in order. There are boxes to pack, junk to clear, a rundown cottage to sell. **But that's not the real reason**.

Megan received a postcard on the day of her parents' funeral. It had a photograph of Whitecliff on the front and a single letter on the back.

'Z' is all it read. Z for Zac.

THE DEATH AND LIFE OF ELEANOR PARKER

'I will never forget the night I drowned…'

Seventeen-year-old Eleanor Parker wakes up cold and alone in the river that twists through her quiet village. She remembers a hand on her chest, another on her head, water in her throat, those final gasps for air…

Her brother's girlfriend was drowned in the same river the summer before, held under the water by an unknown killer.

Determined to unlock the mystery of what really happened that night, Eleanor can't escape the feeling that something terrible links her to the previous summer's murder. But will she discover the shocking truth, before it's too late?

TEN BIRTHDAYS

There are going to be so many things I wish I could've told you in person, Poppy. I won't get the chance to do that, so perhaps this is my only way...

It's Poppy Kinsey's birthday.

She should be blowing out candles and opening presents – but hers falls on the type of heart-wrenching, agonising anniversary she would far rather forget.

The worst day of them all. The day her mother died.

But this year is special because the person she misses most in the world has left her a set of letters, one for each of her next ten birthdays.

As Poppy opens them year by year, she discovers that no matter how tough life gets, her mum will always be by her side, guiding her along the way.

Printed in Great Britain
by Amazon